SLEEPING MALLOWS

THE WATER STREET CHRONICLES BOOK 2

TAMMERA COOPER

BRACKISH ROMANCE PRESS

AUTHOR'S NOTE

This story and all the characters in it are purely fictional.

The city of Washington, North Carolina is a real and fantastic place. Many of the places my fictional characters visit in my book are real and open for your business. I hope you feel the need to visit our charming Southern town.

Abram and Selah are fictional characters based on the heroes of the Washington Underground Railroad. Hundreds were secretly smuggled through the Port of Washington to freedom in the North during the period before and during the Civil War. Without the conductors risking their lives every day, the dreams of freedom would not come true.

Locals will be tempted to guess who my contemporary characters are inspired by. Please know that every person in this book lives only in my imagination.

ACKNOWLEDGMENTS

I would like to thank the people who have made this book possible. There are many behind the scenes.

Thank you:

~to Patrick, who literally put a roof above my head so I can continue this crazy journey and building 14ft in the air

~to Marcia Koenig and the Cadaver Dog Facebook group for sharing your knowledge and training incredible furry heroes everyday

~to Jeni, who makes my thoughts shine

~to Joan and Lisa for reading it chapter by chapter and pushing me to finish so they would know the ending

~to Leesa, who did the research to uncover Washington's hidden past

~to Sabrina who answers my texts at 1a.m.

~to the Beaufort County Sheriff's Department for keeping our county safe in good times and bad

Most importantly, my readers who asked for the next part of the story.

QUARTERING THE WIND

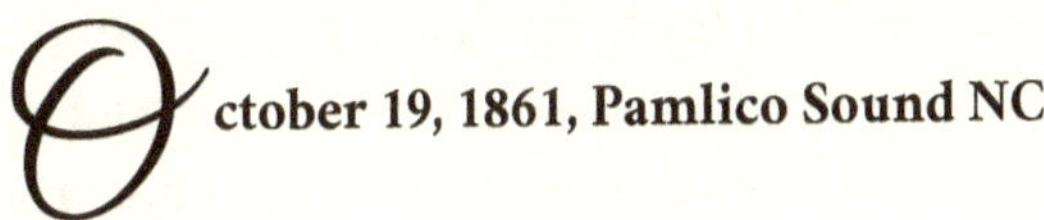

October 19, 1861, Pamlico Sound NC

ABRAM LEARNED a long time ago silence serves a man well. It kept you out of trouble, and if you listened in the silence, you learned an infinite amount. He steered the workboat against the tide, listening silently. The tide descended quickly, which meant only one thing: the storm over his shoulder gathered strength and would soon arrive.

As Abram stood, he listened for changes in the sounds of the waves and altered the boat's course as necessary. He was an expert navigator and knew the shoals like the back of his hand, but they were dangerous and changed almost monthly. A storm like this could place debris in his path where nothing had been for centuries. He had rescued many ship captains boasting about their experience, only too loudly to hear the sea. Tonight's pickup was too important not to miss. His precious cargo did have monetary value, but not to him. This voyage was one of the heart, and he never felt emotion like this for anyone. Selah was waiting for him, and the year it took to get back to her had dragged on like an eternity.

He turned his eyes to the heavens, praying God would see them through this. They picked this date a year ago but had no way to know a hurricane would be barreling down on the Outer Banks. The wind picked up. He didn't feel like an expert at the moment. Every bone in his body told him to seek shelter, but it would not get him closer to the port of Washington, where she waited. He needed to press on.

The boat gave a sudden jolt and dragged along the bottom. Abram jumped into the shin-deep water and checked the hull. No holes meant nothing solid. Without his weight, the boat traveled easily across the sandbar. He pulled out his spyglass and peered into the distance. He was almost to the turn. The river water would be easier to navigate, but the tide would be working against him. His determination pulsed harder than the tide. His love for Selah inspired his strength.

The setting sun darkened the sky. He'd better make good time across the sound if he was going to meet her at their decided time. Seafoam built on the sandbars, making it easier for him to move past them. Seaspray soaked through his shirt, causing it to cling to his well-sculpted chest. Droplets of salty water stung his skin. His muscles throbbed from the exertion. Thoughts of her pushed him harder across the water, and soon he fought the current to enter the river. The trees on the bank bent and fell to the ground as the wind tore them from the rain-saturated soil. This storm was bad. It already showed its strength, and he knew the worst was still to come.

He found himself alone on the river. It would normally be filled with schooners and other freight ships on their way to the next big port from Washington. But the worsening storm kept all the smart captains in port waiting out the storm. He told himself he would make it in time, but they would not be able to leave until after the storm passed. He knew the backside of the storm would be worse, making the tidal surge deadly. The small boat skimmed the waves, but as utter darkness fell, he tied the boat in the harbor. Soaking wet and exhausted, he slipped through the streets, cutting between the warehouses lining the bulkhead, and turned down Water Street. Staying in the shadows, he headed toward the grand house at the end of the street. His pace quickened when he saw the waves licking the edge of the front porch. He fought against the waist-deep water and rounded the house to find the small shed at the edge of the yard gone and Selah nowhere to be found. He thought maybe she hid in the garden. He jumped the garden gate. Leaning against a big oak, he gave up his silence and yelled her name.

"Selah? I'm here, Selah." But there was no answer. Anger filled him. *Where was she? Had she changed her mind? No, she wouldn't. Not after all she had written. She was ready for him.* His anger turned to anguish. What happened to her?

He ran to the front door of the house. Not caring what they thought of him, he beat on the door. "Open the door," he yelled. "Ya know where she is. Open up. Selah?"

A branch from the large oak fell in the side yard only to fall on a pile of debris. The wake it caused threw river water onto the porch. He beat on the door again. He spied a lantern through the window come closer to the entrance. Slowly the door opened.

"What do you want? You know better than to come to the front door. You should come to the slave entrance in the back." An older black man dressed in a suit stared at Abram with disdain. "You should not be out in this storm. Go away."

Regaining his composure, Abram calmed himself then yelled only loud enough to be heard above the wind. "I am looking for a young woman who stays here. Selah is her name. I'm worried about her and want to make sure she's safe."

"There is no woman here, slave or free, by that name. Now go away." He closed the door.

Abram stood on the porch, stunned. He knew she stayed here. Why would he lie? The saltiness of his tears diluted the rain on his face. Where was his precious Selah?

With a crack of thunder and a flash of lightning, his heart broke into a million pieces.

CHAPTER 1

FOCUSED SPECULATIVE

"*Every day I remind myself: For us to have a great assignment, Someone else is having the worst day of their life. Closure is the ultimate goal.*"

Captain Savanna McCormick, cadaver Dog handler

OCTOBER 8, 2014

Deputy Tim Whitaker sat at his desk sorting through the notes of his interview with Beth Pearse. He hadn't made much progress on the kidnapping case despite the culprit sitting in the county jail. It wasn't strange she didn't remember many details, considering her ordeal, but it had been a week since Beth had identified his childhood friend and fellow deputy, Bill, as her kidnapper.

He needed a break in the case to help him find the scene of her confinement. The photos from her house displayed footprints from a large man walking through the house. The dark flooring showcased the print of a hiking boot tread in what forensics determined was finely crushed limestone. They had checked all the fertilizer storage facilities in the county.

"Hey, Mae," he yelled through the open room to the woman sitting at the reception desk at the front of the building. She put her hand up in the air and then pointed toward the phone headset at her ear. "Okay, okay." He turned back to his notes. He spread a map out on the table behind his desk. Sharpie dots marked spots on the paper. In his mind, he drew a circle. There were so many possibilities. He knew she swam to safety and was rescued in the river, but the scratches and cuts on her legs were similar to those attained in the woods. His finger ran over the swamp on the south bank of the Pamlico. It was a definite possibility.

He turned back to his desk and made a quick note to check the abandoned warehouses in the swamp area on his next patrol. There were no fingerprints other than those of the workers doing the renovation. Her canvas tote had never been recovered. She stated the tote was the reason she had walked back to the house on the night she was abducted. He needed to touch base with Sam since now he was no longer a suspect. Maybe he knew where the tote was. His ink pen made a tapping noise as he hit the desktop next to his notepad.

"Ahem." Someone cleared their throat. "Ahem."

He looked up, startled as Mae stood, peering over his shoulder.

"Oh, hey Mae. Whatcha need?"

"You needed to ask me something a minute ago." She smiled at him.

"Oh, yes. I was going to ask you if you could think of any place they used to store lime. I've checked all the stores in town. I'm trying to think of anywhere unusual, maybe deserted."

"I'll think about it. Now, the phone call I was on was about your daddy."

Tim turned in his chair to face her. "What about him?"

"He's been shooting at the church ladies again. He didn't hurt anyone, but it's only a matter of time."

Tim shook his head and massaged his temples with his fingers. "I'll take a ride out there. Why were they on his lane?"

"They were doing their elderly outreach and dropping off some groceries." Mae put her hand on Tim's shoulder and rubbed lightly.

"Okay. Could you call them and apologize for me? Let them know I will make the deliveries for them if they would like to send things."

"I'll let them know. Also, they said you needed a haircut." She walked back to her seat at the desk, her pantyhose swishing as she made her way.

"They did not say that," he protested as he scrubbed a hand through his shaggy hair.

"Actually, their exact words were, 'Tell that tall blond hunk of deputy he needs to stop by the salon for a trim.'"

Tim groaned as he watched her hop up on her desk chair, grab her pencil, and use it to dial a number.

"Okay then. Thanks," Tim mumbled. He made a mental note to grab some groceries and a cheese biscuit from Martha on his way. He couldn't remember the last time he'd been out to see his old man. He'd have to make better efforts if he wanted to keep the warning shots to a minimum.

Mae spun around and winked at him, her chair continuing around until she faced the front door. He turned back to his computer and hit the spacebar to wake it up so he could check emails before heading out for afternoon patrols.

CHAPTER 2

SEARCH BASELINE

October 10, 2014

The sun slid behind a cloud shifting the office into darkness, matching the sudden change in Savanna's mood. "Closure? Let's talk about closure. How fair is it I give everyone the closure I can never have? Every time Max gets close to his target I tense up, and my throat starts to tighten." The large German shepherd lying on the floor next to the chair Savanna sat in raised his head when he heard his name. He listened intently to her rant, his head shifting from side to side waiting for some signal. She rose from her seat and started to pace on the oriental carpet in the middle of the room, winding her long red hair in a bun and tucking it out of her way. "How can I be part of the best K9 team if I can't relax and let him work?"

"Savanna, you need to calm down and focus on why we are here."

"And why is that, Doctor? I thought you wanted to talk about closure."

"And why does closure make you agitated?"

9

"I'm not agitated. I'm pissed. I can't function right now at work without totally shutting down or compartmentalizing as you call it."

"Savanna, shutting down is not the same as taking control and telling your mind you are at work. You don't have to turn everything off."

Max followed Savanna's movement as she continued to pace, waiting for a command. "How can I get anything done without shutting down? Do you see how he is waiting for my cue? He knows I'm upset. He pulls my energy, and I need him totally relaxed and ready to work. So, yes, I need to shut down."

"Okay, we will work on some breathing exercises before you leave today. What do you have on the plate next week?"

"No active cases at the moment. Although, we are on call if they need us. I am going to chaperone Charlie's class trip this week."

"And how do you feel about that?"

"I'm worried I'll screw up. I'm not good at being the 'stand-in.' I worry I will ruin his day."

"You are there for him, I'm sure it will make the day special for him. Where are you going?"

"To Washington."

Her therapist's head rose instantly, and her pen froze on her notepad. "And you don't think it will be a problem?"

"Charlie will be fine. He wasn't here when they brought Mom and Dad's boat in."

"What about you?"

Savanna felt her eyes on her, watching her. "I don't want to think about it. This trip is for Charlie."

The doctor scribbled something on her pad of paper. "Okay. How's his talking?"

"He is still very quiet. Occasionally, he speaks up and surprises me." A smile tugged at her lips as she thought of her little brother and she relaxed. Charlie did not cope well with her parents' disappearance. He'd stopped talking all together at first. She loved him to death, and she wished he was still the bubbly boy she dealt with a year ago. Max laid his head back down on the rug. She sat back down in the big overstuffed chair in the corner beside Max, rubbing his neck again.

"That's great. Does he still have your Mom's phone?

"Yeah. Having something of hers helps. Plus, he can call me if he needs to."

"Is it for you or him?"

Savanna looked up. "Maybe a little of both."

The therapist smiled. "Is he still working with the therapist at school?"

"Yes. The all-boys school is great. They have a lot of extra support for him. Even though he didn't want to change schools, it has helped a lot."

"Is he excited about the field trip?"

"It seems that way. I'm worried I'm going to screw up."

"And what if you do," the doctor asked.

"He won't like me anymore?" Savanna laughed, "I know it seems silly, but I want him to want me there for the next trip."

"Is that what you are really afraid of?"

"Yes," Savanna admitted.

"It's a valid concern. Technically you are a new parent, but you are also his sister. You will have to work out a fine balance. If you need to, we can have a session with both of you. Max can still come."

"Thanks, Doc."

"Now let's work on those breathing exercises," the doc insisted, not letting her off the hook.

~

Session 53: Savanna McCormick

Copy to: Department of Child Services

Client attended session with K9.

Client seems distracted and detached from her anxiety, (i.e., staring into space, not listening to counselor, picking at dog's coat beside her). Reluctant to talk about weekly experience. Listed details but did not elaborate until prompted for further information.

Case this week involved a 20-year-old man found in National Park in a densely-wooded area. Body was in an extreme state of decomposition, likely due to damp, dark environment. Subject was missing for 1 month. Max and Captain McCormick found the male after a 12-hour search. She has admitted to a feeling of jealousy toward the family because of the closure they received after victim's remains were located. This is likely related to the disappearance of her own parents last year. The subject of closure caused agitation in the client (pacing and raising her voice); definitely a subject needing more exploration in a controlled environment.

Personal this week coming: she is chaperoning her brother on a field trip. She is exhibiting anxiety when talking about the trip. She is exhibiting fear of disappointing her brother. She is adjusting to her new role but still is unsure of where boundaries should be set. A follow-up session was offered to discuss things with her brother.

Weekly sessions should continue until panic attacks and anxiety are under control. Client was instructed to practice breathing techniques and compartmentalization during work.

CHAPTER 3

LIQUEFACTION

ctober 13, 2014

WATER DRIPPED onto the plastic covering his computer. Robert sat with his eyes glued to the screen hoping to catch any movement. He felt in control while he watched the quiet house. She was in her bedroom, but there was no light to offer any shadows. The storm covered the moon. He dragged his hand through his hair, closing his tired eyes for only a moment. His dark hair was starting to gray around the edges, and there was no reason to cover it. Over the last month, he stopped saying "only if." His thoughts drifted to the vision of her tied up on the filthy mattress. Beth didn't look like the same woman he left five years ago, but why would she? She had gone through hell, and it was his fault. He couldn't stand the thought of another man touching her, no matter how long it had been. Yes, he had left her, but she had pledged before their friends, family, and God to always be his. Always.

The weatherman predicted the rain would stop, but it still down

14

poured both inside and outside his creek cabin. Resigned to a piece of plastic sheeting over his tech equipment, he growled as rainwater pooled in the plastic. Tonight was bad. Almost as bad as the day she escaped. All the evidence should've washed away by now. He should have released her sooner, but he didn't have the heart to watch her run back to him; the stupid construction worker. How could she fall for him? Hatred coated the back of his throat.

He was brought back to the cabin when a huge wash of water poured into his lap from the suspended plastic above his computer. *Shit.* He jumped up, pushing the chair across the room. Well, at least the equipment stayed dry. He slung the water onto the floor and headed to the bedroom to change the pants. Khakis had become his staple this summer. His abs flexed as he pulled off his sweatshirt and tossed it aside. He went to the closet and pulled out a cotton button-up shirt. His wardrobe had enabled him to fly under the radar all summer. But now they were looking for the stranger in the University of Virginia sweatshirt, so he was stuck in the cabin for the time being. The boat was partially full of water because of the storm, and he would have to wait until things dried out before he headed to the Outer Banks.

There was movement in her bedroom. He could see the monitor through his bedroom doorway. The brunette was standing in the middle of the room talking to open space again. Maybe she hit her head when she escaped from the room, or maybe she was trauma-tized and crazy. Either way, she was not acting normal. He walked over to the screen and adjusted the plastic so he could see the entire screen. Water ran onto the floor beside the table. He looked closer and saw the contractor in the corner taking off his shoes. Damn it, he couldn't watch this. Pulling the plastic over the machine, he turned and walked out the door to the porch over-looking the creek.

He loved a good porch. His house in Aspen had one facing the water. He grimaced. It wasn't his anymore. He knew she sold it last month; the last piece of their past together. Damn this town. Ever since she'd moved here, he could sense it was the beginning of their end. The moon went behind the rain clouds again, and he was left in darkness, listening to the waves beat the shore and the dark thoughts echo in his head. She was his, and it didn't matter what he needed to do to have her back. The wood creaked as he leaned against the porch railing. He pulled out a cigarette and lit it. The embers glowed after several tries. He supposed those were wet too. Everything he owned was wet. The smoked danced around his head. He should quit smoking, but as far as everyone was concerned, he was already dead. He laughed out loud. A cigarette now and then was all he hadn't given up. He lost everything to keep her safe. And a smoke calmed him when his temper simmered.

A shadow crossed the railing beside him, and he spun around but found no one there. His nerves were on edge and making him crazy.

He looked back down at the railing, and the shadow still there. Someone was standing in front of the computers. He took a long drag of his cigarette, slowly blowing out the smoke, and tossed the butt into the river. Thoughts of capture crossed his mind. If they were here and had found him, he would go and end this. He was tired of being afraid for her. He stood there for another moment before he turned, expecting to see an officer in the doorway. All that greeted him was an emptiness in the glow of the monitors. An emptiness that matched his soul.

CHAPTER 4

THERMAL UPLIFT

October 16, 2014

Foam cups bounced on the tile floor of the small gas station. All the other customers turned to watch Tim as he picked up the mess. He held up his hand and gave a little wave and smile, shaking his head. He shifted his utility belt, so his firearm didn't poke him as he squatted down.

"Going to be one of those days." He sat the stack on the counter by the coffee pot. A small boy stepped up beside him as he stirred in his cream. "What'cha need?" He asked as the small child struggled to reach across the counter.

"I'll take one of those," he answered pointing to the extra-long straws.

"Are you sure you're supposed to have one of those this early?" Tim eyeballed the 40-ounce soda the boy was struggling to carry to the front counter.

"What's it to you?" The boy grabbed the offered straw and raced to the counter. He slapped down a crumpled bill and pushed open the door with his back, exiting as quickly as he entered.

Tim shook his head and slid into one of the booths. "Ms. Martha, what is with everyone this week? Seems like everyone ate pissy corn flakes."

"Don't you use language like that in here, Tim. I *will* call your father. You're never too old to show folks respect." She wagged a finger in his direction to punctuate her point.

"My point exactly," he mumbled as he took a sip of his hot coffee, blowing first. His cell vibrated, and he pulled it out of the carrier on his belt to check it then placed it back.

"Come and get your plate before it gets cold, deputy." The older woman slid a Styrofoam plate on the counter in front of her. "You know everyone is getting ready for the cook-off. There has been so much rain, the money hasn't been great. We need it to be a good weekend."

"I know, but do they have to be so crabby." Tim made time over to the plate, grabbing napkins, a fork, and a spoon, sliding into his booth. "Thanks, I'm gonna have to run after this."

"You need to stop in when you have time to chat. I want to hear the news." She took another order from a couple waiting while she cracked four eggs on the griddle. Ms. Martha had multi-tasking down to an expertise, and she still managed to know a little bit more than everyone else in town while she did it.

"You know more than I do; why do you think I stop in here for breakfast?"

"Well, you took a long enough time making it a regular thing. Took Sam settling down for you to drop in."

"I'm glad he is finally happy. Beth's a great woman." Tim took a huge bite of his fried eggs and grits.

Ms. Martha gave him a humph.

"You don't agree?" Tim turned back to look at her over his shoulder.

She stood up straight and peeked over the counter. "She has too much going on. That house is no good. I told him what I thought. Bad things happen every time someone finds happiness there."

"I have no doubt," he said quiet enough she couldn't hear. "Well I think she is great, and he is happy. It's all that counts, right?"

"Even if it kills him?" She announced to everyone waiting for their breakfast.

Tim scraped the last of his grits onto his spoon, choosing to ignore the last comment no matter how loud she was. "Thanks for breakfast. I've got to run. I really think you worry too much." He walked over to the trash can and tossed in his plate as he headed to the front door, stopping for a refill of coffee. "The sheriff has everything under control."

"You find the *other* guy who took her?" She looked right at him.

Tim stopped, turned, and looked at her. His mouth gaped open. "How do you know about the second man?"

"A person of interest is sought in the kidnapping case by the Beaufort Sheriff's department," she mimicked. "You think we're stupid?"

Tim took a step back toward her. "We only want to talk to him, that's all."

"They are still in danger, and you better have his back. He's always had yours."

"Yes, ma'am." Tim nodded and turned back to exit. He pushed open the door and gave her a wave. "See you tomorrow."

Tim looked over the parking lot as he stepped outside. Five kids on bikes flew by, barely missing him. He watched them as they dodged cars at the crosswalk to the school. He remembered trips to school like that, trying to beat the bell. He walked over to the cruiser and opened the door. The radio on his shoulder came to life.

"Dispatch to Whitaker. Come in please."

He juggled his coffee cup and unlocking the car door. The hot liquid leaked onto his hand as he leaned into the cruiser, grabbed the radio and answered, "Whitaker, here." He placed his cup in the console and put his index finger his mouth, seeking some relief from the burn.

"Sheriff Harroll needs you to come by the office after your rounds."

"Will do."

Tim slid into the driver's seat and watched the crosswalk for another five minutes, waiting for the bell. He started the car and dialed his friend, Sam.

"Hey man, you busy?"

"Nope, just grading papers. I could use a break."

"Okay, I'll swing by. Are you at the office or home?" Tim took a swig of his coffee.

"Home."

"Okay. Be there in a bit."

Tim watched a few stragglers cross to the high school as he pulled onto the main road. He could set up a small speed trap and catch some unsuspecting commuters headed toward Greenville and bring in some revenue for the town. He considered it for a second and then decided he would rather see Sam. He headed up the road. The community college was packed for Wednesday morning. Water stood on the road up ahead. Tim slowed the car and turned on his caution lights, parking on the shoulder.

"Dispatch, this is Whitaker."

"Go ahead."

"Broad Creek is over 264. We need some cones and a sign. I'm gonna put some flares out until the crew can get out here." Tim walked around the cruiser and popped the trunk. The flare hissed as he lit it and tossed it out on the pavement.

"Copy that. I will let the crew know."

He walked further up the road and lit another. Hopefully, people will pay attention and not drive through the high water.

He walked past his car and dropped another in the middle of the road. The water had a slight pull as it drained into the creek. Tim checked the flood level sign on the side of the bridge. *2 Feet above.* He pulled out his notebook and wrote down the time and date with a 2.

Jumping back in his car, he pulled over to the left lane on the eastbound side and continued over to Sam's. The rain had stopped this morning, but the water was still rising. The smaller creeks couldn't hold much more. They needed a good week of dry weather. He loved this town but hated the threat the water became during a rainy season.

Gravel crunched under the tires as he pulled onto Sam's driveway and parked behind his friend's truck. He gave the Volkswagon parked under the overhang a once over, texted Sam and headed to the door. After a quick knock, he walked right in.

Sam sat at his desk across the large front room. A huge pile of papers was stacked high enough to cover his face. He raised up and looked at Tim as he crossed the room.

"Hey, man. You getting a lot done?"

"Yeah. I'm a little cross-eyed. How about a cup of coffee?" Sam pointed to the kitchen.

"Nah, I have my 'Martha' coffee. What's with the VW?" Tim drank while he waited for Sam's answer.

"It's a friend's. Wait. You went to the grill? Where's my biscuit?"

"Sorry man. I wasn't originally planning to come by. Plus, Ms. Martha was letting me have it this morning. Coming by here was kind of a spur of the moment decision." Tim grabbed Sam's cup off the desk and headed to the kitchen to pour him a refill.

"What was she giving you a hard time about today?" Sam questioned as he followed behind.

Tim handed him the newly filled cup. "You really don't want to know. How's Beth?"

"She's fine, the gallery is fine. No more dodging, tell me."

"Well, she's going on about how the Water Street house is bad and on and on. Wouldn't let it go."

"She told me the same thing the other day. Like it's out to get me or something."

"Well, you did break your arm."

"True but the house didn't do it. That was me being stupid." Sam stood up and stretched his back, adjusting the sling around his neck. He walked around the desk and leaned over to grab his coffee.

A female voice came from the back of the house. "Hey Sam, where is the map we were marking last night?"

Stopping right in the threshold, Tim looked at his friend. "Dude, who's the chick in the back bedroom?"

Sam turned to look at him. "That's Abbie. She's here working on a project for work."

Tim lowered his voice, "Does Beth know?"

"Abbie drove in a couple nights ago from D.C. and needed a place to stay. It was late, and I told her she could crash here."

"You still haven't answered my question. Have you told Beth?"

"No. She will be fine with it. She's busy with the gallery anyway."

Tim shook his head. "How's that going? The grand opening is this week, isn't it?"

"During the festival. Everything looks good. Beth already has kids visiting from the schools. She loves it." Sam took a long sip of his coffee and leaned against the rail, facing the creek.

Tim looked at his friend over the rim of his travel cup. He wondered if he should ask what he was thinking. They always had each other's back, now was no different. "So, have you told her about Robert hanging out and kidnapping Bill?"

Sam spat his coffee across the rail and turned to Tim. "Where did that come from?"

"I was just wondering. We found out a week ago he was still around, dangerous, and likely connected to her somehow. *You* were going to tell her. Remember?"

"I seem to remember we decided he must've fled and was no longer a danger. I've got this." He leaned back on the railing, this time facing Tim.

"But her last name was floating around every time he was around. He's connected to her somehow."

"You can't prove that." Sam took another sip of his coffee.

Tim slapped his friend on the shoulder, then glanced at his watch. "I will." He took a couple of stairs at a time down to the yard.

"Hey, where you going? You haven't met Abbie." Sam followed him over to the stairs.

"I've gotta go. I'll meet her later. I've been summoned." Tim yelled over his shoulder as he turned the corner of the house.

"So, you came by to give me a hard time?" Sam yelled back.

He opened the car door. "Exactly." He slid in and started the car, pulling the door closed behind him. "And I will prove everything," he muttered to himself as he turned the key.

CHAPTER 5

SCENT POOL

Shouldn't they be out of oxygen by now? Savanna knew she should be able to handle a group of 8-year-old boys. She handled criminals for a living. Her nerves were on edge, and her brain was shutting down. She could feel her curly red hair twisting in knots in the wind blowing through the open bus windows. Maybe this wasn't a good idea. The young boy sitting next to her grabbed her hand and squeezed. She promised her little brother she would chaperone. She would get through this for him, she thought as she smiled down at Charlie with his freckled face and matching red hair. He had talked of nothing else for the last two weeks. Olivia Taylor, his teacher and her close friend, called her and begged her to do it, knowing she would easily pass the required background check because of her job. The teacher at the front of the bus stood up and held two fingers in the air. Suddenly the chaos stopped. It must be some secret code among 3rd graders. She would have to remember it; might come in handy later.

"Now listen up everybody. We have a busy day today full of lots of interesting things. I need everyone to stay with your adult and stay together." Olivia gave Savanna a wink of encouragement. "We will start at the Estuarium. Listen closely to the guides. I don't want to call any parents and tell them their child was eaten by a gator." The bus erupted with laughter, and the boys began shoving each other in the shoulders, inferring someone besides themselves would be the gator snack.

Olivia continued her lecture. "When we go into the art gallery remember your good manners: no hands, only eyes on the paintings." She caught someone's smirk. "No, that does not mean to put your eyeball on the paintings" She pointed at the little boy to her left. "Then we will end the day at the caboose. Who remembers what is there?" Hands went up in the air and butts started jumping out of their seats. She pointed to a small boy in the middle of the bus.

A small voice answered, "The Underground Railroad Museum."

"That's right. Ms. Leesa, the director, has some great activities for you to do. Remember to always raise your hands to answer questions. You will not be noticed if you don't use your classroom manners." She looked through the windshield to check where the bus was on Main Street. As it took a right turn, she leaned into her seat back. "When the bus stops, I want everyone to keep their seats, please." The bus pulled up in front of a green park right on the river and stopped. The dull roar began again as necks stretched to look out the windows on the right side of the bus.

Olivia motioned for Savanna to come to the front of the bus. Savanna grabbed Charlie's hand and obliged. She didn't appreciate the looks he was getting from his classmates but now was not the time. She probably should flash them her badge and scare the shit out all of them, but she wouldn't for Charlie's sake. It was rough on him, not having parents to do stuff with him, much less a busy sister who wasn't good at parenting. He tried to stay under the radar since their parents passed. The twenty-something-year age difference came in handy on days like today when he needed an adult though. Not that she was a good example, but she would try to make a good imitation of one today. How did they teach her to deal with her anxiety: compartmentalize and make a task list? She could do it.

The teacher parked Savanna in the middle of the green grass of Festival Park and then sent a line of boys towards their human marker. The group wasn't a bad lot, a typical group of 8-year-old boys who had been on a bus for 3 hours. No wonder they couldn't stand still. The trip from Raleigh would have gone faster in her car, but she was a chaperone and apparently, the bus ride was one of the job requirements.

Now it was time for assignment number one. "Make sure all kids in your group make it out of the Estuarium with all fingers and toes and without torturing any animals."

Let's see. She crossed her own fingers and toes in hopes she could keep them all alive.

Two hours later, they all survived and were lined up on the green again. The headcount was proof no one was eaten by the gators. The boys still had eyes the size of saucers from the amazement of the alligator feeding. Nothing like blood and guts to get the attention of a boy. *Maybe I can do this chaperone thing.*

On to the assignment number two. "Make sure all charges keep hands in pockets during the art gallery tour, all writing utensils and other implements of destruction are confiscated before entering the building. Ensure all charges are present and accounted for at all times." This one may be a little more difficult. *Although they are still in awe, maybe they'd stay subdued.* Savanna was at the end of the line as they crossed the street to the old house. A sign swung back and forth out front, declaring it a fine art gallery. It simply looked like an old house to Savanna. Charlie stayed close to her side, but she had to grab a couple of the boys to push them toward the door. As they stepped inside, her opinion changed. It was simple and elegant, and the paintings on the walls were fantastic. Charlie instantly left her side, the art pulling him to look closer.

A lady with brown hair stepped out of the back of the house and began speaking. "Thank you for coming and visiting my home and gallery. My name is Beth Pearse. I have a lot to share with you, and if you listen closely, I'm sure you will all get an A on the test at the end of the tour."

There were groans from the group. A smile lit up Beth's face. "I'm kidding, there isn't a test." Cheers erupted from the group with a few fist pumps. "But there *are* some interesting stories about my house. Let's start in the kitchen. Follow me, please." Savanna brought up the rear of the group, the young men acting like it was torture to walk into the next room.

Beth started again, "When we were fixing the house so I could move in, we found a treasure." Heads snapped to attention, and all faces were now facing the guide. There were a few whispers in the crowd. Boy, Beth sure knows how to get a tough crowd's attention. "Who wants to guess what we found?" There were a few who couldn't hold their excitement, shouting out their answers.

"Pirates' gold."

"Diamonds."

"Necklaces."

"Boys remember our manners," the teacher reminded. A few hands popped up in the group, bouncing with excitement.

"Young man in the blue shirt." Beth pointed to Charlie.

Charlie quickly put his hand down, and Savanna squeezed his shoulder with encouragement. "Blackbeard's treasure," he answered waiting for Beth's approval, his nervousness tensing every muscle in his body.

"Not quite, I wish it was the case. This would be a very different museum if I found Blackbeard's treasure." Beth gave him a warm smile, and Savanna felt the tension leave his muscles. "Sometimes, treasure is not money or jewelry. It tells something valuable about who we are and what happened in the past. And that is the kind of treasure we found. The floor in this room had a secret to share, and when we uncovered it, we traveled back in time." Beth stepped to her right revealing a special part of the floor. There was a thick clear piece of plastic covering a hole in the floor. "I want each of you to walk past the opening and look very carefully down the hole. What do you see?" Beth started with the first boy pointing down into the hole. She whispered, "What do you see?"

Savanna watched the little boy squint down the cellar hole, trying to see what the correct answer was. Savanna peered down the hole. Dim lights lit baskets of tools and fabric, leaving lots of shadows to play with the children's imaginations. They each had a look and walked into the big front room. The wall was covered in what Savanna recognized as very expensive classic art.

"We have lots of different styles of art here on the walls," Beth pointed to a couple. "First, I want everyone to stand in front of their favorite painting." Charlie grabbed Savanna's hand and pulled her to an abstract painting in primary colors.

"You like this one?" Savanna looked down at Charlie nodding his head. "I like this one, too. Very colorful." A smile spread across his lips.

There was a group of boys shoving to fit in front of an impressionistic oil, one similar to those you see in fancy museums. Beth continued talking to the group.

"You see, with art there is no right answer. I want you to think about what you saw in the cellar. Think really hard. I'm going to give you a piece of paper." She passed out a sheet of paper to each boy, "This is for you and only you, so there is no right answer. I want everyone to sit down on the floor where you are standing." Boys plopped down where they stood. "There are boxes of pencils and crayons on the floor next to your painting." Savanna looked behind her and Charlie, and there was a box she hadn't noticed before. She pulled it closer to them and opened the box. "I want you to draw what you saw in the cellar." An excitement hummed in the air around the room. "Raise your hand if there is a color you need that's not in your box."

Charlie's hand went up instantly. "What color do you need sweetie?" Beth asked.

"Brown," he answered quickly. Beth handed him a brown crayon, and he went to work covering his piece of paper.

"Is this a good idea?" Savanna asked Beth. "You aren't afraid the art project will stray to the real ones on the wall?" Beth winked at Savanna, bending down to take a look at Charlie's work.

"It will be fine. I promise you. Look at them." Savanna looked around the room. Boys were busy, focused on their own paper. No one was talking to or teasing the boy next to them.

"But we were told to not let them have anything they could write with." Savanna was frustrated, she was failing at her number two assignment. She wasn't used to failing at her objectives.

Beth smiled. "They will not hurt the floor." She stood up, and Savanna watched her walk through the room weaving in between the boys. Savanna watched her comment on one or two as she worked the room. *She is good with kids,* Savanna thought. *I could never do this on a regular basis.* Her hands were sweaty just thinking of the mayhem to come on the bus back to Raleigh.

Savanna glanced down at Charlie, his tongue sticking out at the corner of his mouth as he concentrated on his masterpiece. *He was enjoying this. It had been so long since he was happy.* Savanna wished she could take away his hurt. He had so much before his eighth birthday. Life wasn't fair. She wasn't a good replacement for their parents, not even close. Work pulled her away too much. Her mind drifted, *I need to call and check on Max. He probably doesn't know what to do without me.* Wrinkles set in between her brows, thinking of the dog who never left her side. *One day off wouldn't hurt him.* A pair of shoes beside them brought Savanna back to the room.

"What do we have here?" Beth dropped to her knees, and Savanna focused on Charlie's drawing. "This is very good. And this is what you saw in the cellar?"

Charlie nodded his head, not speaking. Savanna nudged him. "It's ok to use your inside voice, Charlie." She looked at the careful detail of a face. It was an African-American woman with dark, sad eyes. Her head was wrapped in a scarf. Savanna was surprised at an expression of recognition that crossed Beth's face.

"You are a very special boy," Beth whispered close enough for only Savanna and Charlie to hear. "This is my friend, Selah. She visits occasionally, but most people miss her."

Savanna looked at Beth with confusion. She didn't see anyone in the cellar. Beth gave her a knowing smile and rubbed the top of Charlie's head. She stood up and said, "Okay everyone, clean up your supplies. Please put everything back in the box you found them in. Your drawings are yours to keep. Thank you for coming for a visit. I enjoyed having such well-behaved students."

Charlie's teacher took over, and the boys lined up, ready to return to the bus. "We will take our art back to the bus. Then we will walk down the sidewalk to the other end of the waterfront. Our bus will meet us down there."

They walked across the street to the park and boarded the bus. "Make sure you neatly place your art on your seat and then meet me back down here." The boys quickly rejoined the teacher and Savanna.

Savanna's headcount showed a surplus. How could we suddenly have too many kids? Her pulse quickened as she recounted. There were too many. She looked at Olivia and then the faces of each of the children. Who didn't belong? A blond woman crossed the green from the playground, yelling something.

"Phillipe, Jeane.

Phillipe, Jeane. Viens ici vous deux. Pourquoi vous ne venez pas quand j'ai appelé? »

Savanna had no idea what she said, but it looked like the two boys were in trouble. She ran right into the middle of the group and grabbed two boys with hair matching hers. Glancing at Savanna, she apologized in English with a heavy accent and dragged the boys back to the pirate ship jungle gym.

Disaster averted. Savanna took a deep breath and counted the group again. She gave Olivia a thumbs up, and they started the walk down the sidewalk along the waterfront. One boy ran his fingers along the metal railing, and then the others followed. Savanna was surprised someone didn't find a stick so there would be noise involved.

The sunlight sparkled off the river, warming Savanna's face. This was a very different day from the last time she was here. She looked at the boats tied in slips like her parents' when she arrived to claim what was left in the vessel. Only, the things she wanted weren't there, and there was no sign of them to be found even until this day. She had retrieved her mother's cell phone on the table in the galley. A tear threatened to release at the memories, but she brought herself back to the present.

Oh, I spoke too soon. Someone found a stick. Great. Too bad the peacefulness was now gone. Savanna was thankful for the clatter breaking her from the memory. The five-minute walk took about ten, and they crossed the street to another park with a caboose on the far end.

Olivia's fingers went into the air. "Everyone, take a seat on the grass, please, and I will pass out lunches. Savanna, if you will pass out the drink boxes." She handed two plastic bags to Savanna and grabbed the box the bus driver dropped onto the lawn. As Savanna passed out a few boxes, a tall blond officer walked up to the group. Savanna, suddenly self-conscience, ran her fingers through her hair. She knew she looked windblown and tired. The five a.m. start to the day and the open bus windows had taken their toll. His slow saunter only emphasized his height and the boys' eyes got larger and larger as he got closer.

"Well, well, well. What do we have here? I hope you haven't come to town to cause trouble." His whole face smiled, wrinkling the corners of his eyes. The boys quickly shook their heads back and forth. Savanna felt his gaze move up and down her body. She couldn't help but blush. She tried to busy herself passing out the drinks, hoping he didn't notice her red face. His eyes didn't leave her as he asked the group, "Where are y'all from?"

Hands shot up in the air. *Now, they remember their manners,* Savanna thought laughing to herself. *They are probably afraid he will take them to jail.* The handsome man pointed to one of the wigglers on the lawn.

"Raleigh."

"Wow, you guys are from the city? You look like a bunch of city boys. You having fun today?" He looked like he was enjoying himself, Savanna thought.

Hands shot up again, and he pointed to another boy. "Yes, sir."

"Well, stay out of trouble and don't give Ms. Leesa at the museum a hard time this afternoon. She has me on speed dial." He looked at Savanna. "Maybe I'll see you later."

For some reason, the comment made her tongue-tied, and she only nodded at him.

"If anyone needs me, I'm Deputy Whitaker." He waved at the group and strolled down the street and around the corner.

Savanna let out the breath she didn't know she was holding. Olivia came over and nudged her, "You okay? I thought, he was going to ask for your number right in front of the whole group."

"Stop it. He was not. He was just friendly to the boys, that's all." The heat in her face was finally fading, and she took a long sip of her juice box before letting out a sigh.

CHAPTER 6

ACTIVE ALERT

The muddy liquid slowly disappeared down the drain as he tipped his mug into the sink. The sludge resulted from the overheated burned monstrosity that was day-old coffee since no one else in the office made any. He poured the contents of the carafe down the same drain. Putting on a fresh pot, he thought about the pretty red-headed teacher he saw at the museum. *I would have loved school if my teacher looked like that.* He crossed the sheriff's office and took a seat behind his desk. *If Leesa is doing her school presentation, I have a couple of hours before they finish up. I'll swing by then and see if I can get a name.* He looked at the pile of paperwork on his desk. He had better get started if he is going to have some free time later.

"Whitaker!" The sheriff's voice emerged from his corner office.

"Yes, sir."

"Come in here please."

Tim rose from his seat, dreading the conversation he was about to have. The cases he was working at the moment had huge holes, and he was grasping at straws. He squared his shoulders, walked over to his boss's office and stuck his head in the room. "You needed me, sir?" Tim waited for the onslaught he knew was coming.

"Where are we on the Felton case, Whitaker?"

"No new developments. We are still looking for the person of interest. The so-called 'Robert.' We don't have a positive ID yet. The media has been cooperative. "

"Have you touched base with the marina?"

"Yes, they are pulling all the records for the boat he is using. The billing went to Pearse Enterprises in Colorado. I will make some phone calls as soon as I get the contact information."

"Any ideas of his location?" the sheriff continued to grill.

"No, there has been no response to our first release of the photo."

"Release it again. Now, where are we on the Pearse kidnapping? You have really botched this one."

Here it comes, Tim thought to himself. "The suspect's lawyer has requested a psych evaluation. Bill will not tell us the exact location where he kept Ms. Pearse. Ms. Pearse doesn't remember where she was detained. From where she was rescued in the water, it looks like it was on Castle Island or on the far bank of the river."

"For God's sake, get some dogs and start searching. Without that evidence, our whole case is based on the recognition of a voice and the rantings of a crazy man."

Of course, it didn't help the prime suspect was a beloved deputy in town. Tim still couldn't wrap his head around the man who had admitted to the kidnapping, one of his childhood friends. "Who should I call to acquire the loaner dogs, sir?"

"Get with Captain Banks in Raleigh. They have a great K-9 team. Probably save you some time you don't have."

"Okay, I'll get right on it." Tim stood in the doorway for any further direction.

"Now, Whitaker," the sheriff yelled. "Before we get another big rain and your evidence ends up in the Sound."

Tim pulled out his cell and called the Raleigh Police Department. So much for his free afternoon.

The call rang through to the Sergeant's desk, and he waited patiently for them to track down the Captain. He stood in the hallway on hold listening to how important his call was to them and the Sheriff's phone rang. He wasn't really eavesdropping. Just being observant.

"Really? Now? Okay, I'll get him over there." The receiver cluncked onto the phone, and a loud clap made Tim jump.

"Whitaker. Whitaker, get in here."

"I'm on hold" Tim yelled from the hall.

"Come and see me as soon as you finish. There's been a development."

Tim paced. The music went silent. "Captain Banks here."

"Hello, sir. I'm Tim Whitaker from the Washington Sherriff's Department, and the sheriff asked me to give you a call."

"How is Ray doing?"

"He's doing well, sir. We are in need of a search dog team, one specializing in forensic searches preferably."

"I have the perfect team, and she will do a great job for you. I'll have her there tomorrow morning first thing. Make sure you tell ole Ray to stay out of trouble."

"Yes, sir. Thank you, sir." Tim hung up the phone and stepped into his boss' office. "Sir," Tim paused as the sheriff made some notes on his desk calendar. "Sir, the dog team will be here in the morning, and the Captain said to stay out of trouble."

"Phillip better heed his own advice. Sit down, Tim." Tim took a seat. "Our kidnapping suspect has decided he's ready to talk this afternoon. He will only talk to you, so you need to get yourself over there before he changes his mind. His lawyer is just in from Raleigh, so he has representation. He's got a good one, so don't screw this up; keep it strictly by the book."

"Yes, sir. Anything else?"

"Nope. Get over there and get this thing solved. We don't need this hanging over us during the festival."

"I'll give it a shot." Tim stood up and stepped to the doorway. "I won't let you down sir."

"Your career depends on it."

Tim knew he was right. He had to solve this case, as soon as possible.

THE DARK HALLWAY leading to the meeting room created shadows that played with Tim's head. Bill's lawyer stood outside the door waiting. Tim approached the finely dressed African American man taking his outstretched hand.

"Mr. Whitaker, I'm Mr. Felton's lawyer, Mr. Fredrick Brown." He shook Tim's hand, introducing himself. "Just so you know, this meeting is against my advice. He wanted to speak to you by himself. I will be watching closely. My client is clearly unstable, and any type of confession will not be admissible. He feels comfortable talking to you, and I'm afraid it will be his downfall, but he is threatening to hurt himself if he does not talk to you. Tread lightly."

"Will do."

Tim stepped into the meeting room. The white paint on the walls showed yellowing. The room wasn't used often, but it was a necessary evil. Tim had his notepad and his file on the case. It didn't contain much. Beth Pearse's interview about the days she was gone. A picture of a man on a boat in dock at the marina. Maybe Bill would finally fill in the blanks.

The heavy door pushed open, and an officer escorted Bill in to have a seat at the table in front of Tim. His childhood buddy didn't look like himself. The orange jumpsuit was wrinkled, and the beard he was growing for a community play had grown too long and ragged. His hair was mussed. Dark circles under his eyes made him look like he hadn't slept in days. He shuffled to his seat. The officer uncuffed one hand and attached the cuff to the ring on the top of the table. Bill didn't look at Tim and plopped into the seat with a humph.

Tim looked at the one-way mirror, knowing the defense lawyer was behind the one-way glass.

"Bill, how are you today?" He paused waiting for an answer, but nothing came. "I heard you wanted to talk to me. What did you want to talk about?"

"I need to warn you," a small voice emerged from the large man.

Tim swallowed his surprise at how small and feeble Bill's voice sounded. "Can I ask you some questions first?"

"Okay, then I can tell you about the evil one."

Tim shuffled his papers, clicked the top of his ink pen, and looked at Bill. "I need you to focus. Tell me about Beth Pearse."

"Who is that? Do you have a picture of her?"

"Now Bill, I've known you for a long time and I know when you are not telling the truth. I need you to be honest with me. You know who Beth Pearse is, don't you?"

Bill let out a shaky laugh. A smile spread across his face. "Maybe."

"We are not playing games here. I'm trying to find out what happened to Beth and I think you can help me." Tim shifted in his chair. "Bill, I'm going to let you in on a secret."

"What's that?" Bill's eyes stared into Tim's, finally making eye contact.

"When I ask you a question, I already know the answer. So, I know if you are telling the truth. You will be better off if you tell me the truth the first time."

Bill's eyes turned back to his hands. His free hand flew to his mouth, and he started to nibble. Tim noticed his nails had been bitten off to the quick.

"Now, can we start again? Do you know who Beth Pearse is?"

Bill nodded his head.

"Okay, how do you know her?"

"We were dating. Very sweet girl."

"Really? And how long was that going on?"

"About a month."

"Bill, tell me about those dates."

"We would have coffee on the waterfront. Except she likes tea with honey. She doesn't drink coffee."

Tim tapped the tip of his pen against his notepad. "Okay, what else did you guys do together?"

"She likes to jog in the early morning."

"So, you would run together?" Tim's eyebrow rose; he knew his friend wasn't a runner.

Bill's gaze stayed fully focused on the table. "Well, no. She would run, and I was there for support."

"What else did you do together?"

"She likes to walk on the waterfront late at night."

"And you did that together?"

"Well… Not exactly."

"And what does that mean?"

"We didn't walk together. But she knew I was there. She looked so beautiful, the moon shining on her face as she looked out on the river." A sick smile spread across his face.

Goosebumps rose on Tim's skin. "Bill, did you know that she was seeing someone else?"

Bill's shoulders fell. "We never mentioned being exclusive. I didn't say she was my girlfriend."

"In fact, Bill, she has never been on a date with you. Isn't that true?"

"No that's not true. She's mine." Tears started to roll down his cheeks, shaking his head. "She's mine. He can't have her. She's mine."

"Bill, listen to me. She is not yours. She is dating our friend, Sam. Bill, look at me."

The man sitting across from him slowly lifted his head to look Tim in the eyes. The eyes making contact with his were empty like his friend was missing.

"She is dating Sam. You know that, don't you?"

He shook his head again. "She's mine."

"If she is yours, explain to me why you took her. Last time we talked, you said you took her from her house on Water Street. Why would you do that?"

"I needed to show her how much I love her. I could be her hero. I rescued her from the water, and she should love me too."

"But you didn't rescue her, did you? You left her there to drown."

"I would have gone back. I didn't just leave her. That bastard kidnapped me. Took me so I couldn't save her. He wanted her all to himself."

"Who kidnapped you?"

"You know, the guy working in the hardware store. I went to ask him some questions about him being at the college the night Sam's office was vandalized. Some of the students said he was hanging out around the building the office was in and I wanted to ask him about it."

"What day was that?"

"I don't know. It was the same night as the council meeting. I was supposed to talk to Sam afterward, but I got a text message Robert was at the hardware store by himself. I drove over to ask him some questions."

"Then what happened?"

Bill rubbed his beard with his free hand, "He told me we could talk in the back room, so I followed him back to the storage room. He told me to grab a seat. I grabbed one of the folding chairs, and when I unfolded the chair, I guess I turned my back on him, and he hit me in the head with something. The next thing I knew I was in my shed."

"How many days were you in the shed?"

"I don't know. You could ask Sam. He's the one that found me. You were at his house, remember?"

"I do remember."

Tim made a few notes on his pad. Bill had stuck his chewed fingers back in his mouth and had started gnawing on them again staring into the far corner.

"Bill, look at me. I need you to tell me why you went to the hardware store by yourself? I didn't ask you to go there. Why would you go by yourself?"

A loud crunch of his nail and a sigh started Bill's answer. "Do you know what it's like to tell the girl you love you are banished to desk duty? No, of course, you don't. You are the perfect Tim; ready to be sheriff. Doesn't take time off, doesn't make mistakes. Well, you can't crack this one, can you, golden boy? Robert is long gone. Just because you listened to Sam. It's not the first time you've kept a secret for him. Keep listening to Sam, and you won't have a career."

Tim's gaze drifted from Bill's wild eyes filled with contempt and saw the blood running down his hand, making its way down his wrist. Tim stood up and knocked on the door. A guard instantly answered and opened the door.

"The prisoner needs first aid."

The guard entered the room and grabbed Bill's arm to look at his hand. "I will bring the medic. Stay here."

Tim nodded and watched Bill as he jerked his hand from the guard, whipping it through the air. Droplets of blood splattered the floor. The guard was already on his radio when he opened the door to retrieve the medic. Tim walked over to the one-way mirror. He wanted to make sure someone was observing. Bill was clearly not feeling friendly toward him. He gave the glass a quick knock, and there was a returning tap. He let out a breath he didn't know he was holding. Bill's lawyer was still there.

CHARLIE'S small hand slipped into Savanna's. The afternoon had been packed full of fun for the boys. The staff at the museum kept them busy, and now they were out on the lawn. Charlie looked up at her, his eyes sparkling. He was having a ball. He even stepped out of his comfort zone and had left her side for a while, laughing and joking with his classmates. Savanna looked over at his teacher who seemed to be thrilled with his progress as well. He turned loose of her hand and walked over to a group of boys. They were all checking out a new game one of them had. Savanna watched him squeeze in between two other boys. Then it happened. There was a shove, and another, and someone hit the ground. Tears started to roll. There was laughter, and tears grew worse.

Savanna was suddenly overwhelmed by the whole situation. Her breath quickened. Her first instinct was to rush in and apprehend suspects. *This is not the place, Savanna,* she told herself, taking a step backward to reinforce her thoughts.

Charlie's teacher rushed to the group, quickly taking control. Everyone sat down in a circle at her command, so she could check for injuries. Savanna slowly took four deep breaths letting them out nice and slow each time. She had done so well all day. She concentrated on the sound of the air, instead of the voices and yelling happening on the lawn. As her panic subsided, Savanna refocused and scanned the group for Charlie. She looked at each of the boys in the group, but he wasn't there. She looked around, her panic rising again.

Where could he have gone? Savanna checked inside the caboose, and it was empty. The staff was on the lawn with the boys. He couldn't have gone far. It was only a couple of minutes. Savanna headed across the lawn, stopping to whisper in the teacher's ear. "Charlie's disappeared."

Olivia checked her watch. "We have five minutes to check the immediate area. Then we call the police," she explained the policy.

"He has to be close. He probably got spooked by the shoving."

The teacher nodded. "Your time is ticking." She tapped her watch, counting the rest of the boys to make sure everyone else was accounted for.

Savanna felt out of control. If only Max were here. She scanned the old, brick warehouses surrounding the harbor area. He was small and could be hiding anywhere. He tended to like confined spaces when he was upset. She pulled out her cell and pulled up her favorite contacts. As she pushed the button, bile rose in the back of her throat. Her parents' picture popped on the screen as the phone dialed her mom's old number.

Come on, come on, pick up, pick up. No answer. She shook her head as it went to voicemail, her mother's voice requesting a message. She checked for traffic on the street in front of her. *Of course, he wouldn't pick up. He wasn't allowed to have his phone on the school trip. It was back in the car at the school. Now, what should she do?*

She crossed the street and spotted an older couple. *Maybe they saw him run by.*

"Excuse me." She grabbed the older man's elbow. "Have you seen a small boy? He was playing in the park, and now he's run off."

"No, we haven't seen him. What was he wearing?"

"He has red hair like mine, and he was wearing..." Savanna struggled to remember what Charlie was wearing. She couldn't for the life of her remember. "I'm sorry, I can't remember." A tear trickled down her cheek, and her lungs started to constrict. "Keep your eyes open, will you?"

The woman with silver hair nodded, and Savanna could see pity in her gaze. She smiled at her and looked past them down the street. There were more people further down. Savanna ran to ask them the same question. Then out of the corner of her eye, she saw movement down a dark alleyway.

THE GUARD RETURNED with the medic and Tim grabbed his folder and stepped out into the hallway for a breather. Mr. Brown met him in the hall, and he didn't look too pleased.

"It would seem you have made your case, Deputy Whitaker."

"There are still a lot of questions to be answered. Can you make sure he gets the psychiatric care he needs? The stress has affected him. I won't go further until he is more like himself."

"Will do. I've already applied to have him transferred to the mental health facility. They will do an evaluation and make suggestions."

"Good." Tim shook his hand, and his radio at his shoulder blared. "Whitaker, come in, please."

"This is Whitaker, go ahead Mae."

"Whitaker, we have a code Adam at the Underground Railroad Museum. Teacher says they are at 10 minutes. Hurry."

"Do we have a description?"

"4 ft, red hair, blue eyes, blue jeans, and red t-shirt."

"Thanks, on my way." He turned to Mr. Brown. "Gotta go."

"Absolutely. I'll see you again soon."

"Most likely."

CHARLIE PEEKED from around the dumpster full of wood. "Oh, man. Oh man," he whispered. He pressed his fist against his chest. He couldn't see through the tears in his eyes. This wasn't a good spot to hide. A large boom echoed through his metal alcove, causing him to jump. He needed to move. Across the next street, there was a building with no cars close.

Waiting for the workers to go back in the construction zone, Charlie made a run for the large white building. He was careful to stay out of sight. He couldn't let them send him back. The tears were falling harder now, taking his breath and shaking his body. He turned down the alleyway looking for an open door, or a cubby would be even better. He used his sleeve to wipe the tears and snot from his face.

As his eyes cleared, Charlie spotted a ground level window with no glass and climbed in. The space was dark and smelled funky. Now since he was concealed from the world, his crying became sobs. He was a big boy, he shouldn't be crying like this, but he didn't want to leave Savanna. She was the only one left. He gave his face another swipe and started drawing with his finger in the dirt floor under his feet in the only patch of light in his haven.

Charlie hiccupped, and a shadow covered his sketch. A large black hand reached through the opening followed by a smiling face.

"Hey there, young master, what's wrong?" The black man talked funny, but Charlie knew he shouldn't say anything.

"I'm in trouble." Charlie also knew he shouldn't talk to strangers, but he looked friendly.

"What happened? Maybe there is something I can help with."

Charlie shook his head, "Nope, I'll be sent back for sure now."

"I'm a conductor. I help people get where they're headed. Why don't you tell me what happened, and we'll figure it out?" He motioned again with his large hand offering it to Charlie. "I'm Abram."

Charlie grabbed it, shaking it, and then used it to pull against to step out of the crawlspace. "I'm Charlie. One of the boys in my school group got pushed down, and it's my fault." He wiped his face with his sleeve. "I ran away, and now my sister will send me back."

"Young Charlie, even though I don't know your sister, I can't imagine she would do that. She is probably out here lookin' for you." His hiccups slowed as Abram talked. "What else happened today?"

"We saw alligators, then we went to the gallery and saw Miss Selah in the cellar. Then we walked down to Ms. Leesa's museum." Charlie looked away from the man he was talking to, and a rock caught his eye. He poked at it sending it from the crumbling edge of the wall to the rocky sidewalk.

Abram stepped toward Charlie and grabbed his shoulder. "Charlie, who was in the cellar?"

Charlie shrugged off the hand and kept on talking. "Hey, are you one of those conductors like Miss Leesa was talking about?" A shadow walked past the end of the alley interrupting the conversation.

"Charlie," Savanna yelled, her voice sounding funny. Was she angry? "Charlie, Come on out bud. It's okay." She paused a minute and walked a little farther into the shadows of the tall buildings. "Charlie, is that you?"

Charlie froze and stepped back toward the hole in the wall. Abram stepped out of the shadows, and Charlie grabbed his hand, pulling him back toward the wall. Savanna was here to take him back to the Services. His hand started to tremble in Abram's huge palm.

"Charlie, come here please." Her voice seemed huge echoing in the empty space.

"Go on Charlie, you don't want to get a whuppin'." Abram's deep voice filled the alleyway.

The little boy nodded his head, turned and continued toward his sister.

"Charlie, you know you're not supposed to talk to strangers."

He nodded his head. "That's Abram. He found me." Charlie looked at his sister out of breath and face red. "Am I in trouble?"

She made a funny face at him. "Maybe a little."

Savanna felt the man's eyes on her back as she grabbed Charlie's hand and they walked back toward the museum. Her anxiety started to decrease with every step they took closer to their group on the grass. She waved to the teacher, then pointed down to Charlie giving a thumbs up.

One of the reenactors ran to Charlie shifting her skirts out of the way, embracing him in a huge hug. "We are so glad you are safe," her face showed genuine concern. "Where did you go?"

"Over there," Charlie pointed across the park toward the warehouses.

Savanna glanced over her shoulder wondering if Abram was going to return to the museum before they left. She needed to thank him for keeping Charlie safe. He must have been on a break and come across Charlie in the alleyway. That would explain his wardrobe. Thank goodness, he was close by.

"Savanna, I'm afraid I called the police before you got back with Charlie. They are very strict with us you know. I'll call them back."

"Thanks, I'll watch for the responder." Savanna scanned the street adjacent to the park. While she was waiting for the police, she flagged down Ms. Leesa. "I wanted to thank one of your volunteers for finding Charlie. Charlie said his name was Abram. I'm afraid in my panic I forgot to thank him when I rushed Charlie back to the park.

"Abram? I'm afraid I don't have any volunteers by that name. Why would you think he was working here, honey?"

"He was dressed in old cotton clothes. Looked like some of the other men working in the museum. Maybe Charlie got his name wrong. He was very tall and muscular. He had a white cotton shirt and tan canvas pants rolled up to mid-shin. I couldn't see really well in the alley, but he might have been bald. Very large hands."

"Sounds like he would make a great reenactor, but I don't recognize him. If I see him around, I will make sure to thank him. Maybe he is here for the festival this weekend."

"Maybe so." Savanna saw the sheriff's department car pull up and excused herself, thanking her again for the wonderful afternoon. She walked closer to the car and blushed when Deputy Whitaker stepped out. Suddenly self-conscience, the greeting she'd planned wouldn't leave her mouth. Great, this is going to make a great impression. Every muscle in the deputy's face was tight including his full lips. He did not look happy.

"Deputy Whitaker, I am so sorry for your trouble. Thanks for getting here so quickly but we found him."

He relaxed, and a smile crossed his face. "Glad to hear it. I'll have to get a few details from you. What was the student's name?"

"Charlie McCormick," she responded.

"Age?"

"8."

"Have the parents been notified?" he asked looking down at her.

"I suppose. Technically."

He stopped writing looking down at her. "What do you mean?"

"I'm his guardian. He's my brother. So, I was aware he was missing."

A sandy brown eyebrow went up. "So, you teach your own brother?"

"Oh," Savanna shook her head and laughed, "I'm not a teacher. I'm chaperoning."

He nodded and continued to write in his notebook. "Where did you find him?"

"I found him in an alley a few blocks away. He was with a man-- Abram was his name according to Charlie."

"Do you think I could talk to Charlie really quick?" Deputy Whitaker asked.

"Of course, but I don't know how helpful he will be. He's not very talkative usually."

The deputy nodded and followed Savanna over to the group of students. Their teacher had them in a circle talking about the day and what they had learned. Savanna caught Charlie's eye and motioned to him to stand up and join her and the officer. He quickly stood up but slowly walked toward the two of them, his head bowed low. Deputy Whitaker squatted down as Charlie arrived in earshot.

"Hey Charlie, how's your day been? "

Charlie raised his eyes to look at the deputy. "Okay, I guess. I know I was bad. Sorry."

Deputy Whitaker ruffled his ginger hair. "No worries. Are you hurt anywhere?"

"No."

"You want to tell me what happened?"

"Sure..." Charlie's eyed him while looking over the officer's shoulder. "Where's your dog?"

"I don't have a dog. But most people don't bring their dogs to work, do they?" The deputy looked at Savanna.

"Savanna gets to. Why don't you?" Charlie looked at him waiting for the answer.

"I guess she's lucky then." The deputy smiled.

"I guess so. Max goes everywhere with her."

"Sounds like Max is the lucky one." He gave Savanna a wink. Heat flooded her face.

Was he flirting in front of the kid? Savanna wasn't sure.

"Yeah, he didn't get to come today because we rode on the school bus."

"I see, why don't you tell me why you left the group today, Charlie?"

"Billy had his new game, and I wanted to watch him. It was really crowded, and I couldn't see." Charlie looked like he was unsure if he should continue the story. He looked up at Savanna, and she could see the fear in his eyes. "I tried to squeeze in, so I could see, and someone pushed me back. So, I pushed a little harder, and Taylor fell on the ground and started crying. I knew I was in trouble. Savanna, I didn't want you to send me back. I'm sorry I was bad. This was our first trip, and I thought you might not want me anymore if I'm bad, now Mom and Dad are gone."

The deputy looked uncomfortable with the family business unfolding in front of him, but Savanna couldn't worry about it. She had to take care of Charlie.

"Oh, my God, Charlie. I will always want you. This was an accident. Everyone is fine." She gave Charlie a tight hug. "I'm so glad I came today. If Max were here, he would have found you even faster, and Deputy Whitaker wouldn't have to type up his report."

"Oh, don't worry about it, Miss McCormick. You can call me Tim if you want. I'm glad he's safe." A genuine smile crossed his full lips, the emotion showing in the creases at the corners. "I'm going to have to meet the famous Max someday. He sounds like a superhero."

"He is." Charlie nodded his head in agreement the fear and worry leaving his face for the moment. "A real superhero, not like in the movies."

Deputy Whitaker laughed. "I see. Now, I will definitely have to meet him. When are you guys coming back to Washington?" The question was obviously for Savanna as he looked into her eyes. "We are getting ready to have the big BBQ cook-off this weekend. You should come and bring Max."

"Can we, Savanna? Can we? Can we?" Charlie was bouncing up and down, begging.

"We'll see," she responded, and his face fell.

"What's wrong, buddy?" Tim asked Charlie.

"I know what that means. She will be too busy with work, and we won't be able to come."

"She works a lot, huh?" Tim asked him. He was smiling at her now.

She mentally prayed Charlie wouldn't tell him she was a cop. Guys don't like cops, and this guy's cute, plus he seemed interested.

"How about you guys come as my guests and then we will make it a date? That way you have to come."

Charlie grinned returned and widened. "Come on Savanna. Please? We will be Tim's guests. It will be cool."

"But what if Max doesn't like the crowds?" Savanna asked, giving Tim an out if he wanted it.

"Oh, please." Charlie stretched out the syllables, trying to act cool in front of his new friend. "Max will love it."

"Ms. McCormick," Tim interrupted.

"Savanna. You can call me Savanna, since we," she looked down at Charlie, "have decided to call you Tim."

He nodded, "Savanna, I have one more question for you before we wrap up the paperwork information. I need your name and phone number in case we have any more questions."

"Sure,"

He bent down and whispered something in Charlie's ear. Charlie nodded obviously answering some secret question. "And would you mind if I use this information for personal use?"

Charlie giggled.

"Apparently, it has already been decided." She looked down at her brother. This was clearly a set-up. She wasn't used to being ganged up on. She rattled off her information as he scribbled it down.

"May I call you this evening?" He gave her his best southern drawl.

"Don't even pretend this is honorable." She pointed her finger at Charlie and then at Tim. They both broke out in laughter, and then Tim shrugged.

"What?" He asked, pretending to be ignorant of what she was inferring?

Savanna looked past Tim and saw Charlie's teacher waving. "Okay guys, this has been fun, but it's time to head back to Raleigh. It's a long ride, and we don't want to hold everyone up." Charlie groaned. Savanna put her hand on his head and ruffled his hair. She gave Tim a quick smile and directed Charlie with her hand toward the bus. Tim headed back to his car and Savanna watched him slide into the cruiser, his thigh muscles straining against the fabric of his khaki uniform. He was one handsome man.

"Savanna, can we please come on our date?" Charlie asked again.

"I have a feeling we will see Mr. Tim again very soon."

CHAPTER 7

DOWN DRAFT

Another bump sent the kids flying in the air like popcorn, squeals filling the already noisy bus. Savanna would be so glad to make it home. Olivia turned and smiled at her from the front seat as a burger wrapper flew past her face, barely missing her nose. Savanna wondered how the other woman did this for a living, thanking God she was Charlie's teacher and now a close friend. The chime on Savanna's cell rang. She barely heard it over the roar of the bus, but she picked it up and saw his message.

Tim: It was good to meet you today. I'm really hoping you will come this weekend.

Savanna: I'm honestly going to try. Charlie wants to come.

Tim: Good, have a safe trip, there is a storm rolling in.

Savanna: I'm not surprised, it's rained so much. Savanna knew he was probably busy, and she was chatting too much. She tapped out *I'll let you go* and hit send.

Tim: You are totally right. It needs to stop so I can get some fishing in.

She looked over at Charlie on the seat next to her. He was

listening to his iPod, sucking down his soda from dinner, and staring out the window. He had spoken more today than in the last month, especially with Tim.

Savanna: So, you fish?

Tim: Yes, doesn't everyone?

Savanna: No, not everyone. She teased him and added a silly emoticon. *I like boats but not slimy fish.*

Tim: Well, you will just have to work on your tan then.

Savanna: Lol! I'm a redhead. I don't tan.

His reply came faster than she anticipated, and a smile crossed her lips.

Tim: So, you can ride on the boat with many layers of clothes and sunscreen while I fish.

Savanna: Lol! I'll look ridiculous.

Tim: You will look adorable.

Savanna blushed. He was he flirting with her over text now? Warmth seeped through her veins and set her skin on fire. It had been way too long since she'd been flirted with.

Tim: Well, I will let you get back to your boys. I have a report to fill out. Text me when you're home.

Savanna: Will do. Talk to you later.

As soon as she hit 'send' she regretted committing to a later conversation. Was she so out of practice she would come across like a level 9 clinger in their first text exchange? She held her breath and hoped for a reply.

Not even a second later, her screen lit and

Tim: Definitely! His reply flashed across the screen. Her smile reappeared, pulling her cheeks wide. Today was a good day.

Her phone rang in her hand and made her almost take back her happy thoughts.

"Hello sir," she answered, her voice formal.

"Good evening, Captain McCormick. How was your day off?"

"It's still going." Savanna struggled to hear her boss over the bus full of kids. She ducked close to the seat in front of her and pushed her palm against her opposite ear. "How can I help you?"

"I am sending you out on special assignment tomorrow. Washington needs a search dog, and all the other teams are busy. I know it's not ideal considering Max's specialty, but I think you guys can manage because it will be on the river."

"But sir, I will need to drive back to pick up Charlie after school." It was the quickest reason she could think of. She didn't want to do a search on the Pamlico. The memories of her parents' disappearance were still too fresh. Even more so after today.

He interrupted. "Is there a problem, McCormick?"

Savanna paused, looked at Charlie still listening to his iPod oblivious to the chaos around him. "No, sir, I will figure it out." He wasn't going to take an excuse.

"Good. They have you indefinitely. Keep me updated, so I know when you are back in town." And hung up.

Savanna's knee bounced as her chest tightened. *Damn it.* What was she going to do? She wiped her hands on her pants. She motioned to Olivia to join her in the bus seat.

Olivia wove through all the feet and elbows in the aisle, eventually making her way to Savanna's seat. "What's going on?" She glanced at Charlie. "How's he doing?"

"Fine as far as I can tell. It's weird how fine he is." Savanna rubbed Charlie's head making him jump. He looked at her in question but didn't remove his earbuds out to hear her. She shook her head and turned back to his teacher. "My boss called. I have to drive back to Washington in the morning. Can I drop Charlie off at your apartment, so he won't miss school?"

"Sure, no problem. What's going on?"

"Some case they need a search dog on. I don't know what time I will be back though."

"No worries. We will have pizza for dinner."

Charlie turned toward the two women. "Pizza?"

"Oh, now he hears us." Savanna laughed. "Tomorrow, you and Ms. Olivia are going to have pizza for dinner. I have to work."

"Okay." He smiled and turned back to the window.

"And we lost him." Olivia smiled. "Typical 8-year-old."

"You are sure you don't mind?"

"Not at all. How is work going? Any better?" Olivia asked.

"They are still giving me sh... crap," Savanna looked around before continuing, "about having to take time off, but it's what's best for Charlie."

"I'm sure the station is missing its best search team. Do they still only have you on call?"

"Yeah. We've been going out once or twice a week. This is the first time I've had to travel east though. Usually, we're in the mountains. It's going to bring up a lot of stuff from what happened last year." She motioned toward Charlie. "I'm hoping it will be something simple. But it might be too much to hope for."

"He didn't give you any details?"

"Nope, nothing. I guess I will find out in the morning."

Olivia patted her on her knee. "I better head back up front. I don't want them to hassle the driver." She laughed, "Thank you so much for your help today. I couldn't have done it without you."

"No problem." Savanna smiled. She actually had a good time today. She quickly covered her mouth as a huge yawn escaped. *I will definitely sleep well tonight. I don't know how Olivia does it every day.*

The bus soon pulled into the school parking lot. Cars idled as parents waited to collect the kids. Olivia stood at the bus door with a huge trash bag, collecting the fast food wrappers and soda cups left from each child, gently prodding the ones trying to exit without turning in their trash. She greeted each parent as they met their child.

"I'll see you guys in the morning," she said as Savanna and Charlie slipped by her.

"Sounds good." Savanna gave her a quick half hug. "Thanks for the day."

Charlie jumped into their SUV and settled into the rear passenger seat. It looked like he was ready for the day to end too. Savanna turned the key, looked at her disastrous hair in the mirror. She quickly tucked it into a messy bun using the rearview mirror and noticed Charlie was already asleep. The drive home would be her, the radio, and her thoughts; thoughts of a particularly handsome sheriff's deputy.

CHAPTER 8

READING THE DOG

er senses sprang to high alert as she pulled into the parking lot of the apartment complex. The lights were out on the side of her unit, and it was way too dark tonight with no moon. She pulled into her spot and turned off the motor. Music floated from one of the apartments across the grass, but it was the only sound besides the cars driving by on the busy street. The apartment was convenient to her work, but it wasn't ideal for raising an 8-year-old. Maybe when her lease was up, she would look for something nicer, something closer to his school.

She walked around the jeep and opened the door. Charlie was still asleep. "Come on, Charlie. You have to wake up."

He started to stir but was still half asleep.

"Come on, you are too big for me to carry. You have to walk." Savanna reached in and unbuckled his seat belt.

"I'll carry him in." The deep voice came from behind her. Savanna jumped putting her body between the male voice and Charlie.

"Shit, Jeremy. You scared the crap out of me." Savanna looked around to see where he had appeared from and spied his car parked in the shadows of the lot. Her hands instantly checked her hair making sure it was neatly tucked into a bun. "That's not necessary, I will get him."

"He's too heavy, you said it yourself. I'll get him." Jeremy's large hand grabbed her arm and moved her out of his way. His large frame filled the whole passenger side of the vehicle. "Where have you been all day? I thought you took the day off."

The large man was still in his uniform, Savanna noted. She remembered he had been on the morning roster. "How long have you been here?" She knew she didn't have a poker face when it came to Jeremy and all her fear was showing.

"Don't worry about it. Go open the door so I can put him to bed."

She stepped in front of him. "Really, that's not necessary."

"Savanna, I don't want to drop him. Go get the doors." His voice was firm and demanding. Charlie started to mumble something. Jeremy's arms tightened around him. Savanna's spine straightened, and she ran to the front door to unlock it. There was no way she was going to let him in. Leaving the door cracked, she met Jeremy halfway up the walk.

"I can take him, now." Savanna blocked the path as she stood with her arms out. "Really," she insisted as she stepped forward and slid her hands between Charlie and Jeremy.

"Okay. I'm just trying to help you out." He turned loose and Savanna's arms sagged under the weight of the sleeping child.

"I'm fine." She walked slowly to the door, struggling. He was right behind her as she pushed open the door with Charlie's feet. She whipped around as she stepped inside. "You can leave now." And she closed the door right in his face. Adjusting Charlie's weight, so he was leaning over her shoulder, she threw the deadbolt.

Letting out a deep breath, she carried Charlie down the hall to his bedroom. Laying him on his bed, she pulled off his shoes and lifted his legs so she could pull back the Star Wars comforter. If it had been two months ago, Savanna would have believed Jeremy was helping her out because he cared, because he wanted to be a part of their life. But he had made it clear a child was not part of his plans. He was not ready for a family but wanted to date her and only her. Savanna pulled the bedroom door shut and flexed her arms. Charlie was getting big.

She crossed the hall to her room and reached for her phone at her side. It wasn't there. She must've left it plugged in the charger in the Jeep. The tension in her shoulders returned with a vengeance. She went to the front window, turned on the porch light, and looked toward the space where Jeremy parked his cruiser earlier. It was gone, so she unlocked the door.

Grabbing her keys from the side table, she ran out to the SUV and hit the unlock on her key fob. As soon as the lights on the jeep blinked, the hair on the back of her neck raised. She opened the door quickly to grab her things, and his arm reached around her pushing her into the driver's seat.

Savanna knew who it was from his smell. "Why are you here, Jeremy?" her strained voice demanded. "You made it clear you don't want to be here." She looked around the deserted parking lot and wished she had gone by the kennel before coming home.

His hand slipped around her waist. "But I do want to be here." He pulled her closer. "Can't you feel how much I want to be here?"

She could feel every inch of his masculine body as he pressed it against her. Savanna's hands pushed against his broad chest. "Jeremy, no. You don't get this anymore. You need to leave."

"You know you miss me too." His fingers pulled the pins from her hair and wrapped it around his hand. She continued to push against him, failing to escape his strong grasp, her head jerking with every shove. "I could help."

"Help with what?"

"I know the Captain is giving you a hard time about time off so you can take care of Charlie. I could run interference at the office so he won't notice as much." Savanna stopped pushing for a moment, and her eyebrows went up in surprise. A smile crossed Jeremy's face as if he thought she would consider his offer. "Then when you get Charlie back with the foster family who took such good care of him, we can pick up where we left off."

Savanna gave him a huge shove, taking him by surprise and catching him off balance. He tried to catch himself and released her hair letting it fall down her back. Stepping out of his arms, she poked him hard. "Leave now. You are disgusting. That's *my brother*, and he's *my family*. We are a packaged deal now, and if you don't want the whole package, you don't get me." The look on his face suggested no one had ever turned him down before. "Now." She slammed the SUV door and caught his left hand in the door. He screamed in agony. She opened the door again to release the vise, and he grabbed his hand, holding it and writhing with pain. She slammed the door again and walked to the other side, grabbed her purse, Charlie's iPod, and her phone. Her pulse raced as she activated the alarm and headed back into the apartment to lock up for the night, leaving Jeremy still cursing and holding his hand.

She threw the deadbolt and leaned against the door. She slipped off her shoes and padded down the hall, peeking into her brother's room. She sighed when she heard the faint sounds of his sleepy breathing. The muscles in her shoulders loosened, and she could feel relief flood her body.

She pulled Charlie's door shut and leaned against the wall. Tears formed and rolled over her cheeks. Her life was her own now. She couldn't let Jeremy run it anymore. Savanna shook her head, the tears coming hard now. She pulled her hair back and twisted it into a quick messy bun. "Never again."

She returned to her bedroom, set her purse on the bedside table and looked at her phone. Olivia confirmed Charlie's drop off in the morning, and Tim had messaged her again.

She responded to Tim's text first.

Savanna: Just settled in for the night. Thanks for checking on us.

He almost instantly texted back.

Tim: Sweet dreams.

Savanna: Good Night

She cleared the papers and photographs from her comforter, shifting them to one side. The collection of maps and notes from her parent's case covered the queen size bed. She paused as she remembered the easy way Tim talked and joked with Charlie. Her skin started to heat with the thought of the handsome deputy and his easy-going smile. So different from Jeremy. She turned cold at the memory of his comments. She changed into her sleep shorts and a t-shirt; climbing into bed, her mind drifted back to Tim's sun-wrinkled smile and his touch on her arm.

With a huge yawn, she reached over to her side table grabbed her cell and pushed the call button. It went to voicemail. A woman's sweet southern accent filled the speaker.

"You've reached the McCormick's. Please leave your number and a brief message, and we will get back to you."

"I miss you, Mom. Give Dad a hug for me wherever you are. I love you."

She disconnected the call and fell asleep.

67

CHAPTER 9

UPWIND

The darkness suited his mood. Water poured from the bucket he was using to bale and splashed onto his clothes. He felt the chill in the air through his entire body. Everything he owned was damp, and it wouldn't do any good to change before the job was done. He took his time trying not to create too much noise or wake on the creek. If he was going to make it to the barrier islands, he had to get this boat dried out so he could work on the engines. The creek was busy during the day even with bad weather. He couldn't risk being seen. A thick fog was rolling in, and it hid the dock even more than normal. The boat started to rock and threw him to one side.

He looked around and could barely make out a light in the distance, the light on the bow of a boat coming his way. Maybe this spot wasn't as secluded as he thought. He crouched down, hiding, but the wake rocking the boat making it impossible to keep his balance. When the railing rammed his ribs, he wailed in pain, the sound escaping before he could stop it. Blood dripped onto his chin as he bit his lip to prevent any more noise. He listened as a wooden boat pulled up next to his. The wood knocked against the fiberglass hull, sending the sports boat rocking again. The footsteps were almost deafening as a large someone jumped onto the wooden dock. A grunt and then more footsteps moved toward the house. The scent of fresh fish caught the breeze. When he could no longer hear the person, he looked over the edge. There was no boat, only a lantern by the door on the porch. He knew what he heard and felt, but the boat was gone.

He stepped onto the wooden pier and the faint smell of fish filled his nostrils as the breeze blew out toward the creek. Strange, he didn't have fish here at the cabin. He slowly moved toward the cabin watching a shadow against the wall through the window. It was a large figure at least 6 foot tall and muscular. "Shit." There was nowhere to go. The boat still had 3 inches of water, and the motor wouldn't start. As he neared the doorway, the boards creaked under his feet, and the figure stopped, the knife they held frozen in air. The flame flickered in the lantern at his feet. He slowly leaned around the door facing and peeked into the kitchen area. No one was there. He backed up and looked into the window. There he was, slicing away at what Robert could only guess was his fresh catch. Leaning in again, he took a big whiff of the salty, fishy smell.

The sound of running water sent goosebumps over his skin. The sound of metal hitting the bottom of the sink and then running water again. Was this really happening or had he finally lost it? Too much solitude here. He walked into the room and over to the sink. Everything was gone. He turned on the coffee maker and started a big pot. There would be no sleeping tonight. He uncovered the computer, funneling a pool of water in the plastic into a bucket. Plenty to watch. The coffee bubbled and spurted into the carafe. The shadow in the cabin kitchen showed two men as he walked over and sat at the screens to watch her sleep.

CHAPTER 10

TAPHONOMIC AGENTS

ctober 17, 2014

6:30am

The early morning drive was quiet. Max was restless in the back of her SUV. He knew they were going to work. Being by himself all day yesterday was not good for him and Savanna knew it. She didn't like leaving him in the police kennel, but no one else could take him because he was a registered Police K-9.

Max watched out the window as Savanna passed other vehicles trying to make the trip to Washington as short as possible. They had to be there by eight, and she was known for always being on time. Charlie was still asleep when she dropped him at Olivia's, but they parked him on the couch bundled up until he had to wake up for school. Thank God Olivia had come into their lives. The teacher had turned into a good friend Savanna could depend on. They had become fast friends when she went through the break up with Jeremy. She had never had close girlfriends before and to have someone she could lean on was awesome.

Just thinking of Jeremy got her fired up. For him to think he could waltz in and take up where he left off. She was flattered when he paid attention to her at first and then his alpha male act turned into a jealous mess. She couldn't talk to anyone or go out with Olivia. When she finally got custody of Charlie, she had been so happy. She wanted to celebrate as a family, and he showed his true colors. Memories of the conversation made her blood boil. *"Send him back," he said, "He will be happier with the foster family, you don't have time to raise a boy, you don't want to ruin what we have."*

A car flashed their lights at her SUV, bringing her back to the present. She quickly turned down her brights. She needed to concentrate on her driving, so she could get to Washington and back as quickly as possible. Jeremy was not a concern right now. She would deal with him later. She slowed her breathing, letting the air flow in and out between her lips. Max came to the front of his compartment and stared at her, cocking his head and listening to her breathing. He picked up on everything.

"We're almost there, Buddy." She turned up the AC so he wouldn't be too hot. The sun wasn't up, and it was already a sticky warm day. She was dressed in her search and rescue uniform, but she knew today was probably a preliminary meeting for the actual search. She really wanted to get it over with so she could get back to Charlie and figuring her life out.

She pulled into the lot at the Sheriff's office finding a good spot near the grassy island. Putting the vehicle in park, she took a deep breath. "Ready?" she glanced over her shoulder. Max whined and started to dance at the rear hatch. Savanna stepped out and opened the back door, grabbing Max's gear. The bright orange vest helped her spot him when they were in deep brush. She may as well get suited up now. She wanted them to take her seriously. She didn't know if Max's reputation was known here but she was all business and it needed to show. Dropping the vest to the pavement, she opened the hatch, and he stepped out and stood over the vest, his feet in the holes. She could feel the tension in his shoulders as she hurried to fasten the buckles around his chest and back. She double checked her hair, tucking it back into the braid twisting it up and putting it under her cap.

She squared her shoulders and looked around the lot. There weren't many cars, meaning she was probably early. Who was she supposed to meet? She pulled out a piece of paper from the side pocket of her cargo pants. *Sheriff Harroll.* "What do you think, Max, should we get this party started?"

He looked at her waiting for the command. "Okay, let's go. Time to work." The German shepherd instantly moved to her side, she hooked the leash to his collar, and they moved in unison toward the front door of the office.

CHAPTER 11

SHOW-ME CUES

7:00am

Steam rose from Tim's coffee as he tried to wake up. He tossed and turned all night with thoughts of the redhead in the park the day before. He didn't even think about going to bed until she messaged him saying they were home. That Charlie was a character. She definitely had her hands full. He wondered how she did it and what kind of job was flexible enough so she could raise her little brother.

He looked up as someone walked through the door and almost bit his tongue. Savanna's uniform hugged her curves not leaving anything to the imagination. A large, black and tan German shepherd matched her stride as they covered the office floor in no time. The dog's ears stood at attention but had no tips. On her lapel, he saw a badge for the Raleigh Police Department and a K-9 patch on her shoulder. He wondered how she hid all that beautiful long red hair under the cap she wore. Her eyes peeked from under the brim and met his as heat filled him. This woman was ready to kick butt and take names.

"May I help you, Officer McCormick?" Tim asked.

"Well, hello. How are you this morning?" Her eyes darkened as she met his gaze.

"I'm a little tired. You see I was waiting for this hot redhead to text me." Savanna's cheeks reddened. "She kept me waiting till late. Then I had to be here early to meet my help from Raleigh." He left out the fact she was in his thoughts all night.

"I didn't know I would see you today. I was told to report to the Sheriff to discuss my assignment." She walked up to his desk, and her dog sat beside her when she stopped. She was clearly waiting for directions to the Sheriff's office.

"That won't be necessary. Sheriff Harroll will be in at 9, but we may as well go over the case. I like a lady who gets up early."

"Deputy Whitaker, is this going to be a problem?" Her voice was all business matching her posture.

"Not at all. Thanks for the help."

"No problem. Now, why don't you tell me what we have?"

"Okay." He pulled out a map of the waterfront. "The victim was pulled out of the water here. We know she was held in a concrete structure based on the video. In her statement, she said she escaped from the structure when it started to flood and swam toward the clanging of a metal sailboat mast."

Savanna looked at the map of the Pamlico River. The map she fell asleep to every night. She closed her eyes and saw every detail in her head. She looked over at Tim. "Where would you like to start the search?"

"I think the South bank, here, would be a good place to start, then we can expand from there."

"Okay, do we have a boat ready?"

"Yes ma'am, I have one of the local guys on standby. He will be ready at 7:30."

Savanna looked at her watch. It was only 15 minutes after. He had timed it perfect. "Nice planning."

"Thanks. I'm anxious to get this wrapped up. The victim is the girlfriend of one of my buddies. I want them to find some closure." He watched her tense at his words. "Is this the famous Max?"

Her posture eased at the mention of the Shepherd. "Yes sir, SGT Max, introduce yourself." Max stood up and bowed to Tim.

He laughed "Nice one."

"Max, you ready to get started?" The Shepherd looked at Savanna and paused. "Time to work. Let's find it." He started dancing and wagging his tail with excitement. She looked at Tim, "Better show us to the boat, he's ready."

Tim stood up and walked to the door at the front of the building. "After you." He held the door open. She and the dog headed out and across the parking lot.

"I assume you have some items Max can use for a scent article." She looked at him as he joined them walking toward the waterfront.

"I have some bandages with blood from the victim. I thought those might work."

"They will be perfect." The dog was already working, swinging back and forth in the alleyway before they emerged into a parking lot. "He's got something, but we need to redirect him, or there is no telling what we will end up with."

The river was slick as a mirror, and there wasn't a breeze at all. "Oh, man it's going to be a hot one. I don't know which is worse, the rain or the heat this time of year."

"It would be nice to have a little bit of breeze for Max. This isn't ideal."

"The sheriff is worried if we wait too much longer, the evidence might be washed away." Tim put a hand on her arm, and she flinched. She was on edge for some reason. He wondered why. "The sample is on the boat, down there." Pointing down the landing, he unhooked the chain blocking the entrance.

A tall, brown-haired man waited on a boat at the far end of the dock. Max jumped on board and went straight to the duffle parked on the side bench. He started whining.

Savanna smiled for the first time that morning, "I assume our scent article is in there."

"Yes, ma'am. Good job Max." Tim was impressed. She held out a toy and gave it a squeak. The dog jumped around, rocking the boat in the water. Mike's eyes widened as he stepped away from his new shipmate. Tim started laughing. "You okay there?" He stepped aboard. It was going to be a tight fit with the three adults and Max, he thought.

Mike smiled wearily. "I'll be okay. I'm not used to having such an active passenger." He straightened and stepped toward Savanna offering her his hand. "Now, this passenger I don't mind at all. You want to introduce us?" He helped her board the boat.

Tim eyed his buddy, knowing what he was thinking because he had been thinking exactly the same thing earlier. "This is Officer McCormick of the Raleigh Search and Rescue K9 unit. She is going to help us find the crime scene this morning. Officer

McCormick, this is Mike Burwell." Tim was irritated now, and he wanted to sock Mike for acting like that.

Mike's fingers rubbed Savanna's hand, their contact remaining a little too long for Tim's taste. "Welcome aboard. Have you ever been on the Pamlico?"

"Not officially, this will be our first time for a search. We usually work in the western part of the state. I'm going to let Max work independently, I hope you don't mind. He will be loose on the boat. Since we don't have any certain area to search, it will be important for me to follow his cues." Savanna pulled her hand loose to indicate her plan. "I will direct you with hand motions. Please steer the boat in the direction I point, like this."

Mike nodded. "No problem." He eyed Max sideways, and Tim realized he wasn't comfortable with such a large dog, but he wouldn't say. "Should we go ahead and get started?"

"You would probably want to start on the far bank and work this way," Tim suggested.

"Yes, let's get started." She walked over to the duffle and grabbed it. "May I?"

"Of course," Tim said watching her unzip the duffle and pull out a small Tupperware container. He knew what was inside but watched with interest as Savanna popped the seal. Max went crazy jumping around the boat.

"Sit, Max, sit," she commanded, and the dog obeyed, sitting beside her. She lowered it to snout level and let him smell it. "Max?" The dog looked up at her. "Got it?" Max barked once. "Let's find it. Time to work." He went to the bow of the boat and turned toward them. He barked again. "Okay, he's ready. Mike, let's go."

Mike started the engines and Tim untied the boat from the dock. They slowly pulled away, and Max stood front and center with his nose to the water. The speed of the boat cooled Tim's skin, but he knew it was only temporary. Soon as they slowed, there would be no break from the sticky heat. Mike watched Savanna closely. Tim knew she asked him to pay attention to her for direction, but that was not permission to ogle her.

They were halfway across the river when Max moved to the side of the boat. Savanna moved her arm to port and Mike steered the boat to the left. He slowed the boat so he could pay close attention to her movements. Max changed sides again, and she pointed starboard. Mike looked at Tim with a questioning glance.

"Something tells me this is not an exact science," Tim told his friend who nodded in agreement but didn't take his eyes off Savanna.

"He is catching the scent of something," she yelled over the boat engine. "It might be in the air or the current. We will have to follow his alerts."

Mike kept the boat at a slow speed so they could follow Max's movements. Tim had the chart and marked areas where the dog signaled with an alert. He watched Savanna, but she took no notice. They worked their way to the south bank. As they pulled closer to the bank, Tim thought they were headed onshore, but, nope, Max determined they should head back out.

Savanna pointed back out into the river, and it seemed like they were headed back the way they came. Max dipped his head toward the river. He started to lick his lips.

"He has something," Savanna yelled over her shoulder. She grabbed hold of Max by his vest to keep him in the boat. "Cut back across."

Mike increased the boat's speed. Tim looked ahead of them. They were headed straight to Castle Island.

CHAPTER 12

SPIRAL SEARCH

Max was doing great on the unfamiliar boat. His dance was a strong one, and Savanna knew he had the right scent. They were headed to an island in the middle of the river.

"What's this island?" she asked.

Tim walked closer to her so they wouldn't have to yell over the boat's engine. "We call it Castle Island."

Savanna looked at him with an amused look. "I don't see any structures."

"It was a nickname the locals gave it, and it stuck."

"Why castle island?"

"There were large kilns for baking oyster shells for lime. People said the smokestacks looked like a castle."

Savanna gave him a quirky look, wrinkling her forehead. "Yeah, okay."

"Tim, can you move over? I can't see Savanna." Mike yelled.

Tim stepped away from her, and she saw him shoot Mike a knowing look. Max was struggling to get away from her grip, and she was having a hard time holding on. "He's definitely excited. I'm going to turn him loose once we get close enough. Tim nodded his head and then stepped back to Mike at the helm.

The small beach was shaded with cypress trees and Spanish moss. The tide was out at the moment, so there was dry ground in between the cypress trees to walk on. In one leap, Max was out of the boat and tracking the sandy soil, moving back and forth. Mike beached the boat, and they all jumped onto the shore.

Savanna yelled, "Do you have markers?"

"Yeah and tape." Tim pointed to the backpack he slung over his shoulder.

The ground was uneven, and the brush thick. Max pulled away from her, and she knew she needed to catch up in case he needed her. She heard his barking and the bell attached to his collar. Pushing branches aside, a locust bush caught her arm, snagging fabric and she was glad to be in full uniform despite the heat. The trees were wet at least two feet up the trunks and from the moss on the bark, meaning it flooded here often. She listened and heard the guys a good fifty feet behind her. Max's bark changed, then there was quiet. She stopped and listened. Another bark and then silence. He'd found it.

Her throat constricted, and her pulse started to race. Not now. She had to calm down. She concentrated on her breathing, a tingling sensation in her left arm. Damn it, not now. One, short breath, two, a longer one, three, a little longer. Then one, two, three. Her throat eased. She flexed her hand. There, she focused on where she was walking. The ground was muddy, and she could see Max's large prints. She pulled back a branch and found him lying in front of a large concrete bunker. Slowly, she walked toward him. He looked at her and barked, staying in his crouched position. Checking the ground as she eased forward, she watched for any evidence on the ground. She doubted anything would be found without equipment in the mud.

She blew her whistle. "Deputy Whitaker, we are over here." Savanna could hear the men coming behind her but didn't know if they could see her through the brush and trees.

They soon emerged into the clearing in front of the structure. "I didn't know this was still here." Tim looked at Mike. "Remember playing here when we were kids. I used to lock you guys up in the jail." His expression changed like a lightbulb went off. "The iron gate." He put his hand on Savanna's arm. "Let's go take a look."

"This is definitely the crime scene. We want to be careful." Savanna looked at Mike.

"Mike, stay here, will you?"

The other man looked disappointed he wasn't invited along, but he nodded. Savanna checked out the entrance. There was a strong stagnant smell coming from the corridor. She wrinkled her nose.

"That's the brackish water from the river."

"Along with some other things," Savanna commented. "Max, search."

The shepherd stood up instantly, his bell ringing with his motion. He pushed in between the two officers, knowing he should be first down the hall. Savanna pulled a flashlight from her belt to light their way. The beam created shadows around Max. Two minutes in, he stopped and laid in front of a large iron gate.

Savanna shined the light around the spikes at the top of the gate. There were bits of jersey cloth hanging on the tips. "Looks like some blood here." Tim nodded, agreeing with her statement. She turned her attention to Max pulling out his toy. "Good boy, you want this?" He jumped around barking. "Here you go, good job." He grabbed his toy, squeaking the round end. He laid back down enjoying his reward.

"I'll take pictures before we leave." Tim unzipped his backpack and hung the camera around his neck. Pulling out the roll of police tape, he looked around for something he could secure it to.

"You may as well use some of the bushes outside. The walls are so smooth." Savanna shined the light through the gate. There was a dirty mattress leaning haphazardly against the far wall. "Looks like possible blood stains on the mattress. There is a lot of debris in here like it was filled by the river recently." The smell was starting to get to her. She turned to leave. "Max, come." She slapped her hip, and he was there instantly.

"That would match my victim's statement." He pulled out his cellphone and checked the screen. "No signal. Let's step outside."

Savanna was glad to join him. "Who you calling?"

"I have some contacts in Greenville. That's who we usually call for forensics." Tim looked down at Max. "Good job, buddy." He turned to Savanna. "That didn't take as long as I thought it was going to. We actually have time for some breakfast before we meet with the sheriff."

Tim tried his cell again once they were out of the structure. He stepped out of earshot from Savanna. "Come on, Max. Let's get back to the boat." The shepherd followed her as they consciously took the way they came. When they arrived out of the brush, Mike was on the boat waiting for them.

"This was an eventful morning. Max was great."

"Thanks, Mike. It usually goes pretty quick once he has the scent."

"Here, let me help you aboard. Have we met before? When I shook your hand earlier, you seemed familiar." He held out his hand for her to grab. Max leaped onto the deck.

"No, I don't think so." Savanna couldn't recall meeting him before. The only time she had been in town was to help collect her parents' boat and the field trip.

"Where's Tim?" Mike busied himself with the ropes on the boat, keeping things neat.

"He was finishing up running the tape and making a few calls. He should be here soon; said something about breakfast."

"If he mentioned food, he won't be long. So how did you get stuck with this assignment?"

"Apparently, the sheriff called my boss for some help, and I was the one available. It was a nice break from what I'm usually assigned to."

"Oh yeah, what's that?"

Savanna hesitated not wanting to change Mike's good mood. The subject usually tainted any sense of normalcy in casual conversation. "Max is a cadaver dog, so usually we are looking for a dead body."

"Every day?"

"Every workday. I've been on call since my brother came to live with me, so we don't work every day."

"That must be rough." He moved closer to Savanna, and she stared at him while pulling her cap down shading her eyes.

"Sometimes, but I focus on Max's success and not the scene so much." Max perked up at the mention of his name, then settled down on the deck again.

"I bet it gets interesting, I'd love to hear some more about it."

"Ah, it's boring really."

They both heard rustling coming from the bushes and turned to see Tim pushing his way through. Savanna stepped away from Mike and walked over to where Tim was boarding. "Are we all taped up?"

"Yes, I'll come back this afternoon when Greenville gets here."

"What time do we have to be back at the office?"

"In about 45."

"So, where's breakfast?" She chimed in as her stomach growled.

"I thought we would go to Rachel's and grab a coffee. She has good pastries, too. It will be quick enough."

"Sounds good. Mike, you want to join us?" Savanna asked, returning to her place next to the console. She was actually enjoying her conversation with someone who didn't think she was a freak because of her work. He started up the boat and turned toward town. Savanna grabbed her notepad from her pocket and started jotting down notes for her records of the search.

"Nah, I have to get back to work. I'll catch you later, maybe when we aren't busy."

"Sounds good." She felt Tim's eyes on her and turned to look at him. "What is the sheriff like? Should I be worried?"

"He's a good guy. Besides, we found what he wanted this morning. It should be a short meeting."

The boat pulled alongside the dock and Mike leaped to tie it off on the piling. After it was secure, he walked over and offered Savanna a hand.

"Thanks."

"No problem. You should give me a call next time you are in town. I could give you a ride up the river for fun."

"Sounds like a plan. I will see you later."

Tim stepped in between the two of them, interrupting. "Let's head over and get something to eat." He put his hand on Savanna's arm. The action caught Mike's attention and the expression on his face changed instantly to one of displeasure, she thought. Maybe he was enjoying her company as well.

She walked along beside Tim and patted her hip for Max to join them. She looked over her shoulder and gave Mike a wave. His smile returned, and he finished tying the boat in place. Good, that's one friend she made in Washington. She looked at Tim and considered him. She would prefer he be more than a friend but not while they were working. If Jeremy had taught her one thing, it was don't date where you work. Too many complications. The walk wasn't a long one, and when they rounded the corner, a tall, good-looking man ran past them and went straight into the bakery. *That was definitely not a jog.* Her senses went on alert, and Tim unbuckled his holster.

To Savanna's irritation, he placed his hand on her arm and pushed her behind him like he needed to protect her as they entered the building. There was a crowd in the middle of the room. The man, his right arm in a sling, leaned over the body of a woman. Tim buckled his holster and then pushed through the crowd. Max followed him through, pushing his way to the front.

"Sam, what's going on?" he said to the man who had run past them.

Savanna's instinct took over, and she put her arms out. "Can we give them some room, please? I need everyone to back up and give them some space." Tim looked at her and nodded.

One of the clerks started to fill Tim in, while the man who Tim called Sam tended to the woman on the floor. "Did you call the ambulance?'

"Yes, as soon as she passed out, we called 911. They should be here soon."

The sirens arrived outside on the street, and Savanna stepped outside to the curb to meet the EMTs. "We have a woman approximately 37 yrs old that has fainted in the restaurant. She did not hit her head and does not appear to have any injuries."

"Thank you." They followed her in, and Savanna saw Max lying beside the woman. She looked closer at her and recognized her as the owner of the gallery the boys visited the day before. What was her name? "Beth Pearse." *That's right.*

Savanna found Tim. "How is Beth doing?"

"She had a fright and was overcome. She should be fine. She is not going to be happy with Sam though when she comes around."

"Why's that?" She was curious.

"Well, Sam knew something he kept from her. She found out from the TV news which caused her to faint."

"It must have been a shock for her to faint."

"It was. She saw a picture of the man wanted for kidnapping, and she thinks it's her husband."

"What?"

"Yeah, he kidnapped one of the local deputies."

"Holy cow. No wonder."

"Well, that's not the big shock. Supposedly, he died 5 years ago." He paused and gestured to Max. "Looks like she has a companion to the hospital." Max followed beside the gurney headed to the ambulance. When the EMTs lifted it into the vehicle, Max followed as if he was supposed to be there.

"Max, you can't go. Come." He looked at Savanna and barked. "Max, come." He sat down next to the gurney and barked again.

"He can be so stubborn. I don't know why he is acting like that."

Tim stood there deep in thought and said, "He's been tracking her all morning. That's probably why he won't leave her. Beth was the kidnap victim. I think Max is waiting for you to bring out his toy." He started to laugh.

Savanna pulled the toy out of her side pocket and shook it in the air. "Good boy Max. You found her." Max barked and jumped onto the pavement. He ran and grabbed the toy from Savanna, squeaking it over and over.

CHAPTER 13

ANCHOR POINT

8:30am

Tim grabbed their order from the counter and joined Savanna at a table in the corner. The light shined on her hair, and there were glints of gold mixed in with the deep red. Man, she took his breath away. It was making it hard to concentrate on the case. He needed to shake it off and concentrate. He would not mess this up. He was well on his way to being the next in line for sheriff, and this could make it a sure thing. Did he have time for a woman in his life? Maybe he would be better off without her. She looked up and met his gaze, heat passed between the two of them, and he realized he had been standing there staring too long not to be noticed.

Color entered her cheeks, and he continued crossing the room with their drinks. Sam was making it work, so could he. But was Sam really making it work? He had screwed up royally. *I'll call him later to see how things went at the hospital.*

"Here ya go. An iced chai and chocolate croissant," he announced as he placed it in front of her.

"And what did you pick out?" She peeked over his hand delivering her food.

"A cherry brioche." Tim smiled. He couldn't resist the custard.

"Oh, my God I didn't see those."

"I think you were distracted by the chocolate." He said matter-of-factly. She laughed. What a fantastic sound. "So, what do you think of our little town? I promise you it is not crazy like this all the time. It's actually pretty quiet as a rule."

"Everyone seems really friendly. I met Beth the other day at the gallery, and everyone at the Museum was kind. Mike seems nice too."

The last comment hurt. Why did it bother him so much? "Yeah, he's a good guy. Beth is great, one of our newest transplants. Sam loves her to pieces. I hope nothing is ruined permanently there."

"It will probably be okay after the shock of the news wears off."

"I don't know, based on what Sam was saying. She loved her husband a lot. It was a fairytale type thing. He doesn't think he can compete with it."

"So how long have you lived here?"

He wondered at her choice to skip over further comment on Beth's love life. Maybe she had an unsettled romantic past as well. "My whole life. I never wanted to move away. I have the river, work, and my buddies. What else could you ask for?"

She smiled at him. "What about your family?"

"Never really been close to my family. The guys: Sam, Jose, Mike, Alex, and Bill, were who I always depended on. We've been close since we were in school. Sam, you saw, runs the local renovation company and teaches. Jose works for him. Mike has his charter business and does freelance work for the Sheriff's department. Alex is in the Army and Bill, well, he used to be a deputy with me."

"What happened?"

Tim wondered if he should explain but knew she would find out soon enough when the sheriff went over the details. "We are still sorting things out. Has to do with the case we're working."

"I see. So, did you always want to be a deputy?"

"Nope, I've always wanted to sheriff. This is only temporary." Tim watched her as the corner of her lips curled. "This case is supposed to be my big break, put me out in the public's eye, that sort of thing."

"I see." She took a long sip of her chai tea.

He eyed her croissant still sitting on the plate in front of her. He had already finished his. "You better eat up, we don't want to keep the sheriff waiting."

She looked down at the pastry and laughed. "I forgot about it. Tell me about growing up in Washington."

"Nah, I'm talking too much. Where did you grow up?"

"Raleigh, in a typical suburban neighborhood. I was the red-headed tomboy. Mom and Dad were professors." A sadness clouded her eyes. "I was always in the mountains staying busy. They retired and then Charlie was born. A good surprise, Mom always said. It's strange having a brother 20 some years younger than me, but I love him."

"I can tell. Yesterday was scary I bet." He said remembering the relief in her eyes when she told him they had found the little boy.

"Yes, I tried not to panic, remembering boys can be boys, but it's hard after losing mom and dad. He's all I have left."

"We don't have to talk about it if you don't want." Tim wondered where her thoughts were.

She drifted back to him and gave him a small smile. "Thanks."

"So how did Charlie like the museum?" he said changing the subject.

"Oh, he loved it. I'm sure that will be all he talks about for a couple of weeks. And the man who found him, Abram, he made quite the impression. Charlie was only with him for a short time. It's weird how no one knows him."

"I can check around town if you like. Someone will know him."

"It's not really important." She shook her head. "I wanted to thank him. If he hadn't found Charlie, it could have been bad. I wasn't really thinking at the time."

Tim understood, missing kids could cause all types of excitement. "So, are you bringing him back this weekend?" He didn't want to pressure her, but he was excited about them coming to town to have fun. "Max needs a break from working. He told me so."

"He did, did he?" Her face lit up, and he could tell she was now in a better mood. "Well since it's for Max's benefit, I will have to make an extra effort to make it happen."

Tim reached down and scratched Max's head. Content with the extra attention, his tongue popped out of his mouth. "So, what's the deal with his ears? I've been wondering since I first saw him this morning." He stood up and pulled out her chair for her.

She stood up and patted her side. Max joined her standing between her and Tim. "Max was a rescue when he was six months old. He was raised in very poor conditions and, sorry to be gross, the flies had eaten the tips of his ears." She leaned down and gave

Max a hug. "It makes you special, right boy." The shepherd responded with a big kiss.

"Amazing." Tim smiled at the bond they had. Such a pair.

"Yeah, I am so thankful to the rescue group that adopted him from the shelter."

"Let's head over and see if Sheriff Harroll is ready for us."

They walked across the intersection and movement caught both the officers' attention. It was in the alleyway. Tim was tempted to check it out but didn't want to hold Savanna up for the rest of her day.

"That's the alley I found Charlie in," she said.

"Really? Maybe we should go take a look?" He let her take the lead on this one.

"Okay, it won't hurt to look. Besides, Max has something." The dog had his nose to the ground and was working the area. "Is there any reason there would be human remains down this alley?"

She had his attention now. "No. Not that I know of." Tim shook his head. "Why?"

"He has the scent of something." She looked at him. "You ready for this?"

"I'll text the boss." Tim pulled out his phone for a quick message and then followed her into the alley.

"How long has this building been empty?"

"For a while now. I can't remember what was in there last."

"Okay. Max, time to go to work." He jumped straight into the air and then his nose was to the ground again. He started whining and headed into the alley, side to side and then low, crawling toward a small break in the wall of the building. Savanna followed him and looked at Tim questioningly.

"We may as well finish it up." He said as they entered the building. Max walked the perimeter of the room, then came back to the entrance and laid down.

"He says it's right here. It could be small."

"Okay, I'll get the forensic guys to drop by here on the way to the island," Tim said, pulling the tape out of his backpack. No need on missing the opportunity for them to check it out."

"Sounds good," she said looking at her watch. "Good boy, Max. Here ya go." She squeaked his ball and bounced it down the alley. Max rushed to get it, happy to have his reward again. Squeak, squeak, squeeeeak.

"Wow, he loves that thing." Tim laughed.

"He sure does, you can imagine how hard it is to find a replacement. I have backups just in case."

"Basic equipment." He said with a smile.

"Exactly, basic equipment." They crossed the street and headed to the office.

THE SHERIFF WAS in his office waiting for them. Max squeaked his ball down the hall and into the office announcing his presence. The older man behind the desk was annoyed, and there was no mistaking it from his tone. "Officer McCormick, welcome to Washington. Tell me about your progress today."

"Sir, we patrolled the river, and with Max's assistance, we found the crime scene where the kidnap victim was potentially restrained. It was located on what is referred to as Castle Island."

"Really?" he looked at Tim.

She continued her narrative. "Yes, sir. The location was hidden in heavy brush, and we did have to disturb the vegetation to gain access."

"Is the location secure, Deputy Whitaker?" He turned to Tim waiting for the answer.

"Yes, sir. It is marked with tape and the forensics team is already on their way from Greenville."

"Good, we can't afford another storm washing away more evidence. And the alleyway by riverfront?"

Tim answered quickly, "Max signaled a small human scent article. It has been marked, and the forensics team will check it as well when they are here."

"Now, Officer McCormick, I wanted to discuss the possibility of you helping with our fugitive search for Robert no confirmed last name." He waited for her to answer.

"And what can we do to assist, sir?" Savanna wasn't sure what he needed.

"The suspect is wanted for kidnapping one of my deputies, and we," he looked over at Tim, "have not been able to locate him. He has not been seen since the last storm. We know that he was using a boat for transportation, so it is possible he's been bogged in somewhere. But it's only one theory."

"Max doesn't generally do searches for living subjects although I'm sure he would do fine if there has been an injury or something of that nature."

"I wanted to get your thoughts before I called your chief to ask for your assignment."

"He told me you had me until we were finished, so I don't think he would mind if you still need me."

"Sir, Officer McCormick has a young boy she cares for. I think we would need to consider some housing for them if she is going to be here for the investigation." Tim chanced a sideways glance at Savanna and hoped she wasn't angry.

"Your son?" he asked.

"No, my brother."

"Okay, I will see what I can arrange. We have several lofts downtown available on a temporary basis that will probably work. Deputy Whitaker, check on it and get one appropriate for her situation."

"Yes, sir."

"Thank you for your work this morning. I'm pleased it went so quick. Hopefully, it will continue to go that way so you can return to Raleigh."

"It wasn't me, Sir. It was all Max." Max squeaked his ball on cue.

The sheriff looked over desk down at the shepherd on his floor. "Thank you, Max. Now time to take him home." Max squeaked again. Tim looked over at Savanna who was trying to hold in a laugh.

"Sir, did you need anything from me? I would like to walk Officer McCormick out to her vehicle, so we can plan out her return."

He waved a dismissal, "Yes, go ahead. I expect a full report by the end of the day on the crime scene, Deputy Whitaker. I will see you soon, Officer McCormick."

As they walked out to her SUV, Max was content to walk in between them. The sky was starting to cloud, and the shadows danced on the pavement. Tim could feel the rain coming. "It's going to rain again. I hope it's not a bad one."

"So, when do you want to get started?"

"Let's plan on Monday. I will get the apartment lined up for you three, and you can get settled this weekend when you come for the BBQ."

"Okay, that will give me time to get Charlie set with school. You know any good day camps?"

"I'll check on it. I'm sure we can find something. I know Beth's best friend is in from France right now and she has two boys about Charlie's age. They have been hanging out with Jose's kids."

"Awesome. Thanks."

Savanna opened the back hatch, and Max jumped in not turning loose of his toy. She stepped around to the driver's side, and Tim made his move, placing his hand on her door.

"I told myself I would wait for our work project to be over. But I want you to know I intend to ask you out. I just think people shouldn't date at work."

She smiled up at him, taking her cap off and letting down her hair. Red curls fell over her shoulders catching the sun and his breath as she shook it out.

"Wow." His mouth dropped open. "Can I take that back?"

She laughed filling the silence of the parking lot. "I have the same rule. So, no, you can't take it back. We're on the same page. You can call me, though."

Heat ran through him. This week was going to be hard. "Okay, I will. Text me when you are done with your day, and we'll talk."

"Sounds like a plan." She leaned over and gave him a hug. Tim loved the way it felt to have her arms around his waist. He released her to keep her from feeling how much he liked it. It had been a long time since he let a woman affect him that way, but she did every time he saw her. "Now let me go so I can go get Charlie. I have to prepare him for next week."

"Talk to you tonight." Tim stepped out of the doorway so she could shut it, wishing she would stay.

CHAPTER 14

DISARTICULATION

*B*umper to bumper traffic made the trip into Raleigh miserable. *Just my luck to hit rush hour.* The doctor's office was Savanna's first stop. She couldn't miss her appointment. It had totally slipped her mind with everything happening this week. The small shopping center was teaming with customers for the pharmacy which sat next to Dr. Raynor's office. She backed into a parking spot in front of the office, and her knuckles turned white as they gripped the steering wheel. She needed to talk things through with the doc, but she didn't want to. A lot had happened since her last appointment.

"Max, you ready to see Doc?" The German shepherd peeked through the barrier and whined. "I know, buddy, but mom needs to go." She put her SUV in park and turned off the ignition.

Walking around to the back, she jumped as several men came out of the pharmacy yelling, "Shut up, bitch, we didn't want your shit anyway." Savanna unbuckled her holster and cleared her throat. The men turned her way, and Max started to growl behind the glass of the rear window. "And what are you looking at?" They started walking toward her.

"I was just stopping by and heard the yelling. Is there anything I can help with?" Savanna lifted the back window so Max could see what was going on, and the men could see the huge dog in the back. She could see the pharmacy manager looking out of the window talking on the phone.

"No bitch, you can't help me, but maybe you can help him." He pointed at the man next to him who was looking at Savanna with raw lust in his eyes.

"Sorry, I'm not interested. Now you need to move along before you get into trouble." Savanna watched the manager give her a thumbs up and move back into the store. "Max here needs to get out and get some exercise. He's not too friendly." Max growled right on cue. Two cruisers pulled into the lot and pulled in front of Savanna's vehicle. The three men looked at each other, turned, and disappeared around the building.

Savanna stepped into the pharmacy. "Everything okay?"

"Yes. Thank you. They were being vulgar, and I asked them to leave. You heard the rest," the clerk at the register answered, ringing items as she explained.

"You need anything else?"

"Nope, I'm good. I'm busy. Can you thank the officers for me?"

Savanna yelled over her shoulder as she pushed through the front door, "Sure, I got it. You have a good afternoon." She walked over to the officer in the car to fill them in. "Thanks, Tom, for coming so quickly. They were being obnoxious."

"You want us to go ID them?"

"No, it's not worth it. Who's with you?" she asked. She looked over at the other car and froze at the sight of him. Instantly her hands went into her hair twirling and twirling until it formed a bun.

Then the pins came out of her pocket to force it to stay in place. After she was done, she squared her shoulders and nodded at the other car. He smiled.

"Jeremy. We thought you were in Washington today. They release you already?"

She kept her eye on the man in the other car. "Max finished early this morning," she motioned to the back of the SUV, "but they have something else for me to do, so we'll be heading back in the morning."

"How bad was it?" Tom asked.

"Not as bad as our usual. Just a basic search. I've got to go."

"Sure, I know you have stuff to do if you are going to be on assignment." Tom pulled off to the entrance of the shopping center, and Jeremy eased up beside her with his window down.

"Did they send you back or did you get bored and quit?"

"Why do you care? I thought I made myself clear last night. How's the hand by the way?" She scowled at him noticing the ace bandage on his left hand, the public space making her brave.

"You will miss me eventually, and then you will come crawling back. You can't hold out forever."

"Whatever. I have to go. Max and I have an appointment."

"That's right. It's shrink day. Still crazy as ever. I'll see you later. Don't be afraid to call."

Relieved, she watched him leave. What an ass. Thank God she would be out of town for a while. Maybe he would find someone else while she was gone. She popped the back door of the vehicle and Max hopped down to the sidewalk. He sat patiently while she hooked his leash. "Good boy. Let's go see Doc before she cancels on us."

DUE CARE

4:30pm

Tiredness was beginning to overcome Savanna as her early start caught up with her. The subdued lighting in the office didn't help. Max curled up at her feet seemed as tired as she was.

"So, Savanna, tell me about your week." The doc pushed her glasses up on her nose. "How did the field trip go?"

"A lot happened. We enjoyed the places we visited. There was an issue with some of the boys and Charlie went missing for a while."

The doctor wrote something down on her pad. "How long was he missing?"

"About 20 minutes, but it seemed like longer."

"And how did that make you feel?"

"I almost had a panic attack, but I used the breathing techniques we practiced last week. They helped."

"Good. What else happened?"

"I met someone." Savanna shifted in her seat, uncomfortable about mentioning Tim and the doctor jotting down a note.

"Really?" The doctor looked up at Savanna.

"Yes, but he is one of the deputies there in Washington," Savanna said matter-of-factly.

"And what about your new rule about dating at work?" She asked, "Didn't that cause problems in the past?"

Savanna wondered the same thing. "Yes, that's why we have agreed to wait until the assignment is over."

"And he has agreed to wait?"

"Yes. Tim is a great guy and understands."

"Okay, so let's talk about work. Tell me about this week's searches."

"Let's see. We had two this week. One teenage boy had been missing for two weeks. He disappeared on a camping trip with his parents. It was in the National Park out west. Max did a good job even in the dense forest."

"How about you? How did you do?"

"I used the breathing methods you suggested. I let Max do his thing and kept up with flagging as we went so we could record the alert locations. No issues, the parents were not on site."

"So, do you think that helped? Not having to watch the family?"

"Maybe," Savanna agreed flatly. Max put his nose in her lap.

"Okay, what about the second search?" She wrote something else on her notepad.

"That was this morning. Not really our forte. We located a crime scene for the Beaufort County Sheriff's Department." Savanna rubbed Max between the ears, not even looking at the woman sitting across from her. "We are headed back tomorrow to assist further."

"On a Saturday? That's unusual. What about Charlie?"

"Tomorrow will be a transition day. We don't really start the investigation until Monday. Charlie is going with Max and me to Washington."

"And you think that will be okay with Charlie?"

"What do you mean?" Savanna's hands clenched till her knuckles turned white.

"Moving so soon after being settled into your apartment. I'm just asking if you have considered his feelings."

"Of course, I have. It's going to be rough on Max and me too." Savanna's voice raised in volume, disrupting the serene feel of the room. "Do you think I would do anything that would not be good for Charlie?"

"No, I am not saying that. I'm asking if you have asked Charlie about going to Washington yet."

"No, I have not seen him this afternoon to discuss it." Savanna was pissed now and didn't feel like talking anymore. "I will do it this evening when we are packing."

"Do you have a plan on how you will approach it?"

"Actually, I haven't thought about it." Savanna felt the heat in her face. She wanted to scream. "I'm sure he won't mind spending time there with his new friend, Tim."

The doctor stopped writing and looked at Savanna. "So, Charlie has met Tim?"

"Yes. Maybe you would like to come over and supervise the conversation." Her voice rose to a shout.

"Savanna, you need to take a breath. I am trying to help you come up with a plan. Why has this upset you so much? Or maybe there is something else going on?"

Savanna looked at the doctor. "I'm trying to understand why I can't give closure to Charlie. This new search, the one in Washington, is for a woman's husband who is supposed to be dead. And now all the sudden he is alive. How fair is that? She has a new boyfriend, and she finds out her husband is still alive."

"And how does that make you feel?"

"Like we're cursed or something."

"Why do you feel that way?"

"Mom and dad are gone. I've come to grips with it. I know they are never coming back. But what if? This search makes me think, what if?

"Do you think that is realistic?"

"No. I know it's not. But neither did this woman. How do I tell my heart to give up?" A tear escaped from Savanna's eye and ran down her cheek. "I'm just tired, tired of being strong for everyone else."

"And how are you taking care of yourself? Have you done anything fun lately?"

Savanna wiped the tears off her face and looked at the doctor, "We are going to the BBQ festival tomorrow in Washington."

"Is that for you or Charlie?"

Savanna didn't answer right away.

"Think about it this weekend. This is something new moms struggle with all the time."

Savanna started to protest.

The doctor cut her off immediately. "Nope, you are technically a new mom. It's going to take a while to get your life balance back. I have a project for you." The doctor crossed the room from her desk with something in her hand.

Max watched her carefully as she approached Savanna.

"I have something for you to keep. It's small enough to slip in one of your side pockets." She held out a small book.

"Thanks, it's cute." Savanna took it and flipped through the pages. "What's this for?"

"I want you to focus on the good stuff happening with Charlie. So, at the end of each day, I want you to write down one word that reminds you of something good that happened."

"Just one word?" Savanna asked.

"Yes, only one word. You should have enough time for it."

"I guess."

"Okay let's practice your breathing and then we will end the session."

❧

SESSION 54: Savanna McCormick

Copy to: Department of Child Services

Client attended session with K9.

The client continues to be distracted and detached from her anxiety during her session. (i.e. staring into space, not listening to counselor, picking at dog's coat beside her.) Reluctant to talk about weekly experience. Listed details but did not elaborate until prompted for further information.

Case 1 this week involved a 12-year-old boy found in a rocky terrain on the side of a steep incline. Head was removed from torso. No evidence of foul play. Subject was missing for 2 weeks. Decomposition was amplified by heavy rains. Max and Captain McCormick found the male after a 6-hour search. Capt. McCormick has used the compartmentalization technique we have focused on to control her empathy with the victim's parents. She has admitted to a feeling of jealousy toward the parents because of the closure they received at finding the victim. Her lack of closure is maintaining her grief as a barrier when relating to other adults.

Case 2 caused extreme emotional distress to the client because of the reappearance of a woman's dead husband. This has given Capt. McCormick false hope her parents are still alive. She expressed this in the session along with jealousy toward the woman.

Personal this week -- she took brother on field trip. Used new task technique to deal with large group of young adolescents. Seems to have coped well. Mentioned a period of time when brother was missing which caused extreme anxiety. Exhibited signs of panic, client's breathing increased, and legs moved while telling the story. Clearly affected Capt. McCormick and put her in a situation where she was not in control. She does seem to be handling her guardianship well even though she has no experience of being a parent.

Recommend continuing weekly counseling to deal with grief and job-related stress. Client should continue breathing exercises and making lists to deal with situations in which she feels overwhelmed. She has been assigned to start a one-word journal to focus on the good instead of the stress.

CHAPTER 16

SCENT VOID

7:30pm

TIM FINISHED up the report for the morning search and the incident at the bakery. Greenville had turned in a list of preliminary findings. There was bodily fluid on the mattress and gate as Savanna had predicted. There was clothing found and marks on the floor from a tripod. Some footprints in the mud toward the entrance, a male size 12 hiking boot. They were a different size than the prints at the house. Those could be from a tourist, but they could be their perp's. He rubbed his eyes with his thumb and fingers. Time to decompress. He looked at his watch. Maybe the guys were at Down on Main. He decided to walk over. Straightening the notes of the day, he strode over to the front desk.

"Isn't it about time for you to head home?" He asked leaning on the surface of the desk.

Mae smiled at him. "Nope, not yet. Tonight's my late shift. It's been quiet for a Friday. Where are you headed?"

"Down on Main. Maybe play some pool with the guys."

"Sounds fun." She paused for a moment as if she was hesitating. "Listen, I didn't want to say anything this afternoon, but you know that K9 Cop... I would stay away from that situation if I were you."

"What situation?"

"She's been through a lot this year. She lost her parents."

"I know, but, how do you?"

"It was one of our cases last year."

"Here?"

"Yes, they just disappeared, went out sailing, and it was like they never were aboard. I can't remember why you weren't in town for it. Sheriff handled it himself."

"Did they find anything?"

"Nope. You could ask Mike. I think he handled the boat."

Tim scrunched up his lip. "I'll do that." He slapped his hand on the desktop and straightened, heading out the door and down the street toward the restaurant.

THE RESTAURANT WAS PACKED. Tim looked around for the group and wasn't surprised to find everyone standing around the pool table on the upper level. A small blonde sitting next to Sam was the only person he hadn't known most of his life. Customers created a path as he walked through the busy restaurant. He didn't have time to change because of his busy day, and he told himself he would not be drinking tonight because of the uniform. A good impression was always a requirement. As Tim made his way through the crowd of people at the rear entrance, the hum of a hundred conversations was deafening. Then a beautiful laugh broke through. He topped the stairs and discovered it belonged to Sam's companion.

Tim walked straight over to the table against the wall. "Hello there. Sam, are you going to introduce us?"

Sam stopped talking and looked up at his friend. He stood up and playfully punched Tim in the shoulder. "You finally made it."

"Yes, I've made it. It's been busy at work." Tim rubbed his shoulder and then stretched out his hand to the beautiful blonde sitting at the table. "How are you? I'm Tim."

She reached out to take his hand and then a crack of the balls made her jump and look at the table.

"He's always too busy to meet us for a game. Abbie, just ignore him." Mike leaned over the table to take his next shot.

She grabbed Tim's hand still hanging in the air awkwardly. "Hi, I'm Sam's friend from D.C., Abbie."

He shook her hand and released it. "Ah, the other Washington. What brings you down here?"

"Sam and I are working on an inventory for the Historical Registry. There are quite a few unoccupied properties, and I'm making a note of their condition." She took a sip of her drink. Sam sat down in a chair opposite her.

"So, this is Abbie?" He looked down at his closest friend, giving him a look of disbelief. Abbie was what Tim would call a cutie with awesome curves and a smile that lit up the whole room no matter who it was directed toward.

"Yep." Sam checked his phone, shoved it in his pocket and looked up at Tim. "And Beth knows she is staying at the house."

"How is Beth?" Tim flagged down a waitress and ordered a Coke.

"She's okay. They checked her out at the hospital and released her. She's back home at the Water Street house."

Tim pulled up a chair next to his friend. "Did you talk to her about the photo?"

Sam shook his head.

"It obviously upset her." He leaned closer to Sam trying to keep the conversation private despite their company. "You need to talk it out."

"She won't talk to me at all, if you must know, even put her wedding ring back on. She asked for some space, and that's what I'm giving her."

"With a gorgeous woman staying at your place?" Tim eyeballed his friend over the edge of his drink. "Did she say it was him for sure?"

"We both know it's him. She put her ring back on, for Christ sake." Sam took a long swig of his beer, finishing it off. He sat the empty bottle back on the table.

Tim laid a hand on his buddy's shoulder. "You know this is going to make it rough for her. She might want to get a lawyer."

"She has a good lawyer in Colorado."

"Got it." Tim could sense he didn't want to talk anymore. He flagged down the waitress to get Sam another beer. His phone vibrated in his pocket.

Savanna: Hopefully you are having a better night than I am.

He smiled seeing her text before typing back.

Tim: Out with friends

Savanna: Sounds fun, Charlie insisted on packing himself. Ahhhh!

Tim: That must mean I'll be seeing you tomorrow. I'm sure you have it under control. Are you ready for more searches?

Savanna: It's what we do best.

Tim: Is Charlie excited about tomorrow? Mike nudged him with his pool stick breaking the spell of the screen.

"Oh sorry." He moved out of the space his friend needed to line up the cue.

Mike smiled as he looked back at Tim. "What's so interesting?"

"None of your business." Abbie moved past them, and Mike's eyes followed her. "Knock it off, dude."

Mike raised up and shrugged his shoulders. "What?"

Tim shook his head and sat his glass on the table. "I'm out of here. I have to work tomorrow." He smiled at Abbie. "It was nice to meet you, Abbie. Welcome to the original Washington. Don't let these guys give you a hard time." He moved over to the stairs. "Sam," he made eye contact with him. "I'll talk to you later."

He typed out one quick last message to Savanna.

Tim: Headed home. I'll see you in the morning.

CHAPTER 17

SCENT CONE DISTORTION

*O*ctober 18, 2014, 8:30am

Savanna checked the rearview mirror. Charlie's fingers poked through the wire mesh screen separating the backseat and rear compartment; Max's tongue licked the boy's hands. Giggles filled the SUV, and it looked like it was going to be a very good day. She was tired from her late-night packing session, but Charlie was a big help and excited about their new adventure. She might have talked the trip up a bit, but it was important for Charlie to be as comfortable as he could be with the special assignment.

His little head bobbed with whatever song he was listening to, and Savanna smiled with thoughts of meeting Tim on the waterfront. When she rounded the corner into town, the crowd surprised her. Parking was going to be a problem, she could already tell. Charlie's face was immediately stuck to the glass as he pointed at the carnival rides and tents. Savanna rolled down the windows, letting the music and noise of the crowd fill the vehicle. Max started to pace back and forth in the back. She needed to let him out for a break.

"Siri, dial Tim." Savanna scanned the street for a good place to pull over. She felt her pulse increase. The crowds were proving to be a challenge to her good mood.

"Savanna, I want to ride that first," Charlie yelled.

"Okay buddy let's see where we need to meet Tim and we need to let Max have a pee break."

Max barked in agreement.

"We will hit everything. We have all day," she added.

"This is going to be so awesome." He leaned out of the window.

"Charlie, stay in the car." Savanna heard a voice from her phone.

"Hey, Savanna. Where are you guys? Hello, hello?"

"Oh, hey, hold on. Charlie back in your seat, please. Let me put you on speaker."

"Okay, can you hear me now?"

"Yes, that's better. We are down on the waterfront trying to find parking. Charlie won't sit still, and Max has to pee." Max barked again. "This is making me crazy."

"Come over to the sheriff's department, and we can sort some stuff out before we deal with the crowds."

"Are you working?" Savanna pulled down Main Street, the sudden change in wind direction filled the SUV with the smell of smoke and cooking BBQ.

"I'm working tonight, so I have most of the day to spend with you guys."

"Good, I'm coming your way now. I hope you are ready for this."

"I can't wait. See you soon."

The vehicle passed the crowds on the busy street making the final turn toward the sheriff's parking lot. Charlie squirmed in his seat, but Savanna could tell the excitement of the day had taken over. "You need to make sure to stay close to Tim or me. I can't worry about you disappearing today." She looked at him using the rearview mirror. "Charlie, look at me." The little boy slowly made eye contact with her. "Are you listening? No disappearing acts today."

"Okay. Don't forget Max is with us."

"I won't forget Max. I want to have fun today."

He nodded his head and then waved wildly as Tim came into view standing in the front of his cruiser in the lot.

"Look, Max, it's Tim."

Max whined with excitement. Savanna didn't know if it was at the sight of Tim or the grass against the building behind him. As she pulled into the spot next to the deputy, her nerves started. She couldn't believe simply the sight of him made her palms start to sweat. She wiped them on her pants leg. She better set her boundaries now or working with him was going to be impossible.

She smiled and caught his gaze. Heat flooded her face. This was going to be difficult. Charlie was already out of his seat and opened the door as soon as she turned the car off. She let out a sound of exasperation and Charlie turned to look at her. "Thanks for waiting for the car to shut off." He shrugged and ran to Tim.

"Wait till you meet Max."

"I met him yesterday, bud. We got on great."

Charlie smiled up at him and yelled over at Savanna who was unloading Max. "You didn't tell me you saw Mr. Tim yesterday."

Savanna grabbed Max's collar and hooked his leash. "We've been busy." She walked Max over to a small patch of grass.

"Come on, Savanna. We are going to miss it."

"I hardly think the festival is going to disappear in a matter of minutes. Can you help me out here?" She looked over at Tim for some support.

"What? I'm as anxious as he is to get down to the waterfront." He gave her a charming smile.

"Thanks a lot." She kneeled down and gave Max a hug. "Looks like it's you and me, Max," she said so everyone could hear her. He gave her a huge lick and then strained against his leash to get to Charlie. Savanna turned him loose, and Max ran to Charlie giving him a huge kiss before stepping back to relieve himself in the grass.

Tim let out a loud laugh, his smile touching every inch of his face. "Looks like it's three against one."

"Oh, I see how it is. Charlie, you are in charge of Max then. Don't let him eat too much people food."

"Awesome. Come on Max, let's go." The little boy grabbed the leash and wrapped it around his hand. The dog gave Savanna a look, and she nodded. The dog was instantly on his feet and following Charlie across the parking lot.

"Charlie, hold up," Tim yelled after him. "We have one stop before we head down to the waterfront."

The little boy's face fell, and he turned. "Are we ever going to get there?"

"It's a quick one. I thought you might want to see where you will be staying in case you need a break later."

"Who's going to need a break?" Charlie asked.

"I might need one if I get hot," Savanna added trying to support Tim.

"Okay, but just for a minute. Max really wants to play some games."

"We need to go down the alley and then turn left." Tim gave him some directions since they were leading the way. Charlie pulled Max to go down the alley, and Savanna noticed the dog resisted.

"Can we go down another alley, maybe?" Savanna tried to relay her concern to Tim, but he didn't seem to pick up on it.

"Sure, we will go down the next one. Hey, Charlie let's go down to the next one and cut over."

Charlie shrugged and pulled the German shepherd down the block to the next alley. Max happily followed and to Savanna's relief he had no trouble heading down the alleyway. As they turned down Main, the street was full of people. Max walked closer to Charlie.

"Charlie, we are going to stop at 532." Tim let him know ahead of the time.

Charlie checked each number on the buildings, stopping in front of an antique store. "What is this?" He looked in the large display window at porcelain and pottery. "Max can't go in there. We will break something for sure."

Tim handed Savanna a key. "We are actually going to go in this door." He motioned to a small door next to the shop. "You have the pleasure, Ma'am."

"Okay, cool." Charlie pushed in between Tim and Savanna, as she stretched to reach the lock. When she finally unlocked the door, he ran up the stairs. Savanna quickly stepped out of the way, watching him and Max head up.

"Thank you for this." She said to Tim.

"For what? It's going to be a great day." He looked down at her a smiled.

Savanna thought he was going to kiss her, or maybe she wanted him to kiss her. Then Charlie appeared at the top of the stairs. "Savanna, you have got to see this. It is so cool. Do I get my own bedroom?" Then he disappeared again.

"Thank you so much for finding us a place." Savanna was disappointed Charlie interrupted them, but thankful at the same time.

"It's no trouble. It's fully furnished, but I let the landlord know you have a boy. So, it's been tween-proofed. There is Wi-Fi and cable. I think you will really like your room if Charlie hasn't already claimed it." He reached down and grabbed her hand, sending shivers up her arm. "Are you cold? I didn't think I turned the AC up that high."

"No, I'm good." As they climbed the stairs, Savanna was amazed at the artwork on the wall. A beautiful mermaid curved against the banister and swam to the top floor. On the ceiling, shells and starfish were peaking from behind pieces of seaweed. Fish covered in gold leaf almost jumped off the wall on the top landing. Charlie's voice echoed through the hall that led to additional rooms. It sounded like he was giving Max the grand tour. Tim tugged on her hand pulling her toward a back room.

"And this is your room."

Savanna could not believe her eyes. The window covered the south wall with a view of the waterfront. She could see the festival in full swing. "Charlie, come and see my room."

His footsteps were noisy coming down the hall. "Oh, man. I thought my room was the coolest. Look at yours." He jumped on the king size bed bouncing high into the air. Max watched him from the bedroom floor, the dog's head bobbing with every jump. Savanna leaned over to Tim and whispered, "I hope we won't be too loud for our downstairs neighbors."

"I'm sure you guys will be fine. They have very limited hours. Charlie, show me your room."

"Okay." The boy jumped to the floor, planting his landing like a gymnast. "Come on." He grabbed Savanna's hand and led the way down the hall. He pushed open the door to reveal an underwater diver's paradise. The walls were a deep blue with a mural of a distant sandcastle.

"Can you swim?" Tim asked.

"Yes, my mom taught me how."

"Well, this is the perfect bedroom for a young man who loves to swim."

"I don't go swimming anymore."

Savanna stopped and looked at the pair talking in the corner.

"Really? Why is that?" Tim looked over at Savanna. She didn't want to answer the question and wondered how Charlie would.

"It makes Savanna worry if I get too close to the water."

That was a good answer, maybe Tim won't dig, Savanna thought.

"Are you a good swimmer?"

"The best, I can put my head under and everything."

"Maybe I'll take you out of the river one day." He ruffled the little boy's hair.

Savanna interrupted, "I don't think that would be a good idea. Come on, you don't want to miss the games."

Charlie didn't miss a beat, grabbed Max's leash and headed to the stairs. Tim looked over at her and Savanna felt uncomfortable under this scrutiny. Charlie wouldn't keep their secrets long. He was too comfortable with Tim. A dark cloud washed over her suddenly, and she felt her excitement for the trip begin to fade. Tim watched her without saying a word. He opened his mouth to say something, and then a head poked around the door facing.

"Savanna, come on. We're gonna miss it."

Savanna looked at her brother and smiled. He was the one person she could always count on, and she really needed to shake this feeling off for him. He was enjoying life again, and she couldn't ruin it.

"We can bring boxes up later," Tim commented as he headed down the stairs. He was already on the sidewalk when the other three closed the entry door.

"I appreciate the help." She forced a smile and checked for traffic as she grasped Charlie's hand. The smell of smoked meat drifted in the wind luring the three people and their furry companion toward the waterfront. It was still early for the crowds Tim had promised, but it suited Savanna. Booths lined the grassy area along the water.

Today is a day to have fun, Savanna reminded herself again as Tim agreed to buy Charlie a huge ice cream cone before he ate his sandwich. *Just breathe.* She started to regulate her breaths in and out and closing her eyes focused her mind. Then a giggle broke into her zone. She opened her eyes, and all the boys were staring at her. Max cocked his head and didn't even blink. Tim had an amused smirk on his face, and Charlie didn't try to hide his laughter as his cheeks exploded with more laughter.

"Do you need a yoga mat?" Tim asked. She shook her head. "It's not that bad. He will burn the sugar off."

"You're not the one will be with him this evening after you go to work." She elbowed him, giving him a smile. The long line slowly disappeared as the attendant filled the orders one cone at a time. Tim continued to tease Savanna as they neared the end of the line.

"No Max, we need to stay close to Savanna." Charlie was getting flustered. Max pulled on the leash hard enough to pull him off balance, and it made his hand hurt. He looked over at Tim and his sister laughing and having a good time. He didn't want to ruin her day. "Max, stop it." Max pulled harder. He yanked him back, shortening the leash like Savanna had taught him.

Then, a figure caught his eye at the corner of the truck. He stared to see if he was right. Abram popped out again, peeking around the corner. It was him. He looked worried as he made eye-contact with Charlie. Max pulled against Charlie's hand toward Abram. This time, he followed. Abram motioned for him to come to the back of the food truck. He loosened his grip on Max's collar and followed the dog in between the booths.

As Charlie stepped next to a loud generator, Abram grabbed his arm making him jump. He couldn't hear anything. Abram looked him in the eyes and said something. He concentrated as Abram tried again. Charlie followed his lips. *Someone needed help. Take Max and follow him.*

The threesome walked up the waterfront to a garden. Max pulled toward one of the bushes along the fence line.

"There, Charlie. He's lost. Get him and take him to your sister. They will know what to do." Abram pointed to the corner bush.

Charlie nodded and followed Max. They parted the branches, and a small toddler looked up at him. Tears were running down his cheeks. "Doggy," was the boy's shout as he reached up to touch Max's tongue. His blue shorts were dirty from playing in the garden, and his arms were scratched up.

Charlie turned back to Abram to ask him how to get the little boy back to the ice cream truck, but he was gone. Taking the little boy's hand, Charlie helped him gain his balance and then turned to Max. "Max, not too fast. This guy can't walk very well. We need to find Savanna, quick." He looked down the walkway, trying to figure out how far they had come. It wasn't far. "Find Savanna." Max barked startling the little boy making him cry again. Charlie looked around, no one was there to help. The garden was on a small hill and Charlie could see the ice cream banner blowing above the crowd.

Leaning down to look at the little one's face, Charlie reassured him, trying really hard to get him to stop crying. "Come on buddy, let's find your mom." Charlie took a big breath. "I wish someone would find mine," he half whispered not caring who heard.

He stood back up and wrapped Max's leash around one hand and grabbed the boy's hand with the other. They followed the railing along the boat slips back up the walkway. He could hear Savanna's panicked voice now. "Charlie, Charlie, where are you?" Oh, man I'm in trouble again. He yanked the leash toward the ice cream truck and squeezed between the booths, being very careful of the little one as he passed the trailer hitch.

"We're back," Charlie announced. Tim stood there, ice cream dripping down his hands and Savanna twisting her hair in a bun like she always does when she is worried about something. There were so many people, and they were all looking at him. "Savanna, this guy is lost, and Abram said you would know what to do."

Savanna rushed over, hugging him. "Where did you go? I thought we promised you wouldn't do any disappearing acts today." She leaned out, looking at him and waiting for an answer.

"Abram asked Max and me to save this boy." Charlie pulled the toddler toward Savanna.

Tim ditched the ice cream cones in the trash can. "Next time you go on a police mission you might want to let someone know where you're headed. You're making a bad habit of this, dude."

Charlie nodded his head. "So, what do we do with this guy? He won't stop crying."

Tim grabbed the little boy into his arms and leaned down to Charlie. "We are going to take him to the sheriff's tent, where all lost boys should go to find their parents. Great job dude, finding the kid."

Charlie took a deep breath. "Thanks, Tim." He followed the adults, Savanna holding onto the tail of his shirt like he held onto Max's leash. The sheriff's tent came into sight and a lady with braids, screaming her head off, ran toward Tim.

"Benjamin, where did you go?" She grabbed the small child sitting him on the ground. She ran her hands over him. "You are absolutely filthy." She gave him a tight hug, and he pointed to Max. "Doggy."

She turned to Tim. "Where did you find him? I was in line one minute and the next he was missing out of his stroller."

"Max actually found him." Tim pointed at the German shepherd. "He was playing in the garden up on the hill."

"How in the world?" She shook her head. She walked over and gave Max a scratch between the ears. The toddler grabbed an ear when his mom leaned down. "Thank you, Max." She looked at

Charlie. "You have a very special dog." The mom headed back to the tent behind her.

Charlie was so proud of what they had done. *Sometimes, I guess it's okay to take a risk.* "He is a great dog." He turned to Tim. "Now, can we get some ice cream." He jumped up and down. "I'm hungry."

Tim let out a big breath, biting his bottom lip.

"Sandwich first, then ice cream and no more running off." Savanna poked Charlie's shoulder.

Charlie nodded his head wildly and continued to hop.

"Oh boy," Tim breathed, nodding toward the sheriff standing in the shade of the tent. He grabbed Charlie's hand and pulled him to the BBQ tent.

CHAPTER 18

ADIPOCERE

It was three o'clock when Savanna unlocked the door and held it for Tim who carried Charlie as if he weighed nothing. Max did great in the crowd and stayed close to Savanna after his leash master gave up to a nap. They were all exhausted from shopping all the vendor booths. Even Max appreciated the homemade dog biscuit shop.

"Can you watch Charlie while I go get the car?"

"Of course," Tim whispered as he gently laid Charlie in his new bed. He pulled the covers up over the young boy and turned to Savanna. "I will be glad to go get the car, though, if you would rather stay here." He paused for a moment, "in case he wakes up."

Savanna was amazed at how at ease he was around Charlie. "Thanks. I'll be quick. Is it okay if I park right in front?"

"I think it will be fine. We will get you unloaded quick. Then you can park in the lot behind the building."

Savanna pulled the quilt up closer to Charlie's shoulder. She watched his slow breaths moving the blankets. He wouldn't wake up; she was sure of it, but she would take Tim up on his offer anyway. She turned, and he was watching her. His eyes were so gentle, and then it went away.

"Do you know how to get to the car?"

"Yeah, I'm good. Max," she paused listening for his nails on the wood floor. The loud lapping of water in the kitchen stopped, and then he appeared in the doorway. "Come, down."

The dog obeyed lying on the rug in front of the bed.

"Stay. He should be good while I'm gone." She gave Tim a smile, walking past him to the front hall for her keys. She listened, and no one followed her. She slowly pulled the door shut behind her and headed down Main to cut through the alleyway to the office lot.

As she passed the wrought iron sign on the street, the hair on the back of her neck prickled and a familiar feeling ran through her. She looked around, and her hands grabbed her hair, winding it into a tight bun. It pulled the skin of her scalp, but it quickly released without her pins. Her eyes nervously scanned the crowd. Where was he? He was here somewhere. She looked for his broad shoulders and bald head. And there he was standing in a group of people staring at her. His gaze burned her skin like fire.

Savanna stopped, and he started straight for her. Damn it. What should she do? They didn't know anyone here. No one would know she was afraid of him, of how he would man-handle her if he had a chance. Her hands shook, and she tried to will her feet to move toward the car. It was only a block away. *Just walk right past him. Don't acknowledge him.* She didn't have to make a scene.

Before she knew it, Jeremy was standing in front of her. Maybe she should turn around and go back to the apartment.

His hand caressed her cheek and Savanna closed her eyes. "Hey, baby, what are you doing here in Washington?"

"You know I am working."

"So, this is how they dress here for work." His hand went to her hair that was falling down her back now, brushing it with his fingers, so it blew in the wind. His hand traveled down her body, brushing her shoulder and grabbing her butt.

She winced. "Jeremy, let me go. I don't want to make a scene."

"You know you like it."

"I believe the lady said to let her go." Tim's voice came over her shoulder. Her eyes popped open, and she looked up at Jeremy's surprised face. Her whole body relaxed in the shadow of Tim's tall frame.

"Who is this?" Jeremy's smooth voice did not show any fear or surprise. But he dropped his hand in response.

"I'm Tim Whitaker. I'm giving Savanna a hand this weekend." He held out his hand for the other man to shake. Savanna stepped out of the way and looked at Tim. He gave her a wink. Her pulse raced, anticipating Jeremy's quick temper.

"Savanna, I was hoping to have some time alone with you this weekend," was his only response ignoring Tim's hand and turning to her waiting for Tim to leave.

Savanna grabbed Tim's outstretched hand and squeezed it. "I don't think so." She looked up at Tim and held the keys up to him. "Honey, you might need these. I'll be up in the apartment while you go get the car.

Tim nodded, grabbed the keys, and kissed her hand. "I'll be right up."

Savanna turned and went back up to watch the standoff from the apartment window. Tim stepped around Jeremy and disappeared through the crowd without any bloodshed or blows.

~

A TEXT MESSAGE DING SOUNDED, pulling her from her perch at the window.

The car was just around the corner. He should be back by now. What if Jeremy followed him? What if there was an argument? She walked across the hall to her room where her phone was charging, peeking at Charlie who was still sound asleep with Max on the rug beside the bed on her way by.

Jeremy: You are still mine.

The words on the screen made her blood boil. What made Jeremy think he owned her? She had been clear there was nothing left between them. She should call and report him to the Chief. She shook her head. If she did it would mean telling her boss they were dating which is against department rules. What should I do? She squeezed her eyes shut.

The sound of the door interrupted her thought. She poked her head out in the hall.

"It's me." Tim whispered, "And what the hell was that?"

"What?"

"The Neanderthal man-handling you on a public street." His wide gait helped him cross the apartment quickly. He motioned to grab her arm, but she stepped out of his reach.

"Keep your voice down." Savanna glanced over at Charlie's doorway.

Tim nodded. "You called me 'honey.' I think I deserve an explanation."

"Jeremy is not worth worrying about."

"It's obvious you're scared of him. Why won't you tell me?" He reached out again, this time she didn't move. His fingers brushed her cheek and Savanna felt her body relax a bit. "Tell me."

"He's my ex, nothing more. He surprised me, that's all."

Tim's eyebrow went up. "Are you sure?"

Savanna nodded knowing it was a lie. She was afraid of Jeremy and especially his habit of showing up out of the blue lately. His touch was never gentle like Tim's. She snapped back to where she was and the feel of his fingers on her face. She looked up and was drawn into the deep pools of blue. He leaned down and touched his lips to hers, very lightly taking her mouth, possessing it. His kiss deepened, his hunger obvious. His kisses traveled across her neck, and his teeth tugged at her earlobe. A steamy fog closed in on Savanna's thoughts. She couldn't think with him this close. Her determination was slipping away.

"Max, try this," Charlie's voice and the sound of bed springs invaded their embrace.

Savanna struggled to step back, physically shaking her head. "No, we said we wouldn't."

"You're right, I'm sorry. But you are so beautiful..."

"Don't say that." She shook her head again; her eyes dropping to the hardwood floors.

"Savanna, you take my breath away. Don't you know?" He took her hand and kissed it. "I'll wait. Let's go see what Charlie and Max are getting into before I have to go to work."

He didn't let go as he tugged her across the hall. She looked down at their hands woven together and smiled.

CHAPTER 19

SCENT COMMITMENT

4:00pm

Tim scribbled the name and number down on a piece of paper. "Here is Hellen's number. Give her a call. She already said she would love to have the boys play together." He looked up and smiled at her. "I promise you there are people here to help with Charlie."

"I don't know. He can be a handful sometimes."

"He's a boy. Hellen understands. Give her a call." The pen rolled off the table and hit her toe as it fell.

Savanna looked down, and Tim took advantage of the distraction. He wrapped his arms around her and gave her a bear hug, his lips firmly planted on her glistening red hair. She started to squirm, and Charlie started to laugh. Tim loved the way she felt, but he had promised. Promised he would wait till they were finished with this assignment. He released her and grabbed the little boy peeking around the door jamb, ruffling his hair, so it was sticking out in every direction. "I'll see you later, buddy."

"Stay safe Tim. Don't let the bad guys get you."

"I'll be careful. You be good." He gave Savanna a wink, headed down the stairs and stepped through the door onto Main Street.

There was a big crowd this year, he thought to himself. The street was full of people, and not the usual suspects, but tourists ready to spend their money on some good food. He glanced up at the sky as a call came over his radio.

"Deputy Whitaker you are needed at the office ASAP."

"Copy."

The clouds were getting thicker and it looked like the break in the weather would soon disappear. He cut down an alley and heard the footsteps behind him. He turned around to see who it was, but there was no one. He stepped lighter listening for any noise, slowing his stride. The echoes were not his imagination. There was someone in the alley with him.

Tim wondered why someone would be following him and then Jeremy's face came to mind. He didn't have far to go; the office was only another block away. He squared his shoulders and continued his purposeful stance. As he turned the corner, he glanced down the alley and caught a large figure in the shadows. Was it Jeremy? He couldn't tell.

He was too busy for foolishness. He walked across the lot and through the office door. The dispatcher at the front desk smiled at him.

"What have you been doing today, Deputy Whitaker?"

"Enjoying the festival before work. I was headed down to the waterfront when you called. What does he want?"

"He got the call from the National Hurricane Service. They say it's going to be a direct hit on North Carolina, and we need to start to prepare the evacuation."

"They've been talking about it for two weeks. Do we need to plan right now in the middle of the festival?"

A voice came from the far room, "Whitaker, get your butt in here."

Tim didn't waste any time walking to the office. He knew something was up.

"Yes, sir. What can I help you with?"

"The hurricane people are saying we are in for a storm in a day or so. We need to make sure we process the crime scene 100% before it hits."

"Already done sir."

"Good. The man-hunt will have to wait. They say it's a slow-moving storm so we will have time for the festival to finish up and all the guests to go home before we start evacuating. I need you to make some house calls. The usual families will insist on staying. Make sure we have a list so we can check on them as the storm gets closer."

"Yes, sir, and when you do want me to make those."

"Start tonight. Mark can take your shift on the waterfront."

"Yes, sir."

"And Whitaker, it goes without saying if you can change their mind, do it. They say this is a bad one. The storm surge alone is going to flood most of the county."

"Of course, sir. I will do my best."

"Thank you. Now get started."

Tim stepped out of the room and headed out the front door, giving Mae a salute and smile as he walked by. The lot was full of empty cars, and he was glad he was headed to the far end of the county instead of the waterfront. He sent Savanna a text.

Tim: I'm headed to the far end of the county. Might have bad reception. Text if you need me.

He didn't think she would need him, but with her ex in town, he wanted to be sure. He heard the chime on his phone and started the ignition. He made a mental list of a dozen families he needed to visit. The first would be Mitchell Whitaker, his father.

TIM TRIED to think how long it had been since he had been to see his father. The overgrown brush pushing up through the interior of old junk cars lined the side of the driveway. He could remember three times in the past ten years that didn't end in taking one of his brothers to jail. There was usually a call or two a month complaining of shooting or a disturbance. He used to try to bring his father groceries so he would have something in the refrigerator besides beer, but he had given up long ago because of his brothers. He tried to keep his distance so it would not affect his bid for sheriff when the time came, but his brothers had made it impossible to stay completely away.

He parked his cruiser in front of a dilapidated single-story tar-papered house. The porch had started to sag since Tim was there last. He stepped carefully in between the hole-filled boards, knowing good and well he should probably go to the back door for safety. His old man would be in the chair ten feet from the front door watching the soap operas he taped on VHS during the week.

He pulled back the screen door and knocked.

"Get away from that door. I have a gun, and I'm not afraid to use it."

"It's me, Daddy. Tim"

"Try again, my Tim wouldn't come to the front door."

"Daddy, it's me. Don't shoot. I'm going to poke my head in so you can see me."

Tim slowly opened the door, poking his head in first so his father could see who it was.

"You can put that down now."

The old man was sitting in his recliner with a beer in one hand and his rifle in the other.

"Dad, did you hear me? Put it down."

"Why didn't you come through the back? I almost shot you." The old man uncocked the rifle and laid it down on the floor beside him.

"I'm here on official business." Tim stepped into the room taking in the clutter and huge stack of VHS tapes beside the television.

"Your brothers aren't here, and I don't know where they are."

"I'm not here for them, I'm here to talk to you. Is it okay to sit down?" Tim motioned to the one empty spot on the couch.

"Did those church people call you? I only shot at the ceiling, so they would leave and not come back."

"Daddy, you can't be shooting at people."

"I didn't shoot at them. I told you I only shot the ceiling, see?" he pointed at the hole in the drywall above Tim's head.

Tim looked up and shook his head. "Dad they are only trying to be nice. They want to make sure you are eating."

"It's none of their business if I have food. They need to stay away from here."

"It doesn't matter. That's not why I'm here. There is a storm coming, and I want you to evacuate."

The man looked at Tim as if he had slapped him. "I have never left because of a storm and I never will. Humph." He nodded, took a long swig of his beer and tucked his chin into his chest.

"Daddy you need to listen to me." Tim leaned over towards his father. "This one is bad. It is huge and getting stronger by the day. I will come and get you when it's time. We can leave together."

"You're not leaving. You're the sheriff, you can't leave."

"I'm not the sheriff yet, and I will leave with you if you will go."

"What about your brothers?"

"They can decide on their own. You are the one I'm concerned about." Tim stood up and crossed the room looking into the kitchen with a sink full of dirty dishes and the back door standing wide open. "Do you have anything for dinner?"

"I probably have something in the fridge that will do me."

Tim tossed a brown bag into his father's lap. "Ms. Martha says hi and to behave yourself."

The older man opened the bag and licked his lips, "God bless that woman. How is she?"

"She still cares about you no matter how mean you get." Tim smiled at him. "I don't know why."

"Humph." He quickly unwrapped the biscuit oozing with warm cheese. "She's a good woman. Now leave me alone. I'm sure you have a long list of willing evacuees."

"Okay, I'm going, but I will be back for you when the storm comes this way." Tim opened the front door and headed out to the car. He could see a truck coming up the drive and knew he needed to leave now. He double-timed it to the car and started the ignition. As he passed the truck, he threw some fingers up in the air in some resemblance of a wave at one of his older brothers. In response, he received a middle finger salute and a spray of gravel.

So that answered that. Still mad obviously. It isn't my fault they send me out to get you because no one else can handle you. Tim was lucky he was the biggest one of all three of the boys. Otherwise, the county would be in trouble. To them, it was all about getting them back for everything they did during their childhood. To Tim, it was about growing up and being a man. He would show them who the better man was. Next stop would be Ms. Bennington on the creek.

Ms. Bennington lived in a river cabin built over the edge of the creek. Every storm surge, they begged her to come to town. But after 80 years in the same house, she would not desert her family home. She was the 10th generation in the cabin, and she would die there like everyone before her.

That afternoon the creek was already high. The water lapped over the deck surrounding the old woman's home. It wouldn't take much to come up in the house. Tim knocked on the front door, but he knew she already knew he was here. The bottles hanging from the eaves of the porch clanked in the wind. He knocked again.

"Ms. Bennington, may I come in?" he raised his voice over the noise.

She popped around the corner of the house and said, "Of course you can, Deputy Whitaker," startling Tim.

He smiled and took off his hat. "Thank you, ma'am."

"I'm glad you are here. I need to talk to you."

Tim followed her around the porch and bent down to enter the small kitchen on the back of the building. "Really? What can I help you with this evening?"

"Someone has woken up the ghost on the creek, and I need you to make them leave so he can sleep."

Tim looked at the woman with questioning eyes. "I'm sorry I don't think I heard you correctly."

"You heard me, young man. Someone has disturbed the ghost of the creek, and he is wandering where he shouldn't be."

"Ma'am, I don't usually handle the ghost calls. I'm here because of the storm."

"Oh, I'm not worried about that. You need to go see about the others. I will be fine if you can settle that ghost down. Here, sit down and have some tea."

A voice came through the window, "Ms. Bennington, how far up the bank did you say again? I can't seem to find..." the voice disappeared as footsteps rounded the porch to the backdoor.

Tim took the glass overflowing with ice. "Thank you."

"Now what are you going to do about that ghost."

"What?"

"The ghost." The older woman replied as the screen door swung open and Abbie stepped in with her blond hair blowing around her head like it was caught in a tornado.

"Oh sorry, I didn't know you had company. I'll wait outside."

"Don't be silly, child, grab you a glass of tea and relax a minute."

"Where does the ghost normally reside?' He finally gave in. He humored the old woman. She obviously wasn't going to let it drop. He turned and looked at Abbie who was frozen in mid-pour.

"A ghost?" Abbie asked. Tim shrugged and turned his attention back to the complainant.

"His cabin is on Tranter's Creek, and he is all stirred up."

"But Ms. Bennington, that is on the other side of the county. Are you sure?"

"Absolutely, young man. I haven't had him around here for a few decades, and he is making regular trips up the river. There's something going on."

"Maybe it's something to do with the survey," Abbie commented.

"I doubt it. You and Sam are just checking on the old houses. Why would that bother him? Photos of old houses wouldn't bother a soul."

"Okay, I will check it out. I will also check on you when the storm hits in case you would like to come to town."

"Save your time young man. You have better things to do than worry about an old woman."

Tim stood and took one last drink of tea. "I'd better be going. Call if you need anything."

"Will do," she said and busied herself with washing Tim's glass at the large porcelain sink. "We'll talk soon." She waved at him over her shoulder and turned to talk to Abbie.

Tim ducked under the door facing and put his hat back on. The rain had started, and it was blowing hard. The sound of the bottles created a melody that accompanied the sway of the trees surrounding the building.

He checked in with the office and then headed down the road, watching for any locations with high water. His mind wandered as he drove. A vision of Savanna on Main Street with Jeremy touching her popped into the forefront of his mind. It still made his temper flare. She hid her fear well, but he knew she had been scared. His knuckles turned white as he squeezed the steering wheel. An uneasy feeling crossed over him.

What if Jeremy was at the apartment? What if he had come after he left? She would text or call if she needed him, right? But they just met, there was no reason to expect she would call him. She was so beautiful and kind, she doesn't deserve that kind of treatment. He would be good to her, the kind of good that could lead to a long, happy life together. Wait, where did that come from?

He shut his eyes for a moment and shook his head. When he opened them, there was something in the road up ahead.

He needed to be more alert and tonight was going to be another long one. He didn't need thoughts of her clouding his brain.

He slowed and stopped, radioing the office again. "Deputy Whitaker here. Dispatch, do you copy?"

"Copy that Whitaker, go ahead."

"I have a tree down across the highway at the crossroads. We need a crew out here. I'm going to try and move it, so I have one lane open."

"I'll get the tree guys out there as soon as I can."

"Whitaker out."

Tim stepped out of his cruiser and looked the tree over. It was at least twenty feet long. He opened the driver's side and reached in the glove box for his leather gloves.

Oh man, can anything else happen tonight?

CHAPTER 20

CURTILAGE

5:30pm

"But I'm hungry," Charlie whined, jumping on Savanna's bed, narrowly missing her legs under the quilts.

"Charlie, how can you be hungry at all? We ate so much this morning. I'm still stuffed." Savanna rubbed her stomach and stuck her tongue out.

"It's time for dinner."

Savanna looked at her watch and smiled. You could set your watch to this kid's stomach. She was surprised Max wasn't begging too.

"We need to walk Max, and he gets fed first."

"Okay." He dismounted lading on his feet and ran into the other room. "I'll get the leash."

Savanna rolled over and saw Max still stretched out on the floor. So, Charlie was the only one in a hurry this evening. She stretched out her arms and pushed back the quilts. Max was instantly awake and standing when her feet hit the small rug at the side of the bed.

"We're coming."

Charlie was standing at the door tapping his foot. "Come on, we should get some pizza while we're out."

"You and your pizza. I'm not hungry, and you are not going to eat a whole pizza."

"Yes, I will. I'm really, really hungry."

"We'll get some hot dogs tonight and then we will see about pizza tomorrow."

Charlie nodded his head in agreement and bent down to hook Max's collar. "Good boy Max." Soon as the leash was connected, they were both at the doorknob.

"Wait, guys, I have to put some shoes on. Check the window and see if it is raining."

Savanna sat on the floor and tied her running shoes, as the boys ran past her to the closest window.

"Oh man, it's raining. Are we still gonna go?"

"Well, we have to take Max. We will see about going for food. Grab a jacket."

Savanna dug in a box labeled "Savanna's clothes" for a windbreaker.

Charlie was opening every box he could put his hands on. "Which box is mine, Savanna?"

"Everything is labeled. Look for your name."

"But Savanna..."

"Stop the whining and read the boxes."

"But you're faster."

"Charlie, go find your box. You only have two in your room."

The footsteps were deafening as they echoed through the apartment. Charlie stomped and then shuffled to his room. Savanna prayed there was no one downstairs. She needed to look at their hours so she and Charlie would be out of the apartment when they were open. Everyone seemed so nice here, she couldn't torture them with an eight-year-old's tantrums. She thought he would be in a better mood after his nap, but it seemed to make him crankier.

The usual doubts crowded back into her head. *I don't get it. Maybe I can't do this. He needs a real mom. Mom would know exactly what to do. I am not good at this.* Memories of her mom filled her mind. She missed her. She had so much patience with Charlie, with all her students really. Maybe Olivia could help.

Savanna texted Olivia.

Savanna: Help! Charlie is being a pain.

The response was immediate.

Olivia: What's he doing?

Savanna: Stomping around the apartment because I told him to get his own jacket from his room.

Olivia: Normal for an eight-year-old boy. You have to give him some adjustment time.

Savanna: Ok, I thought it was me.

Olivia: No, Believe me. It's not you. Just be there. A smiling emoji popped on the screen.

Savanna took in a big breath and slowly let it out. "Charlie, how's it coming?" Max barked.

"I found it, just trying to get it on over my… help, I'm stuck."

She sprinted down the hall and couldn't help herself when she saw her little brother. She burst out laughing. His head was through the neck hole, and his arms were awkwardly pointed in the air. His jacket was rolled up and twisted so it would not go on right. His hands were waving.

"Savanna help me. Don't laugh."

She tried to stifle another loud laugh. "I'm trying. Hold on, let me get you untangled."

Charlie struggled against the fabric.

"Charlie, stop." He froze like a statue and Savanna started to laugh again. She jerked it off him, and he sighed heavily like he needed oxygen. "Is that better?"

"Yep, can you help me please?"

"Of course. Here I will hold the jacket, and you can aim for the sleeves."

The gangly red-head aimed for the sleeves and hit them after a few tries. When Savanna finally zipped the jacket, Max was dancing at the door with a sense of urgency.

"We better head out before we have to clean up the floor on our first day here."

Charlie laughed, "That wouldn't be good."

"Nope." She grabbed the leash, and they took the stairs two at a time, making it outside just in time. "Charlie, remind me later to bring some hot soapy water for the sidewalk."

"Okay, so which way should we walk?" he peeked from under the hood of his jacket, the rain already dripping into his face from the downpour.

"Let's go down to the park and then we will come back around for hot dogs."

"All right," he jumped as he yelled, landing on the other side of a crack in the sidewalk.

"Nice one." Savanna reached out and pulled the drawstring on his hood tighter to keep him dry. She could do this. She forced a smile, more for herself than anyone else. The grin on her face showed how confident she really was with a little doubt thrown in. The corners of her mouth quivered a bit. She wrapped the leash around her wrist, pulled her own jacket closer to her body and they turned down the alley toward the park. A familiar feeling passed over her and goosebumps raised on her arms, but she told herself it was the cold and let the dog lead her toward the waterfront.

CHAPTER 21

VERTICAL SCENT CONE

6:27pm

Tim's slicker didn't protect him from the rain blowing sideways right into the armholes of the jacket. The tree crew had arrived after he had managed to move the tree to one side of the road. He was drenched and exhausted, but he had one more person he needed to visit before he could call it a night, Mr. Peterson.

He tossed the flares onto the pavement as he waved at the crew and headed down the road. The sun hiding behind a thick layer of rain clouds was starting to disappear behind the trees, and it would soon be dark. He hoped he would be on his way home before sundown. Maneuvering the back-creek roads could be dangerous after dark, not to mention driving up on someone's property when they weren't expecting you. Tim crossed Duck Creek, and the water was over the bridge. The tide must be coming in. He'd better hurry if he was going to make it to the Peterson cabin. He turned down the lane and parked the car. He looked at the already full tidal ditch and grabbed a flashlight. The smell of musty brackish water hit him hard as he stepped out of the cruiser.

Tim could hear the hunting dogs through the trees and knew he needed to announce his arrival. He reached in the car and hit the horn three times, closed the door and started up the drive. The signs on both sides of the drive told any visitors they were in range of the shotgun on the house's front porch.

"Who's there?" A voice yelled through the trees, and the dogs' barking became more agitated.

"Mr. Peterson, it's Deputy Whitaker from the Sheriff's Department. May I approach, sir?" Tim stayed in place waiting for the answer and shining his flashlight on his badge so the man could see.

"Come ahead."

"Are the dogs secure, sir?"

"Um-" there was a pause. "They are now."

Tim laughed, "Thank you, I'm on my way in." His flashlight lit the way as he crossed a small bridge over what was usually a small stream. "How are you tonight?"

"Well. I hope you are." The older man was sitting in a rocker on the front porch, two hounds were peering out of the house through a screen door.

"Yes sir, I'm well. It's been a long day though." Fatigue started to hit Tim.

"I don't normally see people at this time of night. What'cha need, deputy?"

"I thought I would fill you in on the weather situation."

"You mean the storm coming in?"

"Yes, sir. They say it's going to be a bad one and since the water level is already high. We are suggesting people on the creek evacuate."

The man took a long drink of his coffee cup watching Tim over the rim. "What if I don't want to leave?"

"We are encouraging everyone to evacuate when the time comes. We will not force anyone." Tim shifted from one foot to the other. "May I sit down?" the two dogs behind the ancient screen door whined and laid down.

"Of course." He gestured with his cup to the chair beside him. "I would offer you a coffee, but you're driving." He smiled at Tim taking another sip.

Tim smiled back. He had a feeling that cup held more than coffee. "So, how's it been out here?" He took his slicker off and hung it on the back corner of the chair. His large frame completely covering the chair as he sat down.

"Hunters have been on my land this season, but that's nothing new. You sheriff yet?"

"No, not yet." Tim leaned the chair back on its back feet closing his eyes for a minute. The song of the tree frogs and crickets took all the stress of the day from his mind, and a certain red-head entered the picture.

"Your dad seems to think so, brags about you every chance he gets down at the store."

"Really?"

"Yep, can't shut the man up." The old man started to laugh, and it echoed through the moss-covered trees. The laugh turned into a cough, and he had a hard time catching his breath.

Tim leveled his chair and looked over in concern. "You okay there?"

"Oh yeah, it's nothing. All this moisture plays havoc with my lungs. Nothing a good cigar won't cure." And he started to laugh again.

"Well, I will let you enjoy your evening." Tim reached over and offered his hand to the older man. "I need to get back to town. Call me if you need anything." Mr. Peterson took it and shook it firmly.

"Will do. Thanks for dropping by. Maybe next time you can have a coffee."

"I'll take you up on that." Tim smiled and knew the man would never leave no matter how deep the water got. As he stepped over the footbridge, he heard the squeak of the screen door, and the hounds started to bay. They had the scent of something. Hopefully, it wasn't him. His steps quickened, and he made to the cruiser safely.

Savanna took in Festival Park and what was an event earlier now lay littered on the ground. Everyone must have left in a hurry this evening. Charlie ran to the playground and despite the downpour climbed to the top of the pirate ship. Max watched him until he became consumed with finding the perfect spot to do his business. The wind off the river was blowing the rain in sheets toward them, and they were drenched. At least it wasn't cold, she thought to herself. Although, her skin felt chilled.

She looked out onto the river at the sailboats rocking in the white caps. This day was as gray as the day they brought in her parents' boat. So overcast, as if the sun was smothered by clouds of sadness. It was as if they stepped off the boat and disappeared into the mist. Charlie squealed and led her back to the park.

She and Max walked towards the playground to watch Charlie on his quest to find treasure. The kid had such a big imagination when there was no one around.

"Max, walk the plank," he screamed over the storm. Max's ears twitched as he tried to figure out the command. Then, the rumble of thunder made everyone jump. They all burst into laughter and Charlie climbed down.

"We better head to the hot dog place before we get fried."

Savanna patted him on the back, "Good idea, bud." She saw a shadow at first. But then she recognized his wide shoulders trying to hide behind the tree at the corner of the park. Dumb ass, she thought, shaking her head and sending rain dripping from her hood flying.

She scanned the area, and the closest familiar place was the gallery. Would anyone be there? "Charlie let's see if Ms. Beth is home. She wasn't feeling well, and maybe she would like some company."

She grabbed his hand and Max's leash and started across the grass. The sweatshirt-clad figure stepped out into the open and started walking toward them.

"But you don't let people come over when I am sick."

"We are just going to check." She walked faster as they crossed the street and Charlie had a hard time keeping up.

She didn't look back, but she knew he was gaining on them. Savanna climbed the stairs and knocked on the door. She looked behind them, and he was on curb ready to cross the road. She knocked again. A lump started to form in the back of her throat.

She heard movement on the other side of the door. A chain. He was in the street. The knob started to turn. She could hear him on the sidewalk. The door opened, and Beth's smiling face was there.

"I'm sorry we are closed for the day. We would love…"

"Can we please come inside?" Savanna pleaded, and a clap of thunder echoed through the neighborhood. Beth motioned for them to come inside.

They stepped inside, and Savanna looked out the window. Jeremy turned and headed up the street.

Savanna felt Beth's eyes on her back, but she had to make sure he wouldn't try to follow them in the house. Finally turning from the window, she smiled at Beth who turned to Charlie.

"Welcome to my favorite artist." Beth continued to smile but looked at Savanna with concern. "Here, let's get you out of those wet jackets and get a towel for your dog."

A pool of water started to form under their feet. "Sorry, we are so wet. It started to thunder, and I thought we should find someplace to go." Savanna tried to smile but she was now physically shaking, and she didn't quite manage it. She turned back to the window to make sure he didn't return.

"I'll be right back." Beth disappeared upstairs and then came back with a stack of fluffy towels.

Savanna pulled Charlie's jacket off and placed it on the floor by the door. She cringed as she watched the puddle grow bigger. She shrugged out of hers to add it to the pile.

"Charlie, here is one for you and one for your dog." She gave the little boy two towels. "And here is one for your sister." She handed on to Savanna. "Let's get you guys dry and then we will go into the kitchen and get something warm."

Charlie nodded quickly and covered Max with his assigned towel. He rubbed vigorously and started to giggle as Max gave him kisses.

While he was distracted, Beth leaned over and whispered to Savanna, "What is going on? You did not come in here because of the thunder."

Savanna hesitated. "It was. I didn't expect a thunderstorm." She leaned her head toward Charlie hoping Beth would get the hint.

"Okay, we'll talk later." She turned to Charlie. "How about some soup?"

"Savanna, you said we would get hot dogs," Charlie whined.

"That was before the thunder and lightning. Thank Ms. Beth for the offer. If you don't want to eat, that's fine." Savanna mouthed to Beth, 'sorry.' "We have decided to show our bratty side tonight."

"Okay, but Savanna and I are going to have some yummy chicken and pastry. It has big fat noodles. Would you like some paper and pencils? I seem to remember you like to draw."

The little boy nodded and smiled.

"Take your boots off, Charlie. You can have sock feet in the kitchen." Savanna smiled as he sat down and quickly took off his boots. Apparently, Beth found something he liked to do more than being a brat. She looked over at the window again.

Beth touched Savanna's arm startling her. "Come on, he will find his way in. Let's sit and talk." The two women walked into the kitchen. The pot on the stove was bubbling and smelled heavenly.

Savanna glanced down the hall when she heard laughter.

"Don't worry, he's fine. Do you want tea or coffee?"

"I'll have whatever you are having." She motioned to the cup on the table.

"Tea it is. Now, are you going to tell me what has you so shaken up? Did it have anything to do with the man who was in the park with you?" She put the kettle on and grabbed a mug from the hooks on the wall above the kitchen counter.

Savanna didn't want to answer her. She didn't want to admit he was starting to scare her. He had never been so insistent before. Or maybe he had. She had been attracted to his alpha-maleness. He was so in control, especially in the bedroom. Now, it wasn't so sexy after the relationship was over.

"Savanna, honey, you okay?" Beth was standing right next to her with her cup of tea.

"Oh sorry. I must have drifted off." Now she was embarrassed. How could he still affect her that way?

"I noticed. If you need to talk about it, I'm a good listener." She smiled and walked over to a drawer and pulled out paper and colored pencils. "Charlie, come and get your supplies." She put two bowls on the countertop with spoons. When the little red-head popped through the doorway, she stirred the soup.

"Oh, that smells good. Can I have some please?"

"Of course, go ahead and sit down. I'll make you a bowl."

He practically sprinted to the table with Max on his heels. "Max, down." The dog obeyed sitting next to Charlie's chair.

"How are you feeling, Ms. Beth?" Charlie asked as he drew.

"I'm good, how are you? Are you dry yet?"

"Yep, Savanna said you were sick, and we should check on you."

He didn't even look up from his paper, his tongue sticking out as he concentrated.

Beth looked at Savanna with a puzzled face.

"I was at the coffee shop on Friday."

"Oh, I see, I'm feeling fine. I was surprised that's all."

Charlie stopped and looked at her. "Surprises make you sick. That sucks."

"Charlie, watch your language." Savanna quickly corrected.

"I'm sorry, but it does." He shrugged and went back to his picture.

"You're right Charlie. Sometimes there are good surprises and sometimes bad," Beth paused, "I'm still trying to decide which this one was," she added quietly. She stirred her tea adding a stream of honey. Her sweater sleeve slipped down bearing the light pink newly healed scars on her wrists.

Savanna couldn't help but stare and wonder what the other woman had been through. She touched Beth's elbow, and the women's eyes met. Savanna felt like she could trust her for some reason.

"Beth, did you get any new paintings this week?"

"I did. One new piece. Would you like to see it?"

"I would. Charlie, you stay here and draw. Okay?"

"Okay."

Savanna stood up, and Max was instantly alert. "Max, stay," she ordered. The shepherd laid his head back down on the floor under Charlie's chair.

Beth put her cup in the sink and led Savanna into the gallery. She walked over to an oil painting of a fishing village. "I know you didn't have a sudden urge to buy a painting. What's up?"

"I wanted to ask you how you really are." Beth looked at her when she continued, "I was working your case when Max and I walked into the coffee shop on Friday. You didn't seem okay. And I saw this." Savanna reached over and pulled the other woman's sleeves up. "What happened?"

"You said you were working my case?"

"Yes, I'm with Raleigh Search and Rescue."

"Then you know what happened."

"They didn't share the details. Tim is very by the book and only told me what I needed to know for a proper search."

"And did you find what he wanted?"

"Yes, we had a successful search."

"Are you going to tell me what you had you so shaken up in the park?"

"My ex. He's being very persistent. Just being an ass. It's nothing really."

"It didn't look like nothing. You should talk to Tim about it. He's a good listener."

Savanna started to disagree and decided to leave it. She didn't want to scare Tim off with her drama.

"Well, they say my husband is wanted for kidnapping. But he's dead. Then, the sheriff has a picture of him here in Washington." Beth physically shook her head. "I still can't believe it."

Savanna rubbed Beth's shoulder to comfort her. "Have you spoken to him?"

"No. I haven't seen him yet, well not in person."

"Tim said you had a boyfriend. How is he handling the news?"

"Sam? Not well. He's confused as I am. I was just getting used to the idea of us and now this. I'm more angry than anything else. Why did he leave me? Why would he do this?"

"Oh Beth, I don't know what to say." Savanna wanted to give her a huge hug and say but he's alive. What she wouldn't give to see her parents again.

"Part of me doesn't want to believe them. I used to hope for this moment every day. Now, I don't know."

Savanna watched the other woman twist the diamond-studded wedding band on her ring finger. She wondered what decisions were to be made but knew it would be rude to ask. "I know that if I could see my parents again, I would be overjoyed, but missing them is still raw. I've spent a lot of hours with my doc to learn to say 'it's time to move on. It's time to live life for Charlie.' Maybe there was a good reason."

"I know." Beth looked at her and reached over to squeeze Savanna's hand. "Now tell me why you are scared of this ex of yours."

The question took Savanna by surprise. She paused wondering whether she should trust her with the whole story. "Well, he has become more aggressive since we broke up. I've always been the tough girl, able to take care of myself. I don't know what to do with him. He won't listen to me. He wants me to give back Charlie, insisting he has no place in the relationship."

Beth started shaking her head. Savanna put her hand up to stop whatever she was going to say.

"I know, I would never do it. I couldn't even believe he would suggest such a thing." Laughter erupted from the kitchen, and the ladies stopped to listen. Savanna swore Charlie was talking to someone, maybe Max.

They listened to the conversation, and it was clear there was someone else. Savanna walked toward the kitchen and peered in ready to see someone. Charlie kept chatting, answering questions about school.

"Hey, buddy, who you talking to?"

"Ms. Selah, she won't come out because of Max, but she is asking me about school."

Max sat on the floor by the cellar entrance with his head cocked. He turned his head to look at Savanna and then slid to the floor.

"Let's see what you got, boy." Savanna walked over to the opening and peered into the darkness.

CHAPTER 22

PUTRESCINE

7:00pm

The glare on the computer screen was starting to hurt his eyes. He hated being stuck in this God-forsaken cabin. It seemed like a good idea when he picked it. The isolation perfect for hiding. Now he was too far away from her and felt powerless to watch her make decisions about her life without him.

There was a dog in Beth's kitchen with a small boy at the table drawing. Why were they there? The women were in the gallery looking at paintings, perhaps the redhead was shopping. Beth was a gallery owner after all. They moved back to the kitchen to talk to the little boy, and the beautiful redhead got down on her knees to look in the hole in the floor. When she bent over it gave him a perfect view of her sexy ass. Oh, it had been too long.

Movement at the back of the house caught his eye. A man in a dark gray hoodie climbed on a cinderblock to look in a window. He pulled himself up on the window ledge. The dog in the kitchen instantly rose to his feet and started barking.

He couldn't hear what was going on, his hand tightened on the edge of the table. The red-head went to the window and looked out for what startled the dog then turned to tell Beth something, shaking her head. The man outside didn't move. He was right below the window frame. The dog laid down at the boy's feet.

"Don't you see him, you dumb bitch? Call the police."

Much to his surprise, Beth moved to the counter and picked up a cell. She made a short call. The red-head continued to look out the window. His cell phone rang breaking his concentration on the screen. *How did she get my number?* Glancing down he anxiously answered.

"Bonjour, comment ça va?" continuing in French, his voice tense and loud, "Why are you calling?"

"I need to see you."

"I can't get out of this creek. The boat is swamped. Now is not a good time anyway."

"Your picture is everywhere. You need to be more careful."

"Really? Or what?" He wondered where they got the picture. "You need to do a better job keeping him away from her. You said you could keep her safe if I help you."

"I'm doing my best. When is the next shipment coming in?"

"Should be in a couple of weeks. It will come directly to you so you can store it. He is in the house too much."

"Will you stop worrying about that? After her latest trip to the hospital, she hasn't allowed him to the gallery."

He stood up, and the chair slammed to the floor. "She was in the hospital? Why didn't you tell me?"

"She is fine."

"Apparently not if they took her in. I need to get back to town. This isn't working."

"You will stay put and do what you're told."

"But someone has to take care of her. I watched someone try to get into the gallery. I need to be where I can keep my eye on her."

"You do not. You are considered a fugitive. Why would you touch a deputy anyway?"

"He was hurting her, and I took care of the problem. She's my wife."

"Not anymore. I have to go, someone is coming."

"Okay, call me if you find a way to get me back into town. Au revoir."

"Au revoir."

He set the phone down on the desk and put his hands to the side of his head. "Ahh."

He lifted the plastic up and tented it over his head checking each of the screens. The man at the gallery was gone, and the women were sitting at the table eating soup with the little boy. The dog had settled under the child's chair.

CHAPTER 23

ANOSMIA

7:00pm

The storm was getting worse, and Tim was having a hard time seeing the edge of the road as he pulled off and parked. He stepped out of the car, the beam of his headlights bathed the ditch bank illuminating the path to the creek side. The flood gauge on the side of the bridge reflected brightly in the light.

Tim pushed the button on the side of his radio. "Beaufort County Dispatch, come in please." He paused. "County dispatch, come in please, Deputy Whitaker here."

"Go ahead, Deputy Whitaker." The dispatcher's voice came over the radio.

"The Pungo is two feet above stage. I'm going to take a reading at each bridge on my way back in."

"Copy that and recorded, Deputy Whitaker. You are needed at the Pearse house for a possible intruder."

"Copy that. I'll get the measurements tomorrow. Call Beth and let her know I am on my way. Better send another deputy, I'm at least 30 minutes out." Tim jogged back to the car and flipped on the sirens.

The pines flew by in the darkness, his high beams and lights reflecting off the rain pelting the vehicle. Lucky for him, he knew this road like the back of his hand because he couldn't see much. His pulse quickened. "Maybe it's Robert. Yes. I'm gonna get him this time."

Glancing down at the speedometer, 80 registered as his speed. A doe popped out of the brush to his right. He lightly tapped his brakes trying to slow his vehicle. As the vision of the doe flew past, he breathed a sigh of relief until an antler came through his driver's side window.

The cruiser fishtailed and slid onto the ditch bank, rolling over with the incline of the shoulder. Glass flew through the air slicing Tim's face as it fell to the other side of the car. When the sedan found its final resting spot upside down, cold salty water covered the ceiling and bucket seats, covering the top of Tim's head. He struggled to unfasten his seatbelt, but it wouldn't release with his weight hanging upside down. He couldn't focus, what had happened? He reached to his shoulder feeling something sticking out of it, warm sticky liquid covered the stick. "Where the hell did a stick come from?"

Suddenly tired, a deep gasp escaped his lips as he slipped away.

THE TASTE of swamp water startled Tim as he gasped for air. The water filled his airways, and he spewed it in a stream as he found the strength to pull against the seatbelt to find an air pocket. His body grotesquely twisted to keep his head out of the water. Sharp pain radiated through him as he pushed against the car's roof with his right hand. His left wouldn't even work. How long have I been here? He pushed again trying to get the safety on the seat belt to release. There was a foul smell. What was that? Steam, maybe?

A rush of water came in his window, and a flash of blade flew past his face. Suddenly he was falling, all his weight landing on the shoulder he could no longer feel.

A large black hand grabbed him by the shirt collar and pulled him out of the car. When Tim cleared the car, the arm reached under his armpit and another on the other side, pulling him backward through the stream. Pain shot through his entire body, causing a loud moan to escape before he sucked in a breath. Tim watched the red and blue lights reflect in the bushes and cattails along the bank. His car was submerged in the creek. He tried to look up at the man carrying him. He assumed it was a man. He looked up again, but the rain dripped in his eyes causing his vision to blur.

The scene was fading again. He looked at his left shoulder. The lights playing tricks with his head. What was that sticking out of his body? A candy cane? A stick? The creek surrounding him was becoming more shallow, the pain becoming stronger as the water stopped supporting his weight. When the man finally turned loose of him, Tim was laid against the curve of the muddy bank. He tried to push himself up, but he was so weak, and the ground was so slippery.

"You'll want to lie still, sir," a voice intoned from the darkness.

Tim couldn't focus. He tried to turn toward the voice. A hand pressed him hard against the ground. His breath was becoming shallow now. He started to struggle.

"Lie still sir, please. I don't want to hurt you."

Tim saw a flash of steel. He tried to move, but the man put all his weight against him. There was a grinding, sawing noise. It filled Tim's ears. The vibration shot electricity through him. The pain was too much to bear, and then suddenly it all went away.

165

CHAPTER 24

BLIND SEARCH

:15pm

SAVANNA AND BETH sat quietly waiting for a deputy to arrive. The dispatcher said Tim was coming, but he was at least half an hour away. Someone else was also en route and would be here as soon as they could. Savanna saw the man hiding below the window ledge and told Beth to call for assistance. If it was Jeremy, she didn't want to be the person who filed charges. Something told her it would end badly.

Charlie was happy drawing and taking bites of his chicken and pastry in between changing colored pencils. He had no idea there was a threat other than the lightning outside. Max was the first one to the front door when the deputy arrived. He didn't bark like he had earlier. He sat at the door and waited for Beth to open it. Checking the window to identify the person standing on the porch, Beth quickly opened the door and let the officer inside.

"Thank you for coming so quickly."

"No problem, they said there was a possible intruder."

"More like a peeping tom. Someone looking in the back window." She pointed to the rear window in the large gallery room.

"Okay, I will take a look. Stay inside." The deputy touched his hat at Savanna and stepped back outside.

Beth locked the door behind him and set the alarm.

"Come on, we will let him do his thing. Let's finish dinner, then we will go upstairs and visit in the sitting room."

Beth's cell phone rang about five minutes later, and she gave Savanna a thumbs up.

"So, what did he say?"

"Looks like a size thirteen, but no one in sight."

"Well, that's good."

"I requested Tim. He should be here shortly. The other deputy is going to stay out front in the meantime."

Charlie popped his head up from his paper. "Mr. Tim is coming? Alright!" And he went back to his drawing, taking a quick bite.

Savanna felt a little better, but it didn't tell them who the person was. *Maybe there was a clue. Surely Jeremy wasn't stupid enough to pull something like this. But he wasn't acting smart lately, so maybe it was him. Of course, it was him.* She shook her head. Her arm started to tingle, and her breath came faster. She took a deep breath, letting it out slowly. Her hands went up to her hair, pulling it into a ponytail and then wrapping it in a neat little bun. *It was him in the park. I saw his face. Get it together, girl. Maybe Beth is right. I should tell Tim what's going on.*

Beth touched her arm and Savanna jumped.

"Savanna, did you hear me?"

"I'm sorry. What did you say?"

"I asked if you would like a pin for your hair. I think I have some upstairs."

Savanna shook her head and let her hair fly. The rain had given her a nice case of mermaid hair, loose curls, no rhyme or reason. She kind of liked it.

"I kind of like it like this." She looked at Beth waiting for her opinion.

Beth paused a moment, watching her. "It's him, isn't it?"

"I think so." Savanna fought the tears starting to pool. She tried to give Beth a smile, but her lips wouldn't move. She took another deep breath, allowing the air to slowly release.

"We will get through this." Beth rubbed Savanna's arm and then touched her pink wrist, slowly tracing the raised scar. "We will survive."

She gave Savanna a smile and walked over to the kettle. Beth refilled her mug with more steaming water. "Do you want some more tea?"

"Sure." She did manage a smile at that time. "Charlie, are you done with your chicken?"

"Yep. Ms. Beth, Can I have another piece of paper?" he held up his drawing; a boat with the sail blowing in the wind with clouds in the sky.

"Of course, you can. That's awesome. Gather up your stuff, and we will go upstairs where we will be more comfortable."

"Okay." He quickly gathered up the rainbow of colors using both hands. "Can Max come upstairs?"

"Of course." She ruffled his red hair, and his pencils went flying. "Oops, sorry."

Charlie picked them up again. "No problem, thanks for letting me use your stuff. Maybe I can have a picture in your gallery one day, Ms. Beth."

"Maybe so." Beth smiled at him as he sprinted upstairs.

Savanna loved the huge smile on his face. For a fleeting moment, it felt like she knew why they were here, leaving all the day's drama in the back of her mind. The two ladies grabbed their teas and followed Charlie up the stairs. Max took his place behind Savanna, his nails clicking on the wood stairs. Savanna rubbed the smooth wood of the banister with her hand as they ascended.

Beth commented, "One of the few original things Sam was able to keep on the inside of the house."

"It's so beautiful."

"I'll show you something else." She opened the door to a large room and flipped on the light. Savanna would call it a sitting room-slash-office. Charlie ran to the desk in front of a picture window instantly, organizing his art supplies. Max followed him parking next to the chair anticipating the next activity. Beth sat her tea down on an end table by the large overstuffed sofa.

"You can set your tea there, then, take a look at this." She pointed to the table at the opposite end.

"Savanna, look at all the colors," Charlie yelled across the room.

Beth started to laugh. "Okay Charlie, go ahead and steal my surprise."

The little boy looked at her with a weird look on his face. Savanna walked over to where he was standing. He whispered to Beth, "But she doesn't like surprises."

"It's okay. Now, show me what you found." Savanna gasped as she looked at the wall. Charlie touched the clear Plexiglas, his fingers counting the pieces of cloth behind it. "There have to be thousands of pieces." So many different textures and colors, it was like a painting of fabric.

"Yes, and they are original to the house. Sam found them when he was doing demo up here. It is Selah's fabric stash for her quilts."

"But I thought you said Selah was a friend. How can she…"

"She is a very good friend."

"But if this is original to the house, that would mean she is…" Savanna paused not wanting to say what she was thinking. Her eyebrows went up with speculation.

"Dead. Yes, she's dead."

"Your house is haunted. Creepy." Charlie interrupted still touching the glass. "This would be a cool poster for my room. Savanna, take a picture so we can put it in my room." He was jumping up and down unable to control his excitement. Max watched the little boy, his head nodding with every jump.

"Okay, Okay, Charlie. Now, calm down." Savanna pulled out her phone and turned to Beth.

"Do you mind?" Beth was smiling and watching Charlie. Savanna watched her twirl her wedding band around her finger.

"Of course not. It's storage."

"Yes." Charlie jumped up in the air to give Savanna a fist pump, and she totally missed it, trying to take the picture without getting the glare of the outside lights on the glass. "Ah, Savanna, you totally missed it."

"Here you go, Charlie, give me one." Beth held out her fist and Charlie took her up on it.

"What? I was taking your photo. Here, do it again, and I'll take a pic." Savanna aimed the camera, and the two of them did the fist pump in slow motion. All three of them burst into laughter.

"Did you get it?"

"See for yourself." She handed the phone to Charlie, and he hit the button to see the picture.

"Perfect. Look, Selah got in there too." Charlie turned the phone so Beth could see.

"Wait. What?" Savanna was sure she heard him wrong. She reached to take the phone back from him.

"Just kidding." Charlie burst into a loud laugh. "Look at your face, you believed me." Savanna's face started to burn with embarrassment.

"Charlie." Savanna couldn't believe he would do that.

"You are a trickster." Beth joined in. She pulled out some more paper out of the desk drawer. "Here you go, mister. You might want to get busy before your sister kills you."

Charlie sat down at the desk and picked out a pencil to get started. It was good to see him so happy. Savanna looked around the room, eyeing a painting in the corner on an easel. "This one is beautiful. I love the primary colors."

Beth walked over with her tea and swallowed hard staring at the piece. Savanna thought she saw a bit of sadness in her expression.

"This one is by Miró. It was painted in 1925. Very special, Sam gave it to me."

"It really is beautiful; thanks for sharing it with us. You want to sit down?"

"Sure." Beth walked over to the couch and sat down beside her mug. Savanna sat down on the other end. The tea was lukewarm, but it was still warm enough to warm her chest as she took a drink. As she set down her mug, Savanna noticed a picture on the table.

"What a beautiful portrait," Savanna commented, looking at the framed picture of a younger Beth and a dark-haired man. "I know, now I'm being nosey."

"No, it's okay. That was our engagement portrait, Brad and me. We were just out of college, and he wanted to show off his tattoo and my ring." Beth twisted her wedding ring as she stared at the photo.

"What does his tattoo mean?" Savanna looked over at Beth who had drifted off in her thoughts again.

She finally answered, "You know, I don't know. He never said. It was something he got for graduation."

Max stood up from his spot under Charlie's chair, and there was a knock at the front door.

Beth stood up and looked out of the window. Her shoulders fell instantly. "I'll be right back."

"Does Max need to go with you?" Savanna walked over to the window and saw a truck parked on the street.

"No, it's Sam."

NATURAL ALERT

eth disappeared down the stairs, and Savanna snuck to the top of the stairs, so she could eavesdrop. She caught Charlie's eyes as she left the room and put her finger to her lips to tell him not to say anything. He shook his head and went back to his drawing.

She could barely hear their voices, but she heard enough.

The male voice had a sweet southern drawl that matched Tim's when he was holding a casual conversation.

"But Beth, I wanted to check and see how you were. I love you, and you won't return my calls."

"You shouldn't say that. I'm a married woman."

"I don't care. We are good together, and he doesn't matter."

"How can you say that? He does matter. He's my husband." The tears started to fall, Savanna could tell by Beth's voice.

"But he left you. I'm standing right in front of you, Beth. Doesn't that count?"

"I don't know." The sobs came harder.

Savanna came downstairs at that point. "Sorry to interrupt, but I think you need to go." She looked at the tall man standing in the doorway. It was still raining, and the wind was blowing the moisture onto the porch. His short hair was disheveled, and his eyes had circles from lack of sleep, Savanna guessed, but that didn't hide his rugged good-looks.

"I actually stopped by to talk to Tim. Is he here? Dispatch said he was here."

Savanna stepped in between him and Beth. She was a mess right now and didn't need this shit.

"No, we haven't seen him. Look, we have a deputy here. Maybe you could talk to him?"

"Beth, can I talk to you for a minute?" Sam tried to look around Savanna to see the woman standing behind her. He seemed desperate, and Savanna knew desperate men tended to do stupid things.

Savanna turned to the weeping woman. She was shaking her head and incoherent because of the tears.

"I think this conversation is over. Please, go." Savanna grabbed Beth's arm and pulled her into the house, shutting the door behind them and leaving Sam on the front porch. She threw the lock and took Beth to the kitchen.

Savanna flipped on the light and sat Beth down at the table, giving her a huge hug.

"How can I decide?" She hugged Savanna back. "He's right, you know. Brad left me, let me think he was dead. Why would he do that?"

"I don't know why he did it. I do know what it's like to lose someone you love." Beth stared at her. "The thoughts of guilt, 'why wasn't I there?' or 'what am I going to do without them?'"

"You do understand."

"Yes, last year my parents disappeared. They searched for them, and there was nothing left but the damn boat they took out to sea. They wouldn't let me or Max help. I was too close they said." She sat across from Beth, who grabbed her hand.

"I never gave up hope they would show up." She squeezed Beth's hand. "I have to admit I was jealous when Tim told me your husband was alive after all these years. Now I see your dilemma."

Beth grabbed a tissue from a box conveniently parked on the table. "I've been through boxes of these this weekend. I don't know what to do."

Savanna watched the woman across from her. She had no idea what to say to her to take away all the confusion and sadness. "You should talk to Sam. It's obvious he loves you."

"I know, but Brad is out there. Somewhere."

CHAPTER 26

ATROPHY

8:45pm

The rain became heavier, and the tide crept up on the deck. He went out to the woodshed to gather fuel for the fire. There seemed to be a chill in the air despite the heat and humidity of the day. His University of Virginia sweatshirt hood shielded him from the rain as he sprinted across the wooded lot carrying the wood wagon with him. The sound of the rain on the tin roof of the small building deafened him as he tried to fill the small wagon with wood. Hopefully, the river wouldn't rise too far. He didn't have time to replace computer equipment because of water damage. The plastic was a big enough pain. Frustration filled him as he thought of the plastic tent shielding it from the leaky roof. His head started to pound.

He sprinted back to the cabin, pulling the wagon carefully behind him. It wouldn't do him any good to spill it. As muddy as the yard was, he would never get the fire lit. He rounded the corner of the house and noticed a small flicker at the door. The lantern was back. Was his ghost?

176

He slowly entered the front room and heard a moan come from the bedroom. That was different. Usually a shadow or two, the lantern would come and go. The smell of fish hit him as he crossed the room. There was another one. As he walked toward the bedroom, it got louder. He entered the room and could see a figure in the bed. The quilt was pulled up over whoever it was. He shined his flashlight on the person lying there. The face looked familiar although it was badly battered. He couldn't quite place it.

Maybe someone from town? But why was he here?

He pulled back the linen and looked at the man's clothes in shock. A sheriff's deputy in his cabin. How the hell did he get here? He looked closer, noting the blood on the uniform he was wearing. Whitaker was the name on the pocket of his shirt. He didn't come here by himself. Someone must have brought him. But who would even know this cabin existed? Maybe the boss was sending a message. A warning she could do what she wanted. Beth's life was on the line. The man moaned again.

I better get him cleaned up. I don't want him to get worse. I'm already a fugitive. I don't want to be a murderer.

He warmed some river water on the wood stove, staying away from the bedroom. The less interaction with the injured man the better off they both would be. He fed the stove a few more logs to speed up the boil. He was definitely not meant for this rough living. He could see his electric kettle whistling in his sleek modern kitchen in the mountains. He missed it so much. Breakfast in their king size log bed with a crackling fire in the bedroom, her curled up in the crook of his arm, him tickling her nose until she woke and then the morning sex. Man, he missed sex with her.

He walked over to the desk and lifted the plastic. The screens were as he had left them twenty minutes before. Where was she? He needed to see her. He checked again and found her in the sitting room in a rocking chair, wrapped in a quilt, tears rolling down her cheeks. He wanted to hold her and comfort her, but it was impossible right now. He had to keep her safe.

A droplet of water landed on the stove and popped on the hot surface. He came back to reality, an ugly one for sure. Grabbing some towels, he headed in to clean up the stranger lying on his bed. He wasn't sure what Whitaker was saying, but he leaned over to wipe the blood and dirt from his face. He cut the cotton bandage off the shoulder and stood there wondering how he would get the shirt off without causing severe pain.

"Dad, you have to leave. Daddy, listen to me," the man shouted as he rolled to one side.

He took advantage of the movement to remove the bloody shirt Whitaker was wearing. He gave it a quick tug off the man's hands, and the man fell back onto the mattress, moaning something unintelligible. The hole in his shoulder was the size of a quarter and went all the way through to the other side. It didn't look like a bullet hole, but he wasn't an expert.

He filled the hole on each side with a clean rag and tied it tight. As he pulled the fabric, the man moaned loudly and then laid still. Whitaker must have passed out. Better for him anyway. He pulled the quilt over him and made sure there were no gaps in the fabric. The cloth he was using quickly cooled down, and he walked back over to the stove to warm it again. As he stood at the stove, the steam rising from the pot felt good. He held his hands over it to warm them from the chill. He rocked side to side, the floor creaking as he changed feet.

Bending down, his fingers knocked along the knotty pine floor, hitting the board in the middle of the hole under the stove. The board popped and bounced to reveal a hollow in the floor. There was a leather-bound book covered in dust. He opened the cover and on the first page was inscribed. *Captains log of Elizas Light, Abram Willis, captain.* He turned the pages and skimmed the information. There were ports of call, a lot of catch information, freight records, and weather. Each page was a voyage. He ruffled the water wrinkled pages with his thumb. A small windmill caught his eye in the top right corner. Flipping a few more, the small sketch was only on certain trips. He used his hand to roll down the page following the numbers and comments. His eyes drifted to his wedding ring on his finger as the gold glistened in the warm glow of the lights. He would never take it off. This was all to keep her safe forever.

CHAPTER 27

DOWNDRAFT

8:45pm

There was a knock at the front door, and Savanna looked out the window to check who it was. She looked over at Beth, who had fallen asleep in the rocker. Charlie was still drawing at the desk, and Max sat beside him. Only the squad car was out front, so Savanna went down to check and see what the person needed. She looked out of the window to see the deputy standing at the door. He glanced over to her as she moved the curtain.

She unlocked the door and stepped out onto the porch.

"Sorry to disturb you, ma'am, but the sheriff wanted to know if you wanted an escort back to your apartment. I have to stay here so I would need to radio for another deputy."

She appreciated the caring way they were handling this today. "I'll give Tim a call and see if he can pick us up on his way back to the station."

"I'm afraid that won't be possible ma'am." Savanna watched the man shift his weight on his feet. He wouldn't look at her.

"And why is that?"

"I'm afraid I can't say."

"Why is that?"

"Sheriff's business, ma'am."

"Well, currently I work for your sheriff, so you better tell me what is going on."

Her cell rang, and she saw the sheriff's number flash on the screen. A sense of dread filled her as she swiped to answer the call.

"Yes sir, this is Officer McCormick. What can I do for you today?"

The voice on the other side of the line was very business-like. "Officer McCormick, we have a missing person's case that needs immediate attention."

"Yes, sir. Of course, sir."

"The hurricane has taken a turn toward us and will make landfall within 48 hours. This makes this search urgent. Is there anything you need?"

"I will need a scent article for the missing person. Do we know what kind of terrain?"

"Swamp mostly and creek bank."

"Okay. So, I will need access to a boat. The gentleman who helped us on Friday, Mike, knows how Max works. If he is available, that would be great."

"Done. I will make some calls and have someone come and pick you up."

"I am at Beth Pearse's gallery. Our gear is at the apartment."

"No problem. A car will be there shortly."

She hung up the phone and turned to the deputy. "Looks like we are going to work."

She popped back inside and headed upstairs. "Beth? Beth, I need a favor." She headed into the sitting room where everyone was.

She was out of breath. "Beth, can you call Hellen for me?"

Beth cleared her throat and responded, "Of course, what am I calling her for?"

"Max and I have to go to work. I need someone to watch Charlie."

"He can stay here. He'll just need his things." Beth gave a huge yawn.

"No, I don't want to bother you with this. You are tired."

"Bring his stuff by. He'll be fine."

Charlie didn't even look up from the desk. He reached down and patted Max on the head. "Time to go get the bad guys. Stay safe." Max stretched and gave him a big kiss.

Savanna walked over to the door. "Thank you for watching him. Charlie, be good for Ms. Beth."

"Of course, we will be fine. Go on. Besides we have an armed guard on the door, what could happen?"

Savanna laughed. "Good luck with that one. Max, time to go to work." The shepherd followed her out into the hall and down the stairs. She put on her jacket and poked her head out the door. A hand popped out of a sheriff's car on the street, and both she and the dog ran to the car.

"We need to stop by the apartment first. I'll get my vehicle there." Savanna informed him as they hopped in the car.

"We are meeting at the office for a briefing, and then we are headed to the Eastern part of the county."

"Got it."

The deputy pulled up to the entrance of her apartment and Savanna quickly thanked him for the ride. When she let Max out of the backseat, he looked relieved to be out of the small space. She looked over her shoulder, conscious Jeremy could be hanging out. She hated the paranoid way he made her feel now. She needed to be in work mode, and there was no room for one of her panic attacks. She unlocked the front door and headed inside to pack a small bag for Charlie. She changed into full gear, holstering her firearm as well. The sheriff didn't give her much information, so she needed to be ready for anything.

Max's gear was in a duffel by the front door, a habit formed years ago. "Max, you ready?" A bark signaled he was all business too.

They took the quick walk to the SUV and drove back over to the gallery. Savanna pulled up beside the sheriff deputy who was parked in front of the building. She reached down and knocked on the window. He slowly rolled it down and looked at her. His eyes widened when he realized he was looking at the same woman he had spoken with twenty minutes before. She handed him Charlie's bag and asked him, "Can you make sure they get this? Thanks." She didn't wait for him to answer and drove around the block to head over to the sheriff's office.

As Savanna and Max walked into the small sheriff's station, she sensed something big was going on. Savanna wove through deputies and troopers in the jammed entrance to the dispatcher's desk. She smiled at the older woman and got no response. "Hi, I'm Savanna McCormick. The sheriff asked me to stop by to assist."

"Yes ma'am, he's waiting for you in his office. Down the hall." She stood up and tapped on the counter. "Now, gentlemen if you will move out of the way so Officer McCormick can get through." The other lawmen paused their conversations, and the crowd parted.

Well, we know who runs the show around here. Savanna took a double take as she passed the lady. There was something familiar about her. Savanna smiled as she walked back to the sheriff's office. He was on the phone and waved her in without speaking. Savanna stood at attention and waited to be addressed. Max sat her side watching the man behind the desk.

"I don't care what's going on in the mountains. I have a man missing, and there is a hurricane headed this way. I need people now." He paused and let out a humph. Savanna could hear someone on the other end of the line. "Look I appreciate the troopers you sent, but I need search and rescue here now. I have one search team to get started." He smiled at Savanna and rolled his eyes at Max. "Okay, I will expect them in the morning. We will start a search for the wreckage and see if we can have more information before the rest of the team arrives." He hung up the phone and rubbed his palms over his eyes and through the little hair he had. Looking up at Savanna, he started, "Okay, here's what we know."

Savanna pulled out her note pad and started taking notes.

CHAPTER 28

CROSS GRID

9:45pm

The man sitting beside her gave great directions. Max was uncomfortable with the stranger in the passenger seat. The rain made it impossible to see farther than the headlights. Thank goodness for good defrost. The humidity was crazy. Sweat beaded on her skin causing her uniform to stick. Lightning flashed, highlighting the tunnel of pines covered in Spanish moss. Glowing eyes stared as she passed them in the tall reeds on the side of the highway.

"Any idea who we are looking for?" Savanna asked.

The deputy turned in his seat. "One of our deputies was in an accident tonight. He disappeared from the scene. Pull over here."

"Your sheriff told me that much." Savanna maneuvered through the vehicles on the scene.

He shook his head. "He would have told you if he wanted you to know. We don't need your help with this."

Flares and cones blocked off the left side of the road. Lights threw colors over the area's foliage. The shoulder was taped off as a crime scene. Savanna threw the SUV in park. "I wouldn't be here if that were true."

She didn't wait for his response. Time to do what she was best at. Compartmentalize and make a task list. *Breathe, Savanna, just breathe.*

She opened the hatch and took a long deep breath. Max cocked his head. She grabbed his gear and placed the vest on the pavement. "Let's go to work." Max jumped down and placed his paws in the armholes of his vest. Savanna pulled it up and snapped it closed. Standing up, she started to make her list. Survey the scene. *There are a lot of deputies here. I wonder if Tim is here.*

Max took his position beside her as they left the roadside. There was an obvious exit cut through the thick brush along the path to the creek, large enough for a vehicle. Max took the lead signaling for her to follow. She carefully stepped through the reeds. The marshy ground filled her footsteps with water every time she moved her boots. Max jumped into the creek and swam to the cruiser. Savanna followed the splash and saw Max enter the vehicle through an open window.

Savanna waded out to the car and looked inside, Max was on the dash barking when she arrived. A laptop hung from a cord down in the creek water. Her flashlight lit up the ceiling and all the pieces of deputy's essentials, pens, a note pad, chewing gum. She heard a wake behind her as a man wearing a sheriff's department uniform appeared next to her.

"Looks like blood on the driver's seat." She moved the light for a better look at the rest of the car's interior. "Max, come." The dog squeezed out of the window and swam to the shore. He signaled for her to follow, but something caught her eye in the churning water. She swung her flashlight back to the ceiling of the car, her breathing increased. "What was the name of the officer? Nobody has said." She spotted the note floating in the water, the hand-writing familiar.

"Deputy Whitaker. He was out warning people about the hurricane."

Her breath caught in her throat. "Tim?" All the oxygen disap-peared from her lungs. Her hands started to tingle. *This can't happen now. Tim needs us to find him.* She shook her head trying to focus. Make a task list. Assignment number one find the scent target. "Max, time to work, let's find it." Max barked and jumped in the air. He was ready to complete the search, but was she ready for what they would find?

Max ran the banks up and back down, weaving in and out of the cattails that had gone to seed months before. His reflective vest wasn't much help on a stormy night. Only his bell gave Savanna a clue to his location. Then a bark in the darkness called her. Another. Savanna turned on her spotlight and searched the bank for Max. There he was lying as straight as an arrow on the bank.

"Max search." But he didn't budge. He must have a target. She waded closer to him. She could see the drag marks of what looked like a small boat. In the mud, beside Max's paws, was a stick. She cleared the reeds out of her way so she could have a clearer view. "Max" He turned and looked at her whining. The rays of light hit the surface, and she knew instantly it was not a stick. "Deputy, deputy over here." She heard swishing behind her as the wake started to hit the back of her legs. He was beside her in an instant. "Looks like an implement covered in blood."

The deputy shined his lantern closer to Max. "Looks like you're right. I will get the evidence guys over here. Any sign of Deputy Whitaker?"

"Not that I can see. Looks like some drag marks there." She moved her light to highlight the ground beside Max.

"Okay, so he was removed by someone in a boat. Maybe they took him into town."

"We can hope. Max, good boy." She squeaked the rubber ball, and Max bounded towards her, splashing her and the deputy. Assignment two: follow the scent trail to the target. "We're going to need a boat to follow the scent further down the creek."

"Already ordered."

TIM'S HEAD POUNDED. He tried to open his eyes, but every muscle ached. The walls swayed. Am I on a boat? He moved, and the bed squeaked sending another sharp pain across his forehead and behind his eyes. There was a faint smell of fish and wood smoke. He tried to move his arm, but he was wrapped tight in a blanket. "Where am I?"

A scrape of furniture on a wood floor sent shivers through him. He tried to open his eyes again. Shadows crossed in front of his clouded vision. There was definitely someone there.

"You need to rest, deputy," a raspy voice answered from across the room.

Tim turned toward the voice. "Where...?"

"Don't worry about it." The man cleared his throat. "You're hurt pretty bad. I patched you up as best I could." He was closer now.

"How did I get here?" Confusion fogged Tim's brain. "I was driving."

"I have no idea." A pair of hands brushed Tim's face as they reached across his chest. "Why don't you tell me what you do remember?"

Tim tried to open his eyes again. "Damn it, I can't see."

"Your eyes are swollen shut. You're pretty bad off. Can you tell me how you got in my bed?"

"You tell me?" There was a warm glow in the corner of the room creating an outline of the man in front of him. "Are you the black guy?"

"What black guy? I told you. I don't know how you got here. You have cuts on your face and arms. One hole in your shoulder and two swollen black eyes."

"Who are you?" Tim's head ached as he tried to process what the man was saying.

"It's not important at the moment. Are you thirsty?"

"Yes, but I don't think I can sit up." Tim couldn't move his legs under the bedding. Everything felt like it weighed a ton.

"I wouldn't want you to anyway. It took forever to get your arm bandaged." Footsteps crossed the wood floor. "Don't move," came from another room.

Tim tried to open his eyes again. A snapshot of a deer on the side of the road flashed in front of him. A picture of Savanna, then Robert followed. "I've got to get to Water Street. Robert. Beth's in trouble." He pushed up in the bed.

Footsteps pounded towards him. "How do you know?" The voice was forceful now.

"Ahh." Pain shot through him. He could feel a ripping in his shoulder. "Robert, I'm going to get you." It was too much. Wetness ran down his back. He was cold, so cold. His teeth chattered. It hurt to even breathe, and everything went dark.

TIM'S DREAMS WERE VIVID. Water covered the road to his father's house. He swam and swam, but the building was disappearing in the distance. Maybe the current was too strong. His arms lost feeling and the water chilled him to the bone. He tried to tread water, but the waves splashed the brackish water in his face, burning his eyes. *I have to get to Daddy*. The house is unstable in this amount of flooding.

A skiff with open sails came into view. The dark figure at the helm leaned into the wind and steered toward the sloped roof of the front porch. His father clung to the sill of a second story window. Tim floated in the murky water as he watched his daddy release his grip and slide down to the boat. The older man safe in the boat, Tim relaxed and gave into exhaustion sinking down below the surface. The chaos of the weather above disappeared as he found peace in the silence.

CONCERN FELL over his face as Robert watched the man lying in his bed grow suddenly still. He hadn't been responsive since their conversation earlier. A fever had popped up and was hotter than ever. The wild swinging and tossing the injured man did in his sleep had reopened the wound on his shoulder. He didn't know how much more blood loss Whitaker would be able to endure. He stood up and put the log book in the seat of his chair.

He looked over at the cell phone he used only to take orders. He never dialed out. Should he risk it? He glanced back to the man in the bed. He couldn't have another death on his conscience. His boss threatened him with the details of the sail to Ocracoke over and over again to keep him working and show she wouldn't be afraid to get rid of Beth if he made it necessary. But he wasn't the monster she had made him become. Beth had protection right now. This was his one chance to come back from the darkness that had swallowed him.

Who should he call? Someone who would follow his direction, no questions. Someone who didn't know where the cabin was. She was perfect. Crossing the plank floor, he raised the plastic from his table. The cell lay beside the keyboard. He picked it up and signed in, scrolling through the contacts. It had been years since he was on this screen. He touched the name, and her picture appeared on the screen. It began to ring. A chance to hang up. Another ring, another chance to hang up. His finger moved to the red button. He glanced at the man lying in bed. He was so still. Another ring, one last chance to end the call. Click.

"Yes, sir," a female voice answered as if she was on auto.

Silence.

"Who is calling please?" her shaky voice asked.

"Hello," he answered with no emotion.

"Brad, is this you?" She paused. "It is you, isn't it?" Her voice lowered so he could barely hear her. "I knew it. Yes." Then she returned to the phone, "Where are you?"

"Never mind that. I have an injured man I need picked up. Listen very carefully…" He started to pace.

"But I'm in the Virgin Islands. You're…"

"Yes, I know. Listen to me. Call the Beaufort County Sheriff in North Carolina and tell him one of his deputies is floating in a boat in Tranters Creek close to the mouth of the Tar."

"But Brad, you're dead."

"Obviously I'm not. Call the sheriff, now." He disconnected and took the battery out of the phone tossing it onto the kitchen counter. He grabbed the trawling motor and a battery out of the corner of the room. The marine battery strained his shoulder as he pushed the door open and walked down the pier balancing the weight. *I'm gonna have to hurry if I want to beat the police.* Jumping down in the boat, he grabbed the equipment from the dock and hooked up the motor and battery. Sprinting back to the house, he slung the door open. Crossing the floor again, he wrapped the deputy in the quilt stained with blood and lifted him in his arms. The large man's dead weight pushed Brad's arms to their limit as he carried him to the boat. He laid the unconscious body on the pier and pulled the boat he worked all week to empty of water closer. Climbing down, he turned and slid the body onto the deck.

Brad opened the bench seat and retrieved an oar. *I can't believe I am going to set my boat adrift after bailing water all week.* He untied the boat and pushed off into the middle of the creek. There was not much room here to get the boat steered. The large motor was too water-logged to crank. He turned the ignition for the small trawler, praying it would crank. The blood coursed through him as he tried to do something good for the first time in a long time. It turned over and started to push the boat painfully slow toward the river.

Limbs hung over the creek heavy with rain. Their shadows were sluggish as they tried to keep up with the rhythm of the wind pushing them to keep time. Rain soaked his sweatshirt, and he eventually pulled it over his head and slung it to the side. Sweat mixed with the rainwater on his skin as he pushed downstream. Another twenty minutes to the mouth of the river. Hopefully, she made the call.

~

MAX DANCED on the shore as Mike came into view in his small boat. He beat her to the side of the boat as Savanna waded out and Mike gave her a hand up. Once she was securely in the boat, she hooked her hand into the handle on Max's vest and lifted him up beside her. He took his place at the bow of the boat and looked back at her.

"We're ready." Savanna turned to Mike sitting at the motor.

"Any idea where we're headed?"

"Nope." She couldn't tell if he heard her or not. The rain was beating on the hood of her slicker.

Max barked, and Savanna pointed out the way Mike had come. He put the motor in reverse and turned the boat. Reeds and lilies blocked their path as he navigated down the creek. Clouds covered the moon and the spotlight on the front of the boat penetrated the darkness a few feet.

"Mike, you came up this way?" she looked back at him as she pushed a branch out of the way of the boat. The boat barely fit between the overgrown banks. Branches popped and fell as they pushed through. Mike's lantern cast shadows on the vines and Spanish moss.

"I would have been here quicker if it wasn't so dense. Sheriff Harroll called me as you left the office. Seemed to think you would need me."

She turned back to Max, who was lapping up the water as the boat drifted. The trawling motor made very little sound, at least that she could tell. As they emerged on to the river, Max lost the scent for a moment. He danced back and forth trying to find it again. An easterly gust pushed the rain sideways into Savanna's hood.

Max tasted the water and barked. He had it again and was pointing them towards town. Mike pulled the cord to start the larger motor. It sputtered to life.

"I have the larger boat docked up the way."

Savanna nodded and watched Max carefully for any changes in direction.

"Hopefully the rain water won't dilute much," she yelled over her shoulder.

They continued to follow Max's alerts up the river. He had a strong scent despite the weather. His animated dance and barks were stronger on the larger body of water. Mike steered the boat in beside his bigger boat tied to a pier. A quick turn around and everyone boarded the fishing vessel. Max took his position on the bow. Savanna followed him.

She looked back at Mike. The engines were revving, but they weren't going anywhere. He was messing with the controls. Static blared over the radio.

"What's going on?"

"The radio doesn't have a signal for some reason." He shrugged at her and turned on all the lights. Untying the lines, he stepped back to the console and accelerated away from the pier.

As they made their way upriver, the lights of town seemed to act as a beacon. Max tasted the water as they neared the boat slips of the harbor but signaled, they should continue. Savanna gave an exaggerated point toward the east, and Mike increased their speed. She glanced over at the Water Street house and saw the upstairs window glowing with the lamp where she left Charlie drawing. She pulled out her phone and debated whether or not to check on him.

Mike interrupted her thoughts. "Savanna, I'm going to pull in and look at the radio really quick. I don't know how far up-river we're going. Could get dangerous."

She nodded and turned to Max. He was dancing on the bow, most likely confused why they paused. "Max sit." He looked at her and whined as he sat on the deck. She hit the button to call Charlie. It didn't take him long to answer.

"Hey bud, how are you doing?"

"Great, Ms. Beth called Ms. Hellen and Ms. Sophie, and we are having a sleepover. There are a bunch of boys, and we are building a fort, and we have flashlights."

"Sounds exciting." Savanna smiled at his rambling excitement.

"It's great. When are you going to get here? I told everyone about Max."

"I don't know; we are still doing our search. We had a little break."

"Aw, man. Well, hurry up. I want Max to meet all the boys."

"Will do." She glanced at Mike, and he gave her a thumbs up.

"Okay, buddy gotta go. We will be there as soon as we can."

"Really?"

"Yeah. But you know…"

"Alright… Guys, she said she will bring him as soon as she can." There was yelling in the background.

And he was gone just like that. She hit the red button and pocketed her phone. There was no way to leave her mom a message tonight. Her chest tightened. It would be the first time since they disappeared so close to here. Max nudged her hand, and she reached down and scratched behind his imperfect ears.

The radio was blaring. "Burwell come in please, Search Team One, come in, Dispatch to Burwell."

"This is Search Team One."

"Mike, where have y'all been?"

"Mae, on the river. The radio was out."

"Gotcha, we've had a tip. They pointed us to a boat adrift at Tar River and Tranters Creek."

"Copy, headed that way."

He put down the headset and yelled over the engine. "Okay, we are headed upriver. They got a tip. We'll still follow Max in case the boat has drifted."

Savanna gave him a thumbs up and turned to Max. "Ready to work?" He barked in response and moved to his post on the bow. His nose twitched, and he pawed at the edge of the boat. He started his dance again, and she knew he was ready. She pointed in the direction of his signal and motioned for Mike to pull forward.

"Got it," he yelled. He untied the boat and returned to the helm. The engines came to life as they traveled toward the bridge that separated the Pamlico from the Tar River.

IN THE DARKNESS, he steered down the creek toward the river. His boat was too big for the creek, but it was remote, and there was not much traffic. He ran with no lights, and if anyone saw the boat, he would be reported for sure, but he couldn't risk being spotted and this was the best way. The rain helped camouflage the sound of the small motor in the brackish water with a smell he had learned to hate. Maybe the rain will wash some of the smell away. As the creek widened, he passed the few creek cabins. The glow of perfect lives like he used to have with Beth. The blue flicker of a television or the golden light in a kitchen where someone was having their nightly snack took him back to those perfect nights with her. Why did he walk away from all of it? To keep her safe, he told himself. It was the only way.

The tide pulled, assisting his straining muscles and signaling the connection with river water. The bank turned, and the landscape opened up into a watery expanse. He knew it was time to leave the boat adrift. With a glance at the man lying unconscious on the deck, blood soaking thru the makeshift bandage on his shoulder, Brad jumped over the side abandoning his boat in hopes it would save the man's life.

The river water took his breath away as he surfaced. Such a strange difference in temp, the creek water cooler than the humid air. He swam back to the nearest boathouse as the fog started to swirl over the surface. Kayaks were hung on the side. He climbed the ladder to the pier and quietly walked over to the strap that secured them. His breath came quickly as he tried not to break the silence. The canvas strap easily released, and he eased the kayak into the cold water. There were quite a few houses here. Someone would report the boat if she didn't get through to someone. As he paddled away, he gave the owners a silent thank you and a promise to set it afloat as soon as he was close to his cabin.

SAVANNA AND MIKE floated under the drawbridge and Max leaned over the bow. She grabbed his vest to prevent him from diving in.

"The scent cone is strong because of the funnel effect. He was definitely brought this way."

Mike nodded. "This is where the river changes names." His voice echoed against the concrete. A car crossed the metal grate of the drawbridge above them, sending shivers over Savanna's skin.

He increased the throttle. As they emerged on the other side of the bridge, Max danced to the back of the boat. He slipped as he hit the wet deck, hitting the fiberglass surface. He jumped up with his ears pinned to his head. Savanna stood and went back to check on him, slipping her hands below his vest and rubbing his ribs. He looked up, his tongue dangling from his mouth with his panting.

Mike turned and shouted, "He okay?"

She gave him a thumbs up, and he nodded. Savanna went back to Max. "Okay, Max. Let's go back to work." He barked and ran the deck to rediscover the scent.

Savanna passed Mike. He grabbed her hand, making her lose her sea legs for a moment. She gave him a smile, watching Max as he headed back to the bow. "You sure, he's okay?"

"He's just embarrassed," Savanna responded.

Mike let out a huge laugh as he took the speed up a notch.

Rain dripped off Savanna's hood into her eyes. She shook, and it splashed Mike. He put his hands up to block the spray and started laughing, the noise echoing off the trees on the bank. She joined in, and their laughter disturbed a flock of birds, sending them in the air across the river. The boat crossed under a much larger bridge, and fog started to grow thicker with the vegetation. The banks narrowed, and his flood light illuminated both sides of the Tar, Spanish moss swaying in the wind. Max barked and brought Savanna back to her task. She took her spot beside him at the front. She swung her arm toward the north bank of the river and forward. Mike responded by slowing his speed and steering in that direction. She gave him a thumbs up and then the light hit the surface of a boat in the distance.

~

BRAD FLOATED behind the pier at the first house in the creek. The floodlights coming up the river couldn't be missed, casting shadows of leaves on the water's surface. Blue lights reflected off the foggy air as they neared in the larger fishing boat.

An air horn announced their presence and the speaker let out a "Hello."

The larger boat turned off the engines, and they drifted in the water, their momentum pushing them closer to the smaller sports boat. Someone threw a rope aboard and pulled it close. A dog wearing a reflective vest leaped into the boat and barked twice. A figure in a life vest followed him. A female let out a yell. "It's him."

Then, what was that? A squeaky toy. She tossed the rope back to the other boat, and a figure secured it to the rear of the vessel.

Brad let out a breath he didn't know he was holding and started paddling up-creek. The dog's bark started echoing in front of him, bouncing off the boathouses. He paused, drifting, the current taking him back toward the river. A floodlight came on and shined up the creek, the water glowing in its light just short of the kayak. The dog's barking stopped, and the light was turned off. He waited a moment and then started paddling again. He needed to get up-creek before they decided to investigate the dog's interest.

"Mike, we need to go. Let Mae know we need an ambulance."

The shout startled Brad, and his paddle splashed the surface. He cringed as the dog alerted again. The kayak made the turn in the creek before the light was turned on again. He drifted for a moment, beams of light reflecting off the creek surface. Shadows danced at the bend in the bank. His arms ached with exhaustion. There was no moon to light his way, but it also cloaked the kayak with the fog as it turned toward the cabin. He squared his shoulders and paddled toward his lockless prison.

THE BLOOD OOZED between Savanna's fingers as she pressed on Tim's shoulder wound. Max laid beside the unconscious man watching Savanna. He squeaked his toy every now and then, but he didn't move. Uneasiness settled into her stomach. Tim was bad off and in shock. His body shook violently, his teeth rattling. The flashlight in her mouth kept her from talking, but she had nothing to say, not to him anyway. She needed to stay positive, and it was very hard to do right now. She shrugged off her slicker, covering Tim to shield him from the rain, and reached into the first aid kit for another roll of gauze. Flattening the roll, she pressed hard, trying again to stop the bleeding. Tim moaned, and Max whimpered.

There was no bank of trees as they traveled down-river. The fog was thick, and she was glad Mike was familiar with the trip. She looked at the boat towing them, searching for him. He stood at the helm, his hood blown off, his hair whipping in the wind. He had the throttle going full force and was staring toward a shadow of the bridge in front of him. The trip took half the time to return to town and she knew it was because he knew there was a sense of urgency.

"How much longer?" she yelled, but there was no answer. She tried again, her voice echoing under the drawbridge.

He turned and yelled back at her. "Almost there. The EMTs are waiting."

They emerged on the other side and Savanna could see the red flashing lights reflecting in the fog on the bank. He eased up on the throttle and slowed the boats. She maintained the pressure on Tim's shoulder, the blood not showing on the new layer of gauze. Mike slowed them even more. She started to say something but held her tongue when she saw the boat slips emerge from the shadows. He cut the engines and hopped to the pier tying a quick knot on the cleat. The EMTs stood on the pier with a board and their bags ready to come aboard. She prayed they were in time. Leaning over, she whispered, "You're gonna make it, you have to for Charlie." She knew from the way her chest tightened, it wasn't only for Charlie.

Savanna moved out of the way as they quickly shifted Tim onto the board to transport him to the ambulance waiting on shore. Mike jumped aboard and helped pass the board across the water to the pier. They quickly placed it on a gurney and wheeled it to the waiting ambulance. And Tim was gone. She let out a breath and leaned heavily against the railing.

Mike crossed the deck and put his hand on her shoulder. She stood up, leaning into him. She was spent and wanted to run away from everything. He wrapped his slicker around her, protecting her from the wind and the rain. Tears escaped her eyes, blinding her for the moment, making her forget where she was and who was holding her. The only thing in her mind was how she was going to lose another person close to her, and there was nothing she could do about it.

His finger tipped her chin up so he could look at her. "Hey, what's going on? Why the tears?"

She shrugged, embarrassed. She couldn't see a thing.

"We found him." His fingers wiped away the tears that continued to fall. "We found him, and he'll be better in no time."

She nodded. "Yeah right, we found him." She forced out a smile, stepping away from him, the wind sending chills over her skin. "Thanks." She wiped her eyes. "You know, you do seem very familiar. I can't place you." She paused racking her brain. It drove her crazy she couldn't remember. "I need to get back to Charlie." Savanna grabbed her slicker from the deck.

"Max, come on, let's go see Charlie." A bark echoed over the waterfront as he grabbed his squeaky toy and lunged onto the dock. "I'll see you later. Maybe in the morning, I could get a ride back to the car." She walked to the edge of the boat and grabbed the railing, looking back at him.

He walked closer to her and handed her his phone. "Of course, put your number in, and I will give you a call in the morning. Are you going to be okay?" She nodded, typed in her number and hit call. *Stay With Me* played on her phone, and she handed it back to him.

He smiled, a dimple peeking through his five o'clock shadow. "Are you sure you haven't come partying in Washington some time?"

"Nope. I'll call you when we're up. It's been a long day." She gave him another smile, answering quickly on purpose. He was starting to fish, and that made her uncomfortable, but only because she honestly couldn't place him. Savanna followed a now dancing Max to the pier. She looked down at her phone and dialed Charlie. "Max, come." As she walked away, she gave him a wave. She felt awkward when he didn't even see her. He was too busy securing the boats, a roll of police tape tucked under his arm. She quickly put her hand down, and her call went to voice mail.

CHAPTER 29

FALSE ALERT

1:30pm

Shoving her cell back in her pocket, Savanna continued down the brick sidewalk. The walk along the waterfront wasn't so bad. The thick fog created a comforting blanket over the boat slips, and the rain had slowed, so it wasn't blowing in her sleeves at least. Max was enjoying his squeaky toy. Savanna reached down and gave him a pat between the ears. Her face warmed, she couldn't believe she started crying. She wiped her eyes. Hopefully, she didn't look too bad. All the rain and wind on the river during the search probably made her look like a drowned rat. She shoved her hands back in her pockets.

"You did good tonight." Max squeaked in response. "What a good boy." He squeaked some more, then shook the rainwater from his fur.

Savanna let out a laugh, then a 'hey you.' "Let's try Charlie again." She pulled her phone out and tried the number. Max stayed by her side enjoying the free reign on the walkway. It went to voice mail. "I don't know why he won't pick up."

A scream echoed across the dark empty park, the sound bounced off the fog. Max stood frozen in the grass dropping his toy. Savanna tried to decipher where the scream came from. Another one filled the stilted air and Max took off across the park toward the Water Street house.

There was more than one scream now. They were coming from inside the house and Savanna increased her pace to a jog as they approached the front porch. She felt her heart thumping in her chest. The call went straight to voicemail again. As she hit the front steps, she looked for the deputy from earlier. He was nowhere in sight. Where the hell was he?

Another ear-piercing scream- Savanna beat on the door. Max danced on the wooden porch, on her right side and then her left. "What the hell is going on in there?"

Another scream and Savanna threw her slicker to the ground, unsnapped her holster, and pushed the door open running right into a blond woman about her age.

"What is going on?" Savanna demanded as she scanned the room for danger, her hand on the grip of her gun.

"Who are you?" the blond demanded, giving Savanna a shove.

Suddenly a familiar voice came around the corner. "Max." Max ran to Charlie, sitting in front of him.

Savanna stepped around the blond ignoring her question and grabbed Charlie's shoulder. "Why didn't you answer your phone?"

He looked up at her, his eyes starting to water. He stepped behind Max with his arms around his neck.

"I was taking pictures of our fort, and it turned off. Ms. Hellen plugged it in."

Savanna looked at the blonde Charlie was referring to. She

grimaced, realizing how she rude she was busting in, letting the adrenaline take over. "Sorry. I didn't mean…"

"It's okay. I know tonight has been rough. Did y'all find him?"

"We did, and he is on his way to the hospital now." Charlie was still hiding behind Max. "Charlie, give Max a big hug. He did great tonight."

"Oh, Max. Good dog." Charlie tightened his arms around the dog's neck. Max twisted his head around to reach the face of his favorite person with his long, wet tongue.

"I'm Hellen by the way." The blond leaned over towards Savanna. "Anyone I would know?"

Savanna looked at her considering whether to reveal who they had found. "I shouldn't say." She glanced over at the boys who were crowding around the large shepherd, now stretched out on the floor from the weight of the love he was receiving, hinting she shouldn't talk in front of the children.

"That's fine, we can talk later. Hey, you want something to drink?"

"A water would be great. Charlie, you wanna show me your fort?"

"It's our fort," the group of boys yelled in unison.

"Of course, it is. Why doesn't everyone show me the fort." Two hands from what felt like a crowd grabbed hers and led her up the stairs. As she arrived in the landing, she noticed paintings leaned against the wall. The boys ran passed them into the sitting room. The door opened to reveal a room filled with sheets. They had been very busy.

"This looks great, guys. Are you going to sleep in here?"

Charlie's face beamed. "Yep."

The floor was covered in pillows, and there were trucks and cars scattered among them. In the corner was a painting on an easel. She looked around wondering where Beth was. Max looked out of the entrance to the tent, and his tail started to wag. He dove in, and giggles erupted in response. Then the now familiar screams resounded, and Savanna let out a sigh of relief. She turned around to Hellen, "How do you live with this?"

"Oh, it's part of life with boys. Aren't you used to it?" She gave Savanna a questioning look.

"Oh no, this is new to me. I've had custody for only a couple months," she answered as she followed Hellen downstairs.

"That is new. Okay, well if you need any help let me know." She handed Savanna a glass of water. "Are you sure you don't want something stronger?"

A smile spread across, Savanna's face. "No thanks." She took a big drink. "This is great, thanks. Is Beth around?"

"She's working upstairs securing the paintings for the storm." Hellen motioned upstairs.

Savanna glanced around and saw the gallery was empty. The room looked hollow without all the pieces Charlie loved. There were more screams from upstairs. She shook her head as she walked to the kitchen and sat her glass in the sink. Taking a long deep breath, she let it out slowly and returned upstairs. She went from door to door looking for Beth, finding her in the last room toward the back of the house. It looked like a large closet to Savanna, but there were wooden stalls with canvases leaning in them. The brunette leaned over in the last stall, placing a flannel sheet over a piece of framed art. One arm held onto the edge of the wood, and she leaned deep into the compartment, her leg sticking up in the arm to hold her balance. The light pink scar peeked from under her long sleeve shirt, and Savanna's chest tightened.

"Hey, you need some help with that?"

Her head flew up and peaked around the fabric. "That would be great. How did the search go?"

"Good. Turned out it Tim was missing."

"No."

"Yeah. We found him in pretty rough shape. Where's the deputy that was on the porch when I left?" Savanna moved closer to her to position herself.

"He got called back to the station not too long after you left. Something about getting ready for a storm. That's why all the art came upstairs. We will have to board up soon."

Savanna moved toward the fabric, grabbing the corner, and a rumble drew her attention to the doorway. A stampede of footsteps came down the hall and then a huge squeal as the rug started to ruffle outside of the door. She laid the corner down and headed out into the hall.

"Alright guys, you need to settle down. You're being too loud." She yelled.

"But Savanna," Charlie whined.

"No buts. Did you know I almost called the sheriff on you guys? I heard your screaming all the way down the waterfront when I was on the boat." She exaggerated. "Everyone needs to head into the fort and pick a spot to sleep." All five of the boys looked about the same age and just as equally disappointed. "Come on, march." Two of the boys turned to look at Charlie as he started stomping his feet as loud as he could. Two more joined Charlie and then the last two copied the rest of the group. The line headed to the front sitting room. Savanna made eye contact with Beth and smiled. Beth nodded and ducked back into the cubbie she was working in.

The boy's stomps echoed through the house, and Hellen stuck her head above the top of the stairs.

"What is going on here?"

The third boy in line turned to her and said "We are marching to bed. It's cool, Mom. This is the way the cops do it."

Hellen laughed and headed back downstairs. Savanna escorted the crew to their tent, and they snuggled in. She turned off the light and closed the door. A burst of laughter erupted, and Savanna opened the door, turning the light back on. There was immediate silence. She turned the light off, and the giggles started again.

"Okay guys, you really need to try to go to bed."

"We're in bed," came the reply and a burst of laughter.

"Okay. You need to go to sleep."

"Why didn't you say so?" came a smart mouth reply from an unseen Charlie.

"Good night." And she closed the door. A burst of laughter exploded, and she went back to the storage room to help Beth.

"Those boys are a mess," Beth said when she heard Savanna's boots come into the room.

"How are you doing?"

"I'm almost done here. I have to wrap the work in the hall, and then everything will be up here."

"What about the painting in the sitting room? Should we move it in here? I don't know if I trust the boys."

"It will be fine where it is. Besides I don't know if I would open the door again if I were you." She laughed poking her head up to smile at Savanna.

Savanna walked over to where Beth was sitting on the floor. "How bad is the storm going to be?"

"They are saying it's going to be a bad one and the wind is already pushing the water into the sound."

"Should we take everyone to Raleigh?"

"I think we will be okay. This house has been here forever, and Sam did a great job installing the hurricane shutters." A bit of sadness entered her eyes as she continued, "Now if he had only taught me how to use them."

"They can't be that hard. We'll get them closed."

Then, Hellen yelled up the stairs. "Beth, you have a delivery."

"Really? At this time of night?" she looked over at Savanna, who gave her a hand up, and headed downstairs.

The boys were quiet now. Savanna didn't know if that was a good thing or a bad thing. She looked at all the artwork and then heard a scratch at the sitting room door. Max must be tired of boyish attention. She lightly walked to the door and cracked it so he could join her in the hall. Then they headed downstairs.

Beth was at the front door signing a clipboard and then stepped out of the way for the delivery man to pull in a large hand truck with a huge crate.

"Place it in the storage room, Kyle. I'll get you guys the crate after the storm."

"Will do, Ms. Beth." He pulled the hand truck up the stairs with a loud thud for every stair.

Savanna hoped it wouldn't bother the boys. But if they didn't stir when she let Max out of the room, she doubted they would wake for this. Kyle quickly returned with his hand truck in tow and headed out the door.

"Isn't it late for a delivery?" Savanna asked looking at her watch. It was midnight and a stormy night.

"They wanted to get it off the island before the storm blew in. Their warehouse will flood for sure, and the main port has stopped the deliveries at the other end."

"Gotcha, would you mind if I head to the hospital?"

"Sure, no problem. I know you law enforcement folks like to show support when someone is injured."

"Very true," Savanna responded but knew it was more than that with Tim. She had only known him for less than a week and yet there was something there.

Beth smiled at Savanna and motioned toward the front door. "You go on, and I will take care of the boys. Hellen is here with me."

Hellen poked her head out of the kitchen, "I got it."

"One more favor, my SUV is at the accident site, and I don't have a way over."

"Oh, let me get my keys." Beth checked a bowl sitting on an entranceway table.

"Really? I've already been so much trouble."

"Of course. It's no trouble. We will have to move our vehicles when the water starts moving in any way."

A loud thud on the side of the house echoed through the hollow gallery.

"What the…?" Beth jumped as there was a scrape on the same wall.

The women poked their heads out the front door. There was only the delivery truck in front of the house. There was some rustling behind the house. Savanna's first instinct was the peeping tom was back and trying to get into the house. She pulled her flashlight from her utility belt and focused the beam on the side yard. She drew her weapon and placed the light along the barrel. Slowly she rounded the corner of the house and saw a large man on a ladder tugging on a window.

"Police. Hands up," she yelled. The figure froze. "Come down, slowly." The man placed his hands, one in a cast, on the side of the ladder and slowly descended.

"Look, I'm just here to…" His hands started to wave with his explanation.

"Hands above your head," Savanna shouted. She walked closer to the man keeping the light shining on his face.

The man followed her instructions but had a huge smile on his face. "Like I was saying, I'm here to put the shutters up before the storm."

Savanna looked closely at the smiling man and realized it was Sam, who visited earlier that afternoon. "Why didn't you knock and let us know you were here.?"

"I was going to, but I'm not exactly welcome here at the moment. Would you mind?" he asked as he shielded his eyes from the blinding light on his face.

"Sam!" The yell came from over Savanna's shoulder. "What are you doing here?" Beth walked around Savanna who started to holster her gun. "I thought you would be at the hospital with Tim."

"What? Tim's at the hospital?" His smile disappeared.

"Yeah, he was in a bad accident. I would be there myself except my vehicle is at the other end of the county, and I needed to check on Charlie."

"Charlie?"

"My brother. He's staying here with Beth."

"Well, you could come with me. I need to put the shutters up, and then we could drive over." Sam offered.

"Don't worry about the shutters. Hellen and I can get them as long as we can use your ladder." Beth chimed in. "I know how much he means to you. Go ahead. I'll call if we can't get the really high ones."

"You're sure?"

"Yes. Go." Beth walked over and put her hand on his arm.

Hellen appeared around the corner and hooking her arm in Beth's. "Will you get out of here. You are making us crazy. We've got this."

"Okay," he paused. "Let's go. It's a short drive. Forgive me, I don't recall being introduced."

Savanna offered him a hand and then noticed he had one hand in a cast. "Savanna. You visit often I see."

"Not too often. They don't like me there. It's been a rough couple of days." He responded.

"Please don't get him started about going to the hospital." Beth teased him.

"Okay, let's get out of here before they start picking on me." Sam quickly said pulling his keys out of his pocket. "The truck is around the corner."

Savanna gave Beth a quick hug. "Thanks for taking care of Charlie." She handed Beth back her car keys and looked down at the shepherd sitting on the ground.

"No problem. I'll see you later. I assume Max is staying here?"

"Yeah, I think Charlie would rather he stay," Savanna affirmed with a little resignation in her voice. "Max, Stay." Max whimpered as Savanna walked down the path and around the corner out of sight.

CHAPTER 30

GRAVE WAX

October 19, 2014, 12am

Brad's shoulders ached from paddling. The deputy was in safe hands, but now he was going to have to figure out some transportation. The kayak he had borrowed was already on its way downstream with the tide to its real owners. He needed to clean up the mess in his bed so he could get some rest tonight. He stripped the mattress and threw the bloody sheets into the wood stove. There was no sense in trying to save them. Smoke tried to escape out of the door, so he slammed the iron door shut. He opened the flue wide enough to allow the fire to burn hot, ridding the stove of any evidence. He ran his hand through his hair and down to the nape of his neck, kneading the tight muscles.

As he straightened, his eye caught the screens of his computer. Beth had a full house tonight. Five little boys were camped out in the sitting room. Where were the women? Last time he checked Beth was busy in the storage room, and the blond was busy drinking downstairs. A German shepherd was with the boys now. *Isn't that the redhead's dog? So, where is she?* He checked each of the screens and there they all were in the back yard. The redhead had a gun drawn looking up at a ladder. Whoever she was talking to was out of the shot.

Maybe he should risk another call. The last one saved a life. This one may save hers. He glanced at the phone and then back at the screen. He could see light blue fabric descending the ladder. When the figure hit the lower rungs, Brad let out a huge breath. Damn it, it was the contractor. Again. He moved closer to the screen. Beth joined the redhead, who was dressed in a police uniform. No wonder she was so comfortable handling things herself. The police officer had been next to Beth a lot lately. He hoped it was a good thing.

He went back to cleaning so he would have a bed to sleep in. The stains on the mattress weren't budging, but at least they were not running anymore. Maybe he could spread some towels to make a dry surface.

The computer screens were drawing him again. He checked each of them. The blond was pouring herself another drink, and Beth was organizing things outside. The wind was building in town, maybe the storm was blowing in. A lawn chair tipped over, and Beth ran to catch it. The blond sat her drink on the kitchen counter and went out the back door. The construction worker and Red were nowhere to be seen. Blondie ran across the lawn and grabbed the chairs, stacking them.

Brad watched Beth carefully as she moved toward the ladder. What was she doing? She didn't need to be on a ladder with the wind blowing that hard. She rolled up her sleeves, and he glimpsed the contrast of her skin around her wrists. His breath caught. Why had he left her there on the island? Why didn't he set her free? Maybe the scars wouldn't be deep? Movement on the front porch caught his eye. It was the man in the grey hoodie. He looked in each of the windows and then tried the door. What the hell? He went right in.

Where was Beth? He checked the back yard and could see her blue striped shirt blowing in the camera shot. The blond was collecting toys from the lawn. The man in grey continued to move through the house. He looked like he was looking for something. Brad's breath quickened. He watched the women work to clear everything loose in the yard. A hand reached in front of the camera, and a wooden shutter covered the lens, and his outside view went dark. Damn it. He slammed the top of the table. He had to get there fast. Grabbing the keys by the monitor, he sprinted out the door and headed through the woods.

Brambles and sticks grabbed at him as he ran down the non-existent path to where his car was hidden. The beam of his flashlight barely showed the way through the dense undergrowth. He parked it the day the sheriff's deputy spotted it at the Water Street house and hadn't used it since. Doubt started to fill his mind as he thought about how old the beater was and how long it had sat. He brushed leaves and sticks from the hood. It was a chance driving it downtown, but he had to get to town. He had to get to her.

He slammed the car door and turned the ignition key, but his heart sank when the car resisted. He beat the dash with his fist, the vision of the hooded man entering Beth's house entered his mind. He took a deep breath and tried again. The engine sputtered to life, and he hit the gas to force it to a roar. Fastening his seatbelt, he shoved the car into gear and flew down the narrow road. His body jolted from side to side every time the vehicle hit a hole. It didn't take him long to hit the highway pavement and turn towards town.

SAVANNA FOLLOWED Sam in the rotating door of the hospital to find the front lobby deserted. It was after hours according to the sign on the reception desk, and so they were on their own trying to find Tim.

"The emergency room would probably be our best bet," Sam told Savanna motioning to the sign with the big arrow.

Savanna followed him through the corridors. For a hospital, it seemed very quiet.

"What's the deal? There is no one here." She looked over at Sam.

"I'm sure most of the non-essential staff are gone because of the storm." He looked over at her. "People need time to prepare."

"Is that why you were up on a ladder in this wind, with a cast?" Savanna motioned toward his arm.

"I've had it a while, so it doesn't hold me back when something needs to get done. Like securing the shutters before the storm. It's her first storm, ya know."

"We've had lots of rain this year."

"Yeah but it's different with a hurricane. I trust the house, it's been there forever. It's the contents of the house that needs a little extra care."

There might be a double meaning in there somewhere, she thought. They finally ran into a handsome doctor in the hall outside of the emergency room area. Apparently, the doctor that treated Sam, from the conversation between them. Doctor Weldon, from the ID hanging from his lab coat.

"So, when are we going on that fishing trip?" the tall, blue-eyed doctor asked.

"Soon as I get the rest of this cast off, I'll be glad to take you," Sam responded and gave the other man a smile. "Hey Doc, I don't want to put you in a bind but a buddy of mine came in tonight, and I was hoping to get to see him."

Dr. Weldon looked at his watch. "It's way past visiting hours. Most of the staff is at home. I don't think it would be a good idea." He eyed Savanna's uniform. "You guys can't seem to stay out of trouble, can you?"

"Oh, I'm here for moral support," she quickly interjected.

Sam added, "Oh come on, fishing is going to be awesome next month when the red start running."

The doctor looked down at the clipboards he was holding, pausing for a moment. "What's your friend's name?"

"Whitaker."

"Ah, the car accident that came in 30 minutes ago. Let me check and see what room they are going to put him in once we're done with him." He stepped behind the computer and typed in the necessary information.

"It looks like he will be on the 2nd floor, in ICU. They haven't assigned him to a bay yet." He looked up from the screen.

"ICU? He's that bad off." Sam's face changed, showing how anxious he was over his friend.

Savanna placed her hand on Sam's left arm, and he turned to look at her.

She tried to explain what she knew. "He was really bad off when they pulled him off the boat. We don't know exactly how long he was bleeding from his injuries."

"So, you saw him?" he asked.

"Yes. Max and I found him on a boat in the river."

He put up his hand stopping her explanation. "You can tell me the rest while we are waiting. So where do we go?"

"There's a waiting area right off the elevator on the second level. Let the nurses know you are waiting, and when he arrives, they will let you know, and you can ask when you can see him."

"Sounds good. Thanks, doc. I owe you one."

"Just don't lose my number when the fish are biting." He smiled at Sam and pointed them up the hall to the elevator.

THE SPEEDOMETER READ 80 mph as Brad passed the first light into town. There were no cars, and he flew down the four-lane. He flew under the overpass, and blue lights flashed behind him. He wasn't stopping for anyone. His heart pounded with every bump he hit. Sweat poured down his forehead. He hit the corner at Bridge Street and cut the corner, laying on the horn as his car barely missed a car parked in the lot. The rear of his car bounced in the air as he hit the curb coming to the crossroad.

It looked like he gained a couple more cops as he drove, the sirens creating a melody as another was added. Horns blared as he ran a stop sign and another. He was almost there. Five more minutes at this speed. The image of the man entering her house to do God knows what fueled a rage he didn't know existed in him. The last time he felt like this he did something very stupid. Mistakes are going to kill him. May as well do a good job of it. He took a hard right at the bank and made it down to Water Street.

Squealing to a stop in front of the house, the police surrounded his car, blocking any exits on the block. He didn't care. This was exactly what he wanted.

"Place your hands out of your window." The demand came from the speaker on the cruiser directly behind him.

He unrolled the window, pumping the handle up and down. He placed his left hand out as soon as the glass was low enough and continued to roll. The minutes ticked by.

"A little faster, sir," came another command.

Both hands were out the window now.

"Use the handle on the outside of the door and step out with your hands raised."

Brad grabbed the handle and opened the door. A scream came from inside the house catching everyone's attention. Brad took advantage of the distraction and ran toward the house. "There's an intruder. Help them," he yelled over his shoulder.

"Sir, stop. Sir, we're not going to tell you again. Stop and drop to your knees."

Brad made it to the front stoop of the porch when another scream sounded in the night. He dropped to his knees, hands behind his head. It seemed as if he was surrounded instantly. Blue lights reflected on the glistening grass.

"Officer, please, there are children inside." A loud thump hit the other side of the wall by the front door.

"Don't move." The officer motioned to his companion, and his hands were pulled one at a time behind his body so he could be handcuffed. The lead man stepped onto the porch lightly, gun still drawn and walked to the front door. He beat on the front door. "Beaufort County Sheriff's Department. Open up."

"Help me, please!" A shouted cry.

Brad cringed. It was a male voice. Was it the intruder or someone else? Her construction worker? He stayed on the ground, his hands behind his back, totally helpless, a gun pointed at him. There was a female scream, and the deputy tried the door. When it opened, he stepped in the building.

"Everyone remain still, Beaufort County Sheriff's Department," he yelled and then as he disappeared through the opening, "What the hell?"

Brad couldn't see what was going on and it was killing him. "What's going on? Is it her?" He turned his head to look at the man who was watching him. "Come on man. I need to know she's okay." He couldn't make eye contact with the man behind him. He started to shuffle, so he could see his face.

"Don't move sir. I'm sure everyone will be fine now we have the department on the scene."

"I need to see her."

There was a scuffle inside and female voices. Brad listened carefully, trying to decipher what was going on.

"Dispatch, come in. Dispatch, come in please." came across the radio at the deputy's waist.

"Dispatch here. Go ahead."

"Mae, we need animal control here at the Water Street house."

"Which house exactly, Mark?"

There was a pause. "The Pearse gallery. The new one."

"Got it."

"We also need to get ahold of the handler of the search dog. If she can get here ASAP, it could help the situation."

"Savanna McCormick?" the female voice asked.

"Yeah, I guess. She helped with the search earlier today."

"Calling her now."

"We are going to need an ambulance too. We have a male intruder at the property with dog bite wounds."

"I'm on the phone with Savanna now. She's on her way. She says if the scene's safe have Charlie, one of the little boys, tell Max to release. She said he is to say it exactly like that."

"Got it," a male voice.

"Make sure you do it right."

"Mae, I got it. Just get everyone here."

"Charlie," a yell echoed through the house. "Charlie?"

Brad couldn't hear if there was a response. He couldn't stand it. He started to struggle against the cuffs.

"You need to calm down sir. Let us take care of things," the voice instructed him, the shadow shifting on the grass beside him.

"Charlie, I need you to do me a favor."

Another pause followed.

"Charlie, I need you to tell Max to turn loose of this fellow. I know it's scary, but I need you to do it. Savanna says he will listen to you and you are to give him the release command. Do you know how to do that?"

"Dispatch to Officer Boyd, Boyd come in please."

"Mae, I'm kinda busy right now."

"EMTs want to know if there are any other injuries." Brad paused to hear the answer. This was what he needed.

"Nope, Charlie's doing his thing. Can I get back with you?" Brad relaxed at the assurance of the officer's voice. His adrenaline slowly disappearing.

"Okay, Okay. Sorry."

"Yeah, woman, let the man do his job." The comment escaped Brad's lips before he could stop them.

The officer gave Brad's shoulder a poke. "We don't need comments from you."

A child's voice came from the house, "Max, release. Max, come."

A male shriek followed and then a shuffle. The deputy dragged a handcuffed man out onto the front porch, laying him on his stomach and zip tying his ankles. "Ladies, do we have a first aid kit?"

Brad watched as Beth stepped out on the porch. "I'm afraid not. I can get you some towels. I don't think my box of Band-Aids would help with what you have there." She gave the officer a shaky smile.

He released a breath, and a tear rolled down on his cheek. The light of the interior shone behind her giving her the halo she deserved for putting up with his shit. She turned to step back inside and paused. Turning his direction, she asked, "You mean there were two of them? Oh my..." Brad rose up on his knees hoping for a reaction. Her mouth gaped, and eyes glistened in the reflection of the blue lights. She mouthed his name and took a step closer to him.

"Ma'am, you might want to keep your distance. This gentleman is under arrest."

"This is no gentleman, officer." She hesitated but ran back inside, a scream escaping her mouth. "Oh my God, it's really him." She reached back and grabbed the door shutting it and disappearing from his sight. He started to shake as he stared at the front door.

"I've lost her." The whisper escaped him.

A shadow passed in front of him and he watched the construction worker run inside to comfort her. Why was he here? A gust of wind blew leaves past his face, and suddenly time stopped.

Sophie appeared in front of him, poking him in his chest. "You idiot, why are you here? You want everyone to know who you really are?" A hard slap stung his face.

Two men picked him up, carried him to the cruiser, and shoved him in the back seat. Everything disappeared as he felt the vinyl of the backseat rub across his face.

SAVANNA STEPPED out of Sam's truck looking at the scene. Four sheriff cruisers had lights going. As she walked across the lawn, she counted the deputies and the people in handcuffs. Her heart felt like it was beating in her throat. Where was Charlie? She ran up the walk passing one man in handcuffs on his knees. She went to the front door frantically knocking. Her arms started to tingle, and her legs felt like they would give way soon if she didn't see his face. Glancing over to her right she saw Jeremy on the porch bleeding from the arm and legs. He was cuffed and legs tied. She tried knocking again.

"Deputies make sure this one goes straight to jail," she yelled, pointing to Jeremy. She took a step toward him and yelled, "Crazy stalker, the department will know what you've been up to in the morning."

She stepped back to the door and started to open it herself. The door opened, and she stumbled into the open space of the gallery.

Her foot caught the weight of her body, and she righted herself. Beth and Hellen stood there looking at her.

"Are you okay? You don't look so good," Hellen said.

Savanna looked over at her. "You don't look so good yourself. Where's Charlie? I need to see Charlie and Max." They were the only words she could get out.

"Charlie," Beth yelled up the stairs. "Your sister's here!" She turned to Savanna and took her hand. Savanna couldn't tell who was shaking more, her or Beth. "Better sit down before you fall down. I'll get you something to drink." She pushed Savanna down on the bottom stair.

"Charlie, come on down, sweetie. Your sister is here," Beth yelled again turning toward the kitchen. The door flew open, and Sam ran in, taking Beth in his arms. He kissed the top of her forehead and then each of her checks. Savanna could see out into the yard. The officers grabbed Jeremy and toted him to the back of one of the cruisers. Hellen's face suddenly blocked her view and yelled, "Beth, come quick. Sophie's lost it."

"What?" Beth's face was a mess as she turned from Sam's chest toward the ladies.

"She's out front, slapping the piss out of that guy."

"Oh my God, Brad." She paused. "Sam, stay here." Beth wiped her face and took a step toward the door. "I'm sure Charlie will be down in a minute." She said before sprinting toward her friend. "Sophie, Sophie stop it. Let the police have him."

Savanna whistled for Max. "Max, Charlie. Come." She shook her head. "I'm whistling for the dog, not Charlie," she offered up an explanation to Sam who looked lost standing in the middle of the room. He walked to the doorway and watched the commotion out front.

So, no one cared she was whistling for the two of them.

"Maybe I should go," Sam mumbled.

There were at least four sheriff deputies to clean up the mess, they didn't need her help. She headed straight up the stairs to the sitting room. The blanket fort was now dismantled, and the boys were jumping around pointing their fingers at each other like police officers.

"Guys, guys, calm down for a minute." Savanna tried to get their attention.

"Bang, bang," was the response.

"Guys hold on a minute. I need to ask you a question."

"Pow, pow," was the next answer.

Savanna pretended to fall into the pile of pillows, grabbing her stomach. She looked up at them. "Where is Charlie?"

There were a couple of shrugs. Savanna grabbed the arm of the boy closest to her, sitting up so she could look him in the eyes. "Where are Charlie and Max?"

"He left."

"What do you mean he left?" It suddenly felt like a sledgehammer hit her in her chest.

"He said they were going to take Max to jail, so he left to keep him safe."

Savanna scrambled to her feet, "Thanks, guys."

She took the stairs two at a time. "Beth, Beth." She looked in the kitchen and found Beth crying, Hellen giving her a tight hug, and another blonde sitting at the table. "Have you guys seen Charlie? He's not upstairs." They all shook their heads. "He told the boys they were going to put Max in jail. Where would he get that idea?'

"I'm afraid the deputy that arrived on the scene first called for animal control. Maybe he overheard." Beth looked at her apologetically, her eyes glossy. "We honestly didn't know what to do when Max refused to turn loose the burglar."

"Jeremy must've threatened the boys for Max to attack that way."

"You knew him?" Hellen asked.

"Afraid so." Savanna paused, thinking of the second man that was cuffed. "Well, one of them. Apparently, she knew the other one," she said pointing at the blonde sitting next to Beth.

"I don't think we knew him at all," Beth whispered, starting to cry harder and leaning into Hellen.

Savanna looked at Hellen and mouthed Sorry. She rubbed Beth's shoulder. "Do we ever know any of them?" She didn't wait for an answer. "Charlie is missing. Make sure the other boys stay inside." She went out the backdoor into the backyard, eerily dark because all the shutters were closed in preparation of the storm. Trees rustled as the wind gusts started to pick up. The fog had lifted, giving up its fight with the impending storm. She pulled her flashlight from her belt and focused the beam on the perimeter of the yard.

"Charlie," she yelled. "Charlie, come on out bud. The excitement is over, and Max is in the clear." She paused to listen. The sunflowers danced in the strong breeze creating shadows that played with her mind. Maybe he had walked further up the block. He would look for a cubby or a protected area he felt secure in.

Beth stuck her head out the back door. "Do you need some help?"

"Can you get me Max's toy from upstairs?"

"Sure, I'll be right back."

Savanna yelled a few more times. The deputies remaining rounded the corner. "Ma'am, do you need some help?"

"Yes, my brother has disappeared with my German shepherd. Could you give me a hand searching?"

"The one that bit the burglar."

"Yes, the one that bit the guy spending the rest of his life in jail for stalking." She didn't hold anything back in her comment.

"Holy crap." He instantly pulled his radio. "Mae, pick up please."

"This is dispatch, go ahead."

"Mae, we have a missing kid now on Water Street, and the German shepherd from the earlier dog attack is running loose." His voice was shaking as the transmission went through.

The radio squawked back. "Mark, give Savanna your radio and go sit in your cruiser. You will be safe there."

He followed Mae's instructions and ran around to the front of the house.

"Dispatch to Savanna, come in please."

"Savanna, here."

"You doing okay dear?"

"I could be better. Charlie is missing. He is protecting Max from being picked up by the pound."

"Poor guy. Sorry about Mark. He's scared of dogs."

"Dispatch come in, please. Sheriff Harroll to dispatch."

"Dispatch here." Savanna listened carefully as the sheriff contacted Mae.

"Mae, can we please keep the radio clear of unofficial traffic. We have a strong storm coming, and we need to stay clear for emergencies."

"Yes, sir. Attention all available deputies, we have a Code Adam on Water Street near the Estuarium. An eight-year-old boy, red hair, blue eyes, may be in the company of a black and tan German shepherd. Notify dispatch if there are any sightings. Last seen at the Pearse Gallery approximately ten minutes ago."

Savanna glanced at her watch, noting the time and started to walk toward the side yard. Beth ran out of the backdoor and tossed the toy to Savanna as she headed to the sidewalk. "Thanks, the wind is starting to blow. Make sure everyone is safe."

"Will do," Beth agreed and pulled the door shut, eliminating the last of the light.

Savanna looked up at the sky. Everything was hidden, and the sky had turned a dark gray. The lights along the waterfront lit the walkway. Savanna crossed the street to Festival Park. She walked over to the playground shining her flashlight into the pirate ship.

"Charlie, Max, come on out guys. It's me." She continued down the walkway and shined her light under the Estuarium. The solid concrete the building sat on jutted out from the bulkhead. Savanna focused her beam under the building squeaking Max's toy. "Charlie, Max." There was nothing. She thought sure Max would answer. Where could they be?

CHAPTER 31

October 19, 2014, 12:45am

Charlie sprinted down the boardwalk, dragging Max behind him on his leash. He didn't dare look behind him. The grownups were busy with lots of drama and getting ready for the storm. No one noticed him slip out the back door. He couldn't see the red and blue lights anymore, so he paused to catch his breath.

"I'm not gonna let them have you." He wrapped his arms around the large shepherd and gave him a hug. "I'll hide us until Savanna gets it all straight." Max whimpered, and he gave the dog another squeeze. He stood up looking over the railing at the river. Maybe he should go down the bank, no one would see him off the walkway. Staring down the railing, he didn't see a break. Charlie saw a blinking light in the distance. "That way. Come on Max, this way." And he took off down the boardwalk again.

The wind blew in his face so hard, he could barely hear Max's nails on the wood behind him. He could see the light up ahead. *What is that? It's a railroad bridge.* A light was on in the little house right before the bridge. *That would be a perfect spot to hide.* Charlie looked around for a way to get there. The end of the boardwalk faced a large building with tons of wood and stuff to build houses in the chain-link fenced yard. Following the fence, he found a gate with enough give. Pushing as hard on the bottom corner as he could, Charlie made room for Max and pushed him through. He slid under and joined his companion. There was no one there to see him cross the yard and duck into the barn or to see him make his way down to the bank of huge chunks of concrete securing the bank from the whitecaps of the river. He was a boy saving his best friend alone in the night, or so he thought.

"Charlie," came the yell from the water.

Charlie looked around thinking it was the wind playing tricks on him, the rain blowing in his eyes.

"Charlie." This time it was a little closer. He could see a white boat rocking on the water's surface. The waves were high now, and the boat would disappear from sight when it sunk down between them.

Charlie ducked down behind some bushes. Max started to whine. "Max, shh."

"Charlie, it's Abram." There was a pause. "Hallo, hallo ashore."

The small boy popped his head through the branches. "Abram, I need your help."

"What's wrong, young master?"

"The police, they're after us. They are trying to take my dog."

"Okay, I'm coming. Stay there." The boat came closer to shore.

Charlie tried to get closer, but the wind was knocking him off balance. He turned to see where Max was. He turned loose of the leash to hold on to the rock. "Abram, I dropped the leash. Oh my God, I dropped it."

"It's going to be okay. Don't fear young master, he will come to you when you call. Let's get you in the boat first. Then I will run you to the house."

"No Abram," he started to panic. "I can't go back, they will take Max. He's a good dog, he made a little mistake.

"Okay, Okay. No need to panic. Is there anyone with you?"

"Just Max." Charlie pointed to the bushes.

"Okay, Charlie. Ease yourself down to the edge. I'm going to pass you a rope."

"But Max."

"Max will follow you. Come one."

Charlie slid down the cement, the ragged edges of the stone catching on his pants. He looked down and stuck his finger through the small hole. A piece of rope landed next to his feet, then a wave washed it away.

"I'm going to try again."

Abram pulled the rope back into the boat and tossed it again. This time Charlie was ready and snatched it tight.

"Okay Charlie, you're going to get in the water."

"But I'm not allowed in the water."

"It'll be okay. I'm going to get you in the boat. Take the first step into the river, and I will pull you right in."

Charlie nodded and looked back at Max.

"Max will follow you."

Charlie stepped out into the water, and there were rocks under-neath. He stumbled until the ground gave way and he was float-ing, the current pulling him away from Abram. Holding tight to the rope, Abram pulled him to the boat. He reached down under-neath Charlie's arms and grabbed hold, pulling him inside the vessel.

"Okay, Charlie. Now it's your turn. Call Max."

Charlie clapped and whistled for the dog. The dog poked his nose out of the bush. "Max, come."

Max whined and paced back and forth across the top of the jagged rocks. "Come, Max." The waves splashed against the shore. Charlie wracked his brain. *What would work? What would Savanna do? That's it.* "Max, time to work." The dog barked and made the leap in the water, paddling toward the boat. Abram reached down and pulled in Max's front, then reached down again and lifted his backside into the boat.

Charlie smiled at Abram. "Great, now where are we headed?" Max gave a big shake, spraying his companions with water.

"Are you sure you don't want to go back to the house? I heard your sister down the riverbank calling for you."

"Savanna?" He thought for a second. "No, I can't go back to the house. I'm coming with you." Charlie's voice was shrill with fear.

"Okay, okay." Abram looked down at him and then ruffled the young boy's hair. "I have to make a quick trip down-river for some yellow tops, and I'll drop you home on the way back." Abram paused pushing off the rocks toward the channel. "Are you sure? Now's your chance to change your mind."

"No, I can't let them take Max." Charlie shook his head to reinforce his decision.

Abram nodded. "It could get dangerous with the storm. See those gulls on the tracks? They are there for shelter from the storm. They won't move till after it passes. Sometimes it's better to stay put and wait. I wouldn't make the trip if people weren't in worse danger waiting."

"Where are we headed?" Charlie was curious about how many people Abram planned to fit in his small boat. The waves were rocking it back and forth, and he had to hold on to the side to keep his seat.

"Windmill Creek and then Goose Creek. It's a secret trip so you can't share it with anyone." Abram adjusted the sails to catch the wind, and the boat took off toward the hole in the railroad bridge.

"Why is it a secret?" Charlie yelled into the wind blowing against his face. Max was standing at attention on the front of the boat. He seemed to like it there, his tongue hanging out of his mouth.

"Can't tell you. But I need you to watch for the windmills," Abram yelled back.

Charlie nodded, his throat sore from yelling.

They followed the shore until they pulled close to an old tree.

"This tree looks almost dead," Charlie said as Abram lit a lantern.

"It's been here as long as I can remember." He stood and waved the light in the dark night. The boat rubbed the moss-covered rocks as it bounced in the wake.

"Looks like it," Charlie said before he could stop himself.

Abram waved the light again. "There used to be a windmill here, but the tree outlived it. It outlived a lot of us." He paused, then blew the light out. "No travelers this direction tonight." Branches and leaves blew into the river close to the boat. "Charlie, it's a ways to our next stop. You might want to nap."

"Nah, I'm good." His mouth opened wide in a big yawn.

Max looked back at him and then went back to staring straight ahead.

"Well, settle in. That way you won't have to worry about falling out."

"Okay." Abram threw a blanket at him as he slipped down in the bow of the boat. "What's this for?"

"For your noggin. Now lay down."

Then a swell took the boat and Charlie's stomach felt like everything was going to come up. "Ahh"

"Told you. Are you ready?"

Charlie nodded, then tucked the blanket under his head. He watched the clouds blow by in the darkness. There was no moon or stars, only dark grey as far as he could see with the occasional streak of lightning. His eyelids got heavy, and even though he tried to stay awake, everything slipped away.

A RUMBLE of thunder woke Charlie from his sleep. The boat was surrounded by reeds, and it was raining hard now. He sat up in the boat looking around, his body stiff from the trip. Max was the only one in the boat with him. "Max, where's Abram?" The dog cocked his head to listen for a command he understood.

White flowers waved in the wind closed tight against the weather. There was movement in the reeds and the sound of footsteps on wood. Abram jumped in the boat, extinguishing his light as he pushed Charlie low against the hull.

"Charlie, quiet."

Charlie laid as flat as he could. Max joined them. "Max down." He laid next to his boy.

"There are some unexpected men in the marsh. We need to stay very quiet."

Nodding his response, Charlie closed his eyes tight and swallowed hard. Max's breath was warm against his cheek. He strained to listen over the panting. Voices were coming from the reeds.

"Is it her? I didn't hear any motors." A male voice traveled through the reeds on the wind.

"I don't think so. I saw the signal for only a second," another voice answered.

"Aw man, the light disappeared. Where is she at? The mosquitoes are eating me alive."

"Will you shut up. I'm tired of hearing you."

The boat started to rock hard. Abram shifted up to the edge so he could peek through the reeds. The wake roughened and Charlie wanted to see what the man was watching. He pulled up to the edge next to Abram and looked really quick. A big boat was coming into the creek, coming right towards them. He turned loose and slid down next to Abram's thigh. He looked up at the man next to him, his face illuminated by a bright light. The whole marsh was illuminated as shadows danced across the reeds and mallows along the shore. The light blinked off and on three times. Abram crouched back down in the boat putting his finger in front of his mouth and looking at Charlie.

Charlie closed his eyes and listened. There was splashing through the water. Someone fell in the mud, and there was cussing. Charlie started to shake with silent laughter. What a bunch of dorks. Thunder rumbled, and there was a cracking noise. Another splash and laughter. They were laughing at each other. They can't be that bad. He eased himself up to watch.

"You guys suck." A female voice came up from the inside of the vessel. "Get your asses up here."

The men struggled to obey her command. She let out an exasperated breath. Charlie had trouble hearing over the wind, but he could tell she was very angry. She swung her hand over the side of the boat, and there was a flash of light and the sharp pop of gunfire. Streaks of lightning crossed the sky, throwing a spotlight on the scene. The two men lay on the shore.

Charlie grabbed hold of Abram by the waist, hiding his face in the man's wet cotton shirt.

A man's voice questioned, "What have you done?"

"Let's go."

"But..."

Abram bent down to look Charlie in the face. "It will be okay. Stay quiet." He pulled Charlie to him.

"I said let's go." There was a pause. "What? You're worried about them? The river will take care of them. It always does. Let's go." Another rumble of thunder. "Now," she insisted. "I'm going to be missed." The boat motor started and disappeared in the distance.

Abram pulled the blanket around Charlie, sitting him safely down in the bottom of the boat. Charlie couldn't focus. Did she really kill those guys? He looked up at Abram. He didn't even seem phased. This wasn't fun anymore. He grabbed Max's mane and held him close.

"Abram, I wanna go home."

Abram nodded and grabbed his oar, pushing against the pier. He adjusted the sails and pointed the boat back to town.

CHAPTER 32

AUTOLYSIS

October 19, 2014, 3:00am

Savanna's hair curled in the humidity as it blew in the wind. She trudged up Water Street to the house. The adrenaline pushing her an hour ago was now depleted, leaving her exhausted. She didn't know how to proceed without her partner. It was like the field trip. Maybe she wasn't good at her job. Maybe it was all Max. He could operate by himself. He found the target every time, and she was only a crazy disaster following his lead. She left Charlie and him to run to the hospital. *Was that putting family first?*

She shook her head as the thought crossed her mind. They were supposed to be her priority. No one else. Her pace quickened, and she took the steps two at a time. There was a single sheriff's 4x4 left parked on the curb. She had seen two other deputies walking door to door a block away. They were working on finding him. She took a deep breath and knocked on Beth's door. Slowly the door opened, and Beth's face reflected everything she was feeling.

"I'm so sorry," Beth whispered as she wrapped her arms around Savanna. "I should have kept a better watch over them."

"No, I should have been here. I could have handled the burglar, and everyone would have been safe." She gave Beth a squeeze, and the two stepped inside the house and closed the door. Beth threw the latch.

"Max took charge quick. You don't have to worry about Charlie with him around that's for sure."

"I saw the sheriff's truck out front." Savanna motioned toward the front door.

"Yeah, he's in the kitchen. All his deputies are out looking or with the guys at the jail."

"At the jail?"

"Yeah, they are going to book everyone and sort it out later." Beth took her slicker and put it in the closet.

"So, what the hell happened?" Savanna's voice echoed through the empty downstairs.

Beth grabbed Savanna's hand and took her upstairs to her bedroom. The sitting room door was shut, and there was no noise. Savanna looked at her watch, the boys must be asleep. Finally, at three in the morning.

Beth motioned for Savanna to sit on her bed.

"Oh no, look at me. I'm covered in who knows what after today."

Beth crossed the room to her dresser. "You want to change? I have some sweat pants and a t-shirt."

"That would be great." Savanna took the clothes from her. "Where's the bathroom?"

"It's across the hall. Towels are under the sink."

"Has the sheriff heard anything?" Savanna asked as she grabbed the doorknob.

"Not that he's shared. He said he would let me know if they find him."

"Okay, I'm going to change really quick and then I want to hear what happened while I was at the hospital."

Savanna stepped across the hall and closed the door behind her. The reflection in the huge framed mirror above the sink shocked her. The stress of the day showed on every inch of her face. She pulled a washcloth from the cabinet, running it through the hot water. As she wiped away the grime of the day, tears ran down her face. She didn't know if they were from exhaustion or fear. She needed her mother. "Oh mom, I've totally screwed this up. Please help me." She realized she hadn't made her call tonight. Dropping her uniform to the floor, she quickly put on the clothes Beth had loaned her. She grabbed her black pants and reached in the pocket to pull out her cell.

The cell rang a couple of times, she expected a third before the voicemail picked up. She needed to hear her Mom's voice. Then there was a click. She paused and listened.

"Hello?" Her voice was quiet.

"Savanna, is that you?" Her brother's voice came across the line.

"Charlie, you have your phone?" Why didn't she think about calling him?

"Yes, I didn't want you to be mad. So, I grabbed it."

"Charlie, where are you?"

"I'm with Abram on a secret mission."

"I thought we talked about you not going on any more missions with Abram."

"No. Tim said if I go, I need to tell you first."

"Did you call me?"

"Well, no. But they are going to put Max in the pound. You know what they do to dogs there."

"I know buddy, but they're not taking him. I straightened that out. You guys need to come back to the house."

"We can't. We are in the middle of the river."

"You're what? There's a hurricane, Charlie." Panic really sat in. She could hardly breathe. She turned her phone, so the microphone was away from her mouth and started breathing in and out slowly.

"I know, he told me it's dangerous. We are coming as quick as we can."

"But Charlie you would be safest here." She could hear the wind blowing in the phone. The reception started to crackle. The thunder rumbled on the line and then echoed outside the house. He wasn't far away. "Just come on back. They aren't taking Max."

"I told you we are coming as fast as we can. The police said Max had to go, why would he lie?"

"Why don't you tell me what happened, and I will tell you why?" Savanna needed to keep him on the line to reassure herself.

"Okay, Jeremy came in the fort and started cussing." Savanna caught her breath at the mention of his name but didn't want to stop Charlie from talking. As long as he was talking, she knew he was okay. "We all screamed because he scared us. Max jumped on him and then knocked him down the stairs. We heard the sirens outside, and the policeman came in the front door and ordered the dog catcher for Max."

"Okay, then what happened? But first turn around, so the wind isn't blowing in the phone." The sound of the wind changed but still interrupted his words.

"So, the policeman told me what you said over the phone, so I told Max to turn loose." He stopped for a minute and her breath caught in her throat. "He listened and ran upstairs beside me. Then the policeman grabbed Jeremy and dragged him outside. Everyone was watching him, so I told Max we needed to get out of there. And so, we took off."

"Where did you go?" she asked hoping to catch him off guard.

"Hold on," he turned away from the phone. "No, Max, come back. Sit back down. Okay sorry, I'm back. Max keeps running up and down the deck and making the boat rock."

"It's okay, you were going to tell me where you went." She tried again.

"Oh, we are headed through the railroad bridge. I'll see ya in a bit."

"No, Charlie. Wait." But he was already gone. She debated putting her clothes back on. Bending down, she grabbed her uniform, shaking out her pants. She opened the door and poked her head out. Crossing the hallway, she tossed her clothes in the corner of the bedroom. She looked around for Beth and didn't see her in any of the upstairs rooms. She put her boots back on, took the stairs two at a time, and headed to the kitchen. Out of breath, adrenaline pumping, she poked her head in and announced, "Beth, he's on his way. Charlie's coming home."

CHAPTER 33

SCENT CAGE

Charlie closed his phone, and the boat lunged toward the left. His phone went flying into the bottom of the boat as he reached for the side of the boat to maintain his balance. He looked back at Abram. "Sorry, I had to take that." He tried to pretend he wasn't scared, but the waves were starting to splash into the boat.

Abram nodded. "Your sister?"

"Yeah, she's worried as always."

"Well, today is a good day to be afraid."

Charlie held on and stretched as far as he could to retrieve his phone. He shoved it back into his pants pocket. Images of the night kept popping into his brain. He closed his eyes as tight as he could. When he opened them, Abram was bringing the sails down and tying them to the posts.

"The wind is too strong. I will row the rest of the way." He wrapped a rope around the canvas. "Don't worry Charlie, we're almost there."

Charlie wiped the rain out of his eyes and nodded. He could barely see the gulls still hiding on the railroad bridge. The lights blinked on and off on the small shack along the tracks. Its roof was gone. Well, it's a good thing they didn't stay there. Abram moved back and forth, pushing the boat toward town. He motioned for Charlie to look behind him. The bright streetlights of the waterfront glowed. The boat rose and fell in the waves. They rounded the Estuarium pier, now a good foot under water; the only markers were the pylons to tie the boats. Charlie pointed to the sailing school pier, he remembered from the field trip.

"That's right. That's where we're headed." The boats were all missing along the piers. Abram steered the boat to shore. As he pulled next to the wooden poles, he tossed his rope with extra loops. "Okay, Charlie. We are going to have to trust what we know."

Charlie looked at the houses, porch lights glowing on the other side of the street. He knew there should be grass, but all he could see was water.

"Charlie, I'm going to carry you." The boy nodded. Abram stepped onto the wood of the pier, turned and reached for Charlie. With outstretched arms, the boy stretched and climbed into Abram's arms.

Charlie looked over Abram's shoulder. "Max. Come." The dog stayed in the boat. "Aw, he's doing it again."

"Say what you did before."

"Max, let's go to work." The dog instantly lunged, sending the boat out into the river with his back legs, the extra length of rope disappeared into the darkness. Max hit the shore and started to zigzag through the park. He gulped some water and then barked. Charlie scooted around, so he was riding on Abram's back. They followed Max's path. The dog barked again and ran across the flooded lot. When they hit the pavement, it was faster going, and the dog didn't waste any time finding the house. Abram sat Charlie on the porch. "I'll let you take it from here."

"No, you need to come in and get dry." Charlie grabbed his hand.

"Charlie, I can't."

"You can," Charlie argued.

"I'm not welcome here."

"But you're my friend."

"I've been turned away before. I couldn't stand it again." Abram looked sad as he shook his head.

Charlie gripped Abram's hand tight as he walked toward the door, knocking. "I hope she's not too mad." The door opened almost instantly, and Savanna swooped Charlie up, hugging so hard he had no choice but to turn loose.

Savanna pulled back, her face red and blotchy. "Charlie, where is Max?"

Charlie shrugged. "He showed us the way. I don't know where he is." He looked up at Abram. "Did you see where he went?"

She turned him loose and stood beside Abram looking out into the darkness. The water was pushing on the porch now, getting everyone's feet wet.

"Max? Max! Where are you?" she yelled. A bark sounded in the distance, but it was low through the sound of the rain.

"He must be working," Charlie said.

"Charlie, what do you mean?"

"That's how we got him out of the boat. I told him it was time to go to work." There was movement in the sunflowers. "Maybe that's him. Is he following that light?"

Charlie pointed out into the yard at a woman with a lantern. The adults looked in the direction he pointed. It was hard to see through the rainy darkness. A lantern crossed the yard to the big oak. Sunflowers beat against an old weathered shed, then the door opened, the light making the inside glow. As the door shut, he saw her face. *It's Ms. Beth's friend, Selah.* Charlie was sure of it. Couldn't they see her?

Another woman in black ran to the door of the shed and with a large key threw the lock, then ran behind the house. "Who was that? Didn't you see them?"

The adults stood in silence, frozen, staring into the darkness at the shed. They both shook their heads at him. Charlie tugged on Abram's hand. "We need to get Max. Can you help me get him? He needs to come in."

"Call him again, Charlie. He will answer." Abram affirmed.

"Max? Max, where are you?" A bark sounded on the other side of the yard.

Savanna went inside and quickly got jackets for both of them. When she returned to the porch, she handed Charlie his jacket. "Here, put this on."

Charlie threw his arms into the jacket and zipped it up. He grabbed Abram's hand again and pulled him off the porch to the side yard. "Max?" A bark responded. They followed the sound.

Savanna turned on her flashlight, scanning the perimeter. "Charlie, call him again. He's working for you tonight."

Charlie squeezed Abram's hand and looked up at him. Abram smiled down at him. "Max where ya at?" the boy yelled.

A bark came from a patch of sunflowers. Savanna focused her beam to highlight the point of the sound. A nose emerged from between the stems and barked, then returned to where ever he was. The threesome crossed the yard, as the water level rose again. It was knee-high on Charlie. Savanna parted the plants to see Max lying on a patch of bare dirt.

"Looks like we have a target here. Charlie, find something to mark it. Preferably something that won't wash away in the storm."

"Okay," Charlie agreed. "Can I borrow the light?" Savanna handed him her flashlight, and he looked along the ground for something big. Spotting a big rock, he put the light in his pocket and struggled to lift the rock. Pushing his way through the tall stalks, he returned to Max. "Move Max." The dog looked up at him but refused to move. Charlie dropped the rock barely missing Max's paws. Abram bent down straightening the rock into place.

Savanna patted him on the head. "A little close there, bud. Now you have to reward him. Praise him for doing a great job. You have to do a great job because we don't have his squeaky on us."

Charlie nodded. "Good boy, Max. You did it. You found it." He gave the dog a huge hug.

"Okay, everyone inside." Savanna grabbed Max's collar and headed back toward the house.

Abram stood up quickly. "Charlie, do you hear that?"

Charlie shook his head and strained to hear what Abram was talking about. "What is it?"

"Come on help me. There's screaming in the shed."

He knew he should go inside, but Abram needed his help. The two of them ran to the shed. Charlie couldn't hear anything, but Abram was struggling to open the door. He was a strong guy.

There's no reason he couldn't get it open. Charlie helped him tug at the door.

"Help me get it open. The water is filling the shed," Abram's voice yelled above the storm.

Charlie didn't hear anything, but he did see Selah go in there. *If it is her, I have to try to help.* He wedged his fingers in the crack between the door frame and the door, but couldn't get a grip.

"Selah, we can't get it open," Abram yelled through the door.

Charlie looked up at the man. "I knew it was her."

"Okay, Selah, Charlie, stand back," he yelled as he took a step back from the building. With all his strength, he ran full force toward the building. The door and frame splintered causing the building to start to sway. Charlie looked inside, spotting Selah curled up in the corner.

"Charlie, stand back. It's going to collapse," Abram yelled.

Charlie obeyed without thinking in time to see Abram pull Selah from the swaying building. She tried to run back in, but the side-walls started to splinter. Pulling as hard and fast as Abram could, they dove away from the structure as it collapsed into a heap of rubble. Abram wrapped his arms around her, pulling her close. She screamed, "No!." Her arms reaching toward the non-existent building. Abram ran his hand along her neck and tugged the scarf from her head and ran through her curly dark hair.

"Phew, that was a close one," Charlie yelled.

The couple didn't respond. Selah sobbed against Abram's chest. Abram brushed her cheek, tipping her head up, so she was looking at him. "You are really here," he whispered against her mouth. "I've waited so long, my sweet Alizeti." He kissed her and then pulled back. "What's wrong?"

Charlie couldn't hold back anymore. "You guys get a room. You know it's raining out here." The boy hurried across the yard onto the porch and clapped his hands. "Come on everyone, time for the party."

"Wait, Charlie, something's wrong."

Charlie ran back to the two figures kneeling in the flooded yard.

"The baby, I need to find the baby," Selah exclaimed.

"You have a baby? I didn't see any baby." Charlie responded quickly.

"Yes, our son. He was in a basket ready to travel," Selah said.

Abram stood and scanned the yard. Charlie ran over to the pile of wood and rubbish floating in the yard. Then there was a pair of arms that reached out of the sunflowers and grabbed a floating Moses basket.

"There in the bushes." Charlie pointed out the basket as it disappeared into the darkness. "Someone took it."

Abram leaned back down and pulled Selah close. "We will find him. I promise we will." He turned to Charlie. "Thank you for your help tonight. For everything. You were the bravest boy I've ever met. I don't know what I would have done without you." He held out his hand and Charlie took it, giving it a quick shake. "Now, you better head inside." A branch fell from the big oak landing where the remainder of the shed covered the flooded yard.

Charlie jumped with the splash of water. "Will do." He turned loose and waved as he finally made his way to the house.

CHAPTER 34

BACKLINE

October 19, 2014 4:00am

"Beth, can you get us some towels?" Savanna yelled into the kitchen as she pulled off Charlie's jacket. Relief filled her. Max shook the rainwater off his coat. Thank goodness the gallery was empty.

"Charlie, you were supposed to follow me right in."

Beth ran upstairs and returned quickly to throw towels on the floor beside Max and Charlie. "How bad is it out there, Mr.?" she said looking at Charlie.

"Not too bad. The rain is going this way," he karate chopped the air, "and this way," giving another chop.

"I see. Did your friend want to come in?"

"No, I think he was headed home too." Charlie smiled.

"Good deal. It's definitely not a night to be outside. Glad you're home, kid." She grabbed a towel and rubbed his head while Savanna tried to get Max dry.

Savanna smiled as Max shook again. "I don't think your partner likes the water as much as you do, buddy. Are you going to tell me what happened now? The sheriff is here and wants to talk to you and Max. Maybe get some more details about what happened upstairs. Before Ms. Beth and Ms. Hellen came in."

He nodded his head.

"Let's go in the kitchen and talk to him, so he can head home." Savanna grabbed Beth's hand. She whispered in Beth's ear, "Where is Hellen anyway?"

"She had to go lock up their house and make sure it was good for the storm," she whispered back.

"Got it." She pushed the reluctant Charlie to the kitchen where the sheriff was waiting.

As they entered the room, Charlie wouldn't make eye contact with the older man sitting at the kitchen table. His small hands intertwined with Max's fur.

"Young man, I heard you had quite the adventure today. You want to tell me about it? Why would your dog attack a policeman?"

"It was just Jeremy being a jerk. He's not a real policeman."

"That's not what your mom's, excuse me, your sister's boss says."

"Really?" Charlie shrugged. "Well, he can be a jerk too sometimes."

The sheriff laughed. "Is that right? Well, what did Jeremy do?"

"I was asleep in our fort with the other guys and all the sudden the walls fell down on us. We couldn't breathe, so we started to scream. Then we heard him cussing. He got really loud, and so Max started to bark. We poked our heads out to see and then Max was chasing him down the hall, and we heard a loud thump. When we peeked through the bars at the top, Max had his leg at the bottom of the stairs. We were watching, and another cop came through the front door and was on the radio. He called the dog catcher. The radio told him to ask me to get Max off Jeremy, so I did. Max came upstairs afterward." He took a deep breath. "Everyone was rushing around, handcuffing everyone. I knew Max would be next. So, I told him we needed to get out of there. I told the guys we were leaving and not to say anything. They agreed, and we took off."

"Wow, that was pretty scary. Well, because you were honest with me and Jeremy was bad, we are not taking Max in. Does that sound good?"

Charlie nodded, giving Max a hug.

"Now get you a drink of water and head upstairs with your guys and try and get some sleep."

Beth handed him a glass of water, which disappeared quickly. Max gave Savanna a look, and she told him "go with Charlie." He barked and followed Charlie upstairs.

"Wow, what a scary day," Savanna said as she let out a breath.

"Ladies, if you will excuse me. I need to get home while the truck will make it on the street. Glad he's home. I do want to thank you for finding Tim. Whitaker is a good man. I don't know what I would do if I didn't have him to take over for me."

"You're retiring, sheriff?" Beth asked.

"After today, I'm thinking about it. Do you have your emergency supplies?" He pulled on his slicker.

"Yes, we're all set."

"Okay, keep those kids inside." He slowly walked to the front door, Savanna and Beth following him. As the door opened, a gust of wind blew the rain in on them. "You ladies stay safe. I'm going to swing by the hospital and check on Tim. I'll give you an update in the morning. Sam is up there right now so I will send him this way to double check the house for you. Although, you've done a great job for your first storm, Ms. Beth."

"Thanks. We will see you later." The old man waded through the water to his truck. As soon as the ignition turned over, Beth shut the door.

"Are you going let Sam come by?" Savanna asked. She wondered where Beth stood right now with the guys. She definitely hadn't made a decision last time they talked.

"He can if he wants. I could use some help. I actually have no idea if we got everything or not."

"You got all the shutters, right? And I hear the sump pump working."

"I think we're good, but I always second guess myself when it comes to the house."

"Well, I'm sure he's going to come by and check on you." Savanna looked at her and watched her twirl her wedding band.

"I should have talked to Brad while he was here. I was so shocked seeing him, I didn't think about it. I want to know why he left."

"Brad?"

"Yes, the second intruder they arrested; it was Brad. When I saw him, it was weird. I didn't feel a thing. It was like it wasn't him. Like he was someone I didn't know." She shook her head. "I don't know."

Savanna reached over and rubbed the other lady's shoulder. "It's okay. Let's get through this storm and then we will see what the sheriff can do. How about some sleep?"

Beth nodded and led the way upstairs. "I think a good night's sleep would do us good."

Savanna laughed as she looked at her watch. It was almost four in the morning. "Totally agree, let's get some sleep while we can." She knew the boys would be up soon.

CHAPTER 35

CLOSE GRID

*O*ctober 19, 2014, 9:13am

The beep of the heart monitor hurt Tim's head every time it went off. He tried to shift his weight in the bed, but every muscle in his body screamed with the movement. The palm of his hand went to his shoulder where the biggest pang was, but he was tangled in something. He pulled it off his arm, and the computer beside him went insane. He tried to open his eyes to see what was going on, but the light in the room hurt. He shut them as hard as he could to stop the pain.

"Honey, you have to calm down," a female voice chided from the darkness. "Let me get you hooked back up to the monitor." The voice came from the other side of the bed. The alarm turned off, and Tim's shoulders fell back into the pillows behind him. "Can you open your eyes for me?"

"No," he moaned.

A chuckle came from the end of the bed. "Well, you are answering questions. That's good. Do you know where you are, Deputy Whitaker?"

Tim took a deep sniff of the antiseptic smell surrounding him. "The hospital."

"Exactly." He heard some typing. "Now I'm going to go get the doctor, and I want you to work on opening those eyes. I will turn off the lights to help."

"Thanks." He peeked through slits of his lids and saw her shadow and then darkness.

"You're welcome. Be right back." And then she was gone.

He opened his eyes fuller, looking into the darkness of his room. His eyes slowly adjusted, and he saw the tubes and wires running to the monitor. He moved his feet under the blankets. Turning his head, he looked at his left shoulder with enough bandages to stabilize it. He tried to move it, but it hurt like hell.

There was a knock at the door, and then a tall man in a lab coat stepped in. "Deputy Whitaker, I'm glad to see you awake. I'm Doctor Weldon."

"Tim," he whispered.

"What's that?" the doctor asked.

"Tim. Call me Tim, please."

"Okay Tim, do you remember what happened?"

"I was driving on the way back to town. To Beth's." Flashes of the night ran through his mind. "Is she okay? There was an intruder."

"Yes, everyone is safe. I need you to slow your breathing for me." He paused till Tim's pulse was back down to normal. "What else do you remember?

"There were deer, but I passed them. Then something hit the car."

"Anything else?"

Tim was quiet for a while. He searched his mind for any memories of the day. Then he shook his head.

"Okay, let's check and see how you're doing. The nurse said you were sensitive to light earlier."

"Yes."

"Okay. I need to check your pupil dilation, but it will be just a second." The doctor leaned over and shined the penlight in each of his eyes. "Okay, good. Looks like you'll live. To bring you up to speed, you were in a car accident. Something pierced your shoulder, we are unsure what it was. You had heavy bleeding for an extended amount of time and were found on a boat in the river. I will let the sheriff fill you in on any other details they have discovered since I was last updated. Do you have any questions for me?"

"When can I get back to work? I know the storm is blowing in."

"The eye of the storm passed over this morning around five. We are going to see how you are doing tomorrow morning, and then we'll decide. A couple of people are waiting to see you. Are you up to some company?"

"I think so." He tried to scoot up in the bed.

"Stay put, and I'll bring them in one at a time."

The nurse moved around the room, adjusted his bed, so he was sitting up a bit. She made sure he was comfortable, dimmed the lights, and then stepped out of the room, closing the door behind her.

THERE WAS a knock at the door. "Come in," Tim tried to be as loud as he could. He tried to open his eyes, but it hurt to move his lids.

Tim's boss poked his head in the room. "Okay if I come?"

"Yes, sir."

"Wow, you look rough." He took a seat by Tim's bed. "When are they sending you to a regular room?"

"The Doc is going to make decisions tomorrow."

"Keep me posted, will ya?"

"Of course. Tell me what happened. I can remember a few things, but most of it's blank."

"What do you remember?"

"I answered the call to the gallery and was on my way. There were deer on the side of the road. Glass, there was a lot of glass."

"True, the evidence is all over your face," the sheriff interrupted.

"Thanks, there was water, a lot of water. I woke up in an old cabin. There was a guy there. He had me in bed. I could hear the rain on the roof. Then I saw daddy on his roof in the hurricane. A black guy used a boat to save him. Did my daddy evacuate?" Tim struggled to open his eyes and turn his head toward Sheriff Harroll.

"It's okay, keep 'em closed. I don't know. We never did hear from him. I'll send someone out to check." The sheriff tapped him on the wrist. "Now, this fellow at the cabin. Any specifics you can remember?"

"No, my eyes were swollen shut. It was a struggle to see the room. He kept checking my shoulder and offered me some water."

"Did he hurt you or threaten you in any way?"

Tim shook his head.

"Well, according to the fingerprints found on the boat Savanna discovered you on, the man was Brad Pearse, aka Robert."

Tim tensed, a pain shooting up his arm. "How do you know it's Brad?"

"We have him in custody. He was arrested at the gallery."

"Yes." Tim jerked his right arm in the air. "Ahhh. I knew it. Was he the intruder from the call this evening?"

"Not that we know of. He came to the house when the intruder tried to come into the house late last night. A separate stalker case."

"Shit. I should have been there."

"There is something else. Brad's fingerprints were a match for the McCormick disappearance last year."

"Savanna's parents?"

"Yes, looks like he was involved somehow."

"Have you told Savanna?" Tim hoped she could find her answers.

"I will tell Captain McCormick when we have more details. We are waiting for Pearse's attorney to arrive from Colorado, should be tomorrow sometime."

"Hopefully we can break that one."

"You need to rest and not worry about it. This old man has a few more convictions in him." He walked to the other side of Tim's bed. "I need you better. I can't run this department by myself, and after this weekend, I'm thinking…"

"Whatcha thinking sir?" Tim interrupted the pause, wishing he could see the old man's face.

"I'm thinking, it's time to start planning for a transition. Maybe a younger guy to take over this next election."

"I'm your man. Soon as they release me," Tim volunteered.

"I need you a hundred percent though. So, your job is to get better first."

"Will do."

"Now I am going to go see if Sam has gotten back from changing clothes. He was here early this morning after all the ruckus at the gallery, waiting for word."

"I'm sure he has a lot of news." A vision of Sam's face when he thought Brad was Beth's kidnapper came to mind. He was furious then. Now Brad was in jail, he was sure to have a short fuse.

"I'll see you later, hopefully with news of your father." The door opened, and the light in the hallway created a silhouette of his mentor.

"Thanks, boss."

The door shut and Tim was left with his thoughts. He searched for more details of the night. All the trying to remember non-existent memories made his brain hurt. *Why can't I remember? I need Sam here to help me talk it through, see if I can jog something.*

There was a knock on his door.

"Come in." The door opened slowly. "Who's there?"

"It's me, Charlie, can't you see?" Charlie was the first to poke his head in.

"Not very well right now." Tim saw another silhouette come through the door and guessed it was Savanna.

"Boy, you look terrible," the boy said as he pulled Savanna in the room with him.

"Thanks, guy. I missed you too. So, what's been going on while I've been in here?" Tim tried to give them a smile. The scent of Savanna's shampoo drifted through the hospital room, invading the turf of the antiseptic smell that Tim had started to hate.

"Charlie did his first HRD this morning." She was close enough for him to feel her warmth, but her facial features were blurry.

"Really? Way to go Buddy." Tim held up a fist for a fist bump. Charlie was happy to run around the bed so he could hit.

"It was so cool. Max was listening to only me and found some bones." Charlie was bouncing up and down as he talked.

"Hmm sounds cool. I heard the hurricane blew through. Was that scary?" Tim was trying to follow him and having a hard time of it.

Savanna chimed in, "Hey Bud, Tim can hear you better if you stand still." She gently placed her hand on Tim's hand.

"Okay." He was still almost instantly. "I didn't hear a thing."

"But what time did you go to bed?" Savanna asked.

"I got to stay up super late. Abram had me out on a boat during the storm."

Tim tried to raise an eyebrow, but the stitches on his face kept it from moving. "Was that smart?"

"Probably not, but he was bringing me home, well, not home, but to Ms. Beth's. And I needed to get home before it was really bad. He said it was the quickest way."

"Okay, but you know not to do it again, right?"

Charlie smiled shyly as he shrugged it off. "Pfff, of course."

"Anything else?" He looked at Savanna.

"I think that's enough news for now. Can you handle another visitor?"

"Sure. Will you stay?"

"Of course, let me see if he is still out here." She crossed the room and peeked out the door. Waving him in, she stepped out of the way so Tim could see Sam's silhouette. He stood there and didn't say a thing.

"What's up with you, guy?" Tim guessed he already knew what was wrong.

Sam walked over to the bed and bent down to hug him then resisted, looking at his shoulder. He held out his hand, and Tim grabbed it. "It's been a long night. I'm glad you're okay."

Tim looked at Sam's hand, pulling it close so he could see it scraped and cut.

Sam looked across the bed at Savanna and Charlie. He shook his head at Tim.

"What? I'm curious. Charlie, here, did his first human remains search. I have been filled in on everything except your night."

"Have you ever put hurricane shutters up with only one good hand?" Sam responded raising his arm in the cast.

"Can't say that I have." Tim's lips tried to form a smirk, but it hurt.

"Plus, Beth had some unexpected visitors last night during the storm." Tim could hear the disappointment in Sam's voice.

"Some guy and Jeremy," Charlie added, "and Max bit him."

"Max bit someone?" Tim asked.

Charlie nodded. "Yep, Jeremy, because he was being an ass."

"Charlie, you shouldn't say that." Savanna corrected him.

"But he was." Charlie turned around to look at Savanna.

"I know, but you can't say it."

Sam held out a fist across the bed for Charlie to bump. Charlie smiled and took him up on it.

"And the other person?"

"It's not important." Sam quickly responded.

"Sam." Tim turned his head to look at his dearest friend, feeling sorry for him because he knew what he wasn't saying.

Tim turned to Savanna. "How many were arrested last night?"

"Two. Brad and Jeremy."

"Max almost went to jail, too," Charlie added.

"He certainly did, but you protected him, so we got him off." Savanna praised him.

Tim smiled, then yawned big. "Excuse me."

Savanna brushed his hand, and his smile widened. "I think we better go, guys. We'll let you get some rest."

"No, it's okay."

Sam, as he made is way toward the door, quickly said, "I've got do some storm clean up over at the house. I'll see you later."

"Yeah, we need to go check on Max. Charlie and I will be back later." She leaned over and gave him a quick kiss on the cheek. Charlie giggled, shaking his head.

"Oh, I almost forgot. I drew you something this morning." Charlie ran back around the bed and set a piece of paper on Tim's bedside table.

"Thanks, dude. I'll look at it a little later."

"Okay. Hope you like it." And Charlie disappeared out the door.

Tim lowered his hospital bed, and as the door shut, he closed his eyes and fell asleep.

CHAPTER 36

REFIND

October 20, 2019, 10:00am

Brad sat at a metal table. Handcuffs attached his arm to the metal table. He stared at himself in what he knew was a two-way mirror. His hair gray at his temples and the beard he grew out over the summer made him look like he belonged here, a room with peeling paint and concrete floors. His legs didn't make noise as they shook against the edge of the chair.

The door opened, and an older rotund man carrying a folder of paperwork stepped into the room. Walking over to the table, he slapped the folder onto the surface. "I'm Sheriff Raymond Harroll, and what are you going by today?" He paused waiting, staring into Brad's eyes. "Should I call you Robert or maybe I should call you Brad Pearse?"

Brad swallowed hard. "I'm not going to say anything without my lawyer."

The sheriff sat down opposite him and opened the folder. "I have something I want to go over with you. You don't have to say anything." The man laid pictures of a sailboat on the table. "I've heard your request for your lawyer, and he is on his way. He's landed in Greenville, so he's thirty minutes out." Brad studied the pictures and watched him add more, his sport boat and pictures of the older couple from his first summer in Washington. "Now I know you recognize these photos, we'll talk about those later." He placed a portrait of Whitaker on top of the pile. "Let's talk about him."

Brad looked down at the photo. He knew this was going to bite him in the ass.

"First, I want to let you know I have talked to Whitaker." Here it comes. "I want to thank you for saving his life."

"Wait, what?" Brad was taken back, his head jerking up to look at the sheriff.

"I want to thank you for taking care of him, and I have an offer for you."

"Shouldn't we wait for the lawyer to get here?" Brad looked back down at the photo of the deputy.

"I don't have a problem with that. Just make sure we don't wait too long. My appreciation does have an expiration." The sheriff pushed the chair back from the table. "Send me a message at the office when you're ready to deal." He started placing the photos back in the folder.

Brad's eyes watched the man's hands as they grabbed the deputy's photo and placed it gently with the others. He held it differently. *Something's up with that.* The older man crossed the room to the door, knocking three times.

"We will talk soon."

"Absolutely." Brad needed to clear his head. The door shut behind the sheriff. Was he ready to cut a deal? Was Beth safe enough? He ran his free hand through his hair, tucking it behind his ear. Leaning back in the metal chair, his arm pulled against the metal of the handcuff. Yanking at it, the sting of pain reminded him where he was. "Damn it," he yelled. I can't keep her safe in here. I need to know she's safe before I give them anything.

The door opened quickly, and Richard Wolfe stepped into view with his briefcase. He was talking to someone in the hall. Brad strained to hear but couldn't make out the words. Wolfe nodded and then threw his briefcase across the room hitting the table, the impact echoing in the room. He stepped in and shut the door behind him.

"Why the hell am I in this little town?"

Brad opened his mouth to respond, but the next question came too fast.

"Why would you talk to the sheriff without me? You know better than to talk to any police without a lawyer."

"But…" Brad tried again. The lawyer paced back and forth in the small room.

"Are you an idiot? I thought I taught you better than that. I set you up with this persona when you asked me to. The least you can do is explain to me how we ended up here."

Brad pounded the table. The startled lawyer stopped staring at him. "Can I talk now?"

"I'm waiting."

"Okay, first of all, the reason I am here is the same reason you are, to keep Beth safe. It's always been the reason for me leaving and is what we need to remember before we do anything."

"You obviously have a next step. I can tell by your voice."

"I need you to talk to the sheriff. He mentioned a deal."

"What kind of deal?" Wolfe asked.

"He didn't say. I told him I needed to talk to you first." Brad closed his eyes, a headache coming on. He needed a smoke.

"You're smart every once in a while. Why don't you tell me what we're dealing with, so I can see what I need to consider?"

"What do you want to know?"

"Start with why Washington, NC, then we'll go from there."

CHAPTER 37

TARGET ODOR

*O*ctober 21, 2014, 3:55pm

Beth and Savanna stood at the window and watched the SUV pull up in front of the house. The sheriff's vehicle didn't even pull in the driveway. Savanna reached for the other woman's hand. The fingers trembled as they gripped hers. Their lock tightened as the two men emerged and the figures grew closer to the porch. They stopped short of the steps, and surprisingly the sheriff uncuffed the other man. He rubbed his wrist and nodded, his beard rubbing his chest through the open collar of his shirt. The two women stepped out onto the front porch. He eyed her and took one step at a time.

Savanna ran her fingers across the knuckles of the other hand in hers. Beth released her hand and closed the gap between her and the man.

"Brad?"

"Yeah, baby, it's me."

She tipped her head back and looked up at him. She looked back at Savanna and then placed her hand on his chest, pressing into the fabric. Her other hand found its way to his chest. Suddenly, her hands formed a fist, and she started punching him. The sheriff made a movement to intercede, but Savanna shook her head.

Beth continued to punch Brad as hard as she could. Tears rolled down her face. Her pounding slowed.

"Are you finished?"

A hard slap landed on his face. "No. Why?"

"I can't tell you."

"Why?" she shouted into his chest.

"To keep you safe."

She shook her head. "No. I don't believe you.'

"I did what was best."

"Best for who? You, maybe." She sobbed into his cotton shirt.

"Believe what you want."

She looked up at him. "Who are you?"

"I'm your husband."

"No. Brad would not do the things they say you've done. He would not have left me and let me think he was dead. He would have come to me and let me help him deal with whatever caused this."

She paused for a moment and then. "It was you on the island. You were there. And you left me again." She slapped him again. "Sam was right; you left me. You don't deserve my love."

His jaw tightened and started to twitch. Savanna watched him carefully, her hand moved to her holster, unbuckling it.

"Do not mention him in my presence. You are mine, not his." He grabbed her wrist.

"But that's where you are wrong. You left me. It took me a long time to heal, but I started over. This is my new start, and Sam is part of it. I'm not yours anymore." She jerked her arm trying to free herself.

Savanna drew her weapon and pointed it at Brad. "Step away, Mr. Pearse. I think this conversation is over. Sheriff, you need to come and get him."

Brad turned loose of her arm. "So, I've lost you forever? You are giving up on us?"

"I've learned to live without you. You are the one who gave up." Beth turned around and went back into the house. The sheriff stepped forward, cuffed Brad and led him back to the cruiser. He bent down and slid into the backseat, his head leaned on the back of the seat, and he let out the scream of a wounded man.

Savanna followed Beth into the house after everything was secure out front. She found her in a room in the back of the gallery unpacking boxes. "Are you okay?"

"Yes, I'm fine." She didn't sound right. Savanna watched her struggle to pull the brown paper off a painting. Her hands shaking.

"Are you sure?" She squatted down so she could see Beth's face. There were tears running down her checks.

"Yes, I need to get this order ready to go out." Beth reached and brushed Savanna's arm. She looked down and noticed Beth's ring was missing.

"Did you lose your ring in the paper?" Savanna started to dig through the mounds of brown paper.

"No, I – it's okay. I took it off." Savanna wrapped her arms around her. The tears came heavier now. "Thanks for having the sheriff bring him by, I know it wasn't exactly procedure."

"I didn't have anything to do with it."

Beth wiped her eyes, leaned back, and looked at Savanna. "You are a terrible liar." She laughed. "I know you asked him."

"I just mentioned it in passing, how you could use some closure. I didn't think he would make it happen." Savanna smiled over at her. "Closure is what I do."

Beth smiled. "And you do it very well. Don't you need to get to the hospital to see someone?"

Savanna nodded. "Yeah, I'm gonna leave before I make you cry again." She took a step towards the door and then remembered Charlie's bag upstairs. "I'm gonna run upstairs and get Charlie's stuff."

"Okay," Beth yelled from the closet.

Savanna headed upstairs and looked around the room. Something was missing. She couldn't place it, and then it hit her.

"Beth, I see you decided to move that painting after all," she yelled down the stairwell. Savanna went back to the room looking for Charlie's bag, checking behind the furniture. She heard Beth's steps up the stairs.

"I'm sorry what did you say? I couldn't hear you.

"Nothing important, I said, you moved the Miró after all," Savanna said casually as she finally found Charlie's bag under the desk.

"The what?" Beth stuck her head in the sitting room. She stood there frozen. "I didn't move—" As if someone had cracked a whip behind her, she repeated Savanna's trail from looking for the bag.

"Maybe it's in the storage room," Savanna offered.

Beth's breath came faster as both the women went into the storage room across the hall. She didn't bother to offer the white gloves Savanna saw her usually wear when handling the canvases. They flipped through the paintings, Beth from one corner and Savanna from the other.

"No luck here," Savanna announced.

Beth looked around, her face muscles twitching as she figured out the answer. Then it was as if a terrible thought hit her mind and anguish took over her features. "The Miró is gone."

The End

October 21, 2014, 6:26pm

Savanna knocked lightly on Tim's hospital door as she cracked it and peeked in. "Are you up for a visitor?" It took her forever to find his new room. She was glad to finally see him, and he was smiling, even better.

"Sure, come on in." He looked at her with opened eyes, still purple and green, but he was able to open them.

"You sound much better. How are you feeling?" He didn't have as many monitors now that Tim was in a regular room. Savanna knew all the beeping was driving him crazy.

"I'm still sore, but it's better than I was. I can at least open my eyes all the way."

She crossed the room and sat in a chair next to his bed. "That's good." She leaned close to him, careful of his shoulder.

"How's Charlie?"

"He's playing with the guys. Still head honcho after the hurricane."

"Bet he's loving that." Tim smiled at her and put his hand on hers. "I'm dying to get out of here. The doctor says at least another week."

"That's not too bad. I know the sheriff could use your help. He just got a big break in my parents' case."

"Really? I hate being out of the loop. Has he shared any details?" He gave her hand a squeeze.

"No, not to me anyway. You know the rule, family is too close." She rubbed the palm of his hand with her fingers.

"We'll find out what happened. You have to trust me." He closed his hand around hers and raised it to his lips. "You have to be patient."

"I know. I'm tired of being patient, though, you know?" She looked at him, her eyes turning glossy. "We're also working on a smuggling case on the river," she added trying not to cry.

"No tears now, look what Charlie drew for me. He left it last time he was here. It's fantastic. Look at this detail."

Savanna looked over at the piece of paper that Tim was unfolding. He was right, it was an amazing portrait of Abram on his boat. The wind was blowing his white cotton shirt behind him like a cape, and there were two figures behind him standing in the marsh surrounded by white mallow flowers. Tears finally broke through and ran down her face.

"Savanna, what's wrong? I showed you this to cheer you up." He shoved a tissue in her hand. "I suck at this stuff, but I can't be that bad."

She wiped her cheeks. "It's not you." She wiped her nose with the tissue. "Really, it's not."

"Then what?"

"It's the picture. Those two in the back are my parents. Charlie has our parents in the marsh. It's good that he can remember them happy like this."

"Oh." Tim took a closer look at the smiling couple in the reeds. "Well, he did a great job. Make sure you tell him. Won't you?"

"Of course."

"So, when are you headed back to Raleigh?"

"I thought we might stay a while. Max and I are needed here, and Charlie has settled in. We've only been here less than a week, but it's been good for him. Hopefully, we will break him from this running away thing."

"I could probably help you out when I get out of here."

"That would be great. I can't wait till everything is back to normal."

"Wait, I didn't say I could work miracles." Tim stuck his tongue out at her.

"Well, our normal." Savanna laughed and gave him a smile.

"What are we going to do about the not dating at work thing? If you are thinking about staying, I don't know if I could stand it."

"We'll figure it out." Savanna leaned over and kissed him on the lips. "Besides I need some cheering up, and you are actually very good at that."

"Oh, really." Tim slid his good hand up behind her neck and tugged at her hair, causing it to fall over her shoulders. Pulling her closer, he kissed her with smiling lips.

"Yep, the best. In fact, I might stay indefinitely," she said in between kisses.

"That, Captain McCormick, can be arranged."

Washington D.C., October 13, 2014

Abbie walked through the garden of one of her wealthiest donors. Fairy lights twinkled in every tree as they swayed in the light breeze. What a perfect ending to the summer. This fundraiser was already a success with ticket sales, and now she would work her magic to bring in the big checks. The sequins on her light blue dress shined as she walked through the crowd, smiling, making small talk, and shaking hands with everyone on her list. She felt awesome tonight, and it showed. The invitation was the talk of the town.

"Abigail, you look fabulous." A female voice came through the crowd.

She turned to see her favorite benefactor. Giving her a huge smile, she walked across the grass. "Thank you, Samantha. How are you doing tonight?"

"I love these things, but I wish some people would rethink their dress choices." She scanned the crowd and then patted Abbie on the arm. "Thank goodness you have some fashion sense. Your dress is to die for. Have you seen the senator yet?"

"No, not yet. He will be fashionably late as usual. So glad he RSVP'd. It helped build the rest of the list. Samatha, can I order you a drink?"

"I'll get something in a minute. Why don't you go get something for yourself? You need to enjoy your success tonight. I'm sure we will surpass our goal."

"From your lips to God. I'll talk to you later." She gave Samantha a quick hug and walked toward the bar.

"What can I get you, ma'am?" the female bartender asked in her slow southern drawl.

"I'll have a white wine. You are doing great." Abbie smiled at her. Ruth, her intern at the office, had come to her asking for help finding some extra money for school. This was perfect for her. She was cute as a button, and this crowd loved her if the tip jar was proof.

"Thank you, ma'am. It's not too bad yet."

"I'm glad. Let me know if you need anything."

She handed Abbie her wine. "Will do." She smiled and turned to the next guest in line.

Abbie took a drink of her wine, squared her shoulders, and walked across the lawn toward the temporary stage. This was the part of her job she hated.

Grabbing the microphone, she tapped the end, and speakers rang through the night. Some of the crowd turned to listen. She tried again.

"Welcome everyone." She paused and then tried again. "Welcome everyone to the 10th annual fundraiser for the National Society for Historic Preservation." Loud applause rose from the crowd. "Thank you so much for coming tonight. If everyone can please take your seats, they are getting ready to start dinner. While you are taking your seats, I wanted to share with you what tonight means. Your generosity tonight will give the Society another successful year of restoration and preservation. The history of America's architecture depends on your donation tonight." She got a thumbs up from Samantha in the back of the crowd. Her smile widened. "Enjoy yourself tonight and don't forget to fill out the donor card at your table before you leave. Thank you." She turned off the microphone and placed it back in the stand at the corner of the stage. As she made her way down the stairs, she saw the senator arrive at the garden gate.

The waiters made their way through the exceptionally dressed tables, placing the beautiful china in front of the diners. Abbie shook hands and smiled, giving a few a little waves while stepping around the waiters and attempting not to disrupt their well-rehearsed dance. The senator rose and gave her a light hug as she arrived at his table.

"Thank you so much for coming, sir," she gave him a dazzling smile motioning for him to sit back down in his seat.

"Thank you for the invite. Looks like it's going to be a fantastic night. Good for fundraising." He returned her smile. "I hope you don't mind me bringing my entourage. You know I can't leave the house without these guys."

"Of course not. Let me get someone to grab them some plates." Abbie raised her hand motioning for the head waitress that was standing in the corner observing.

"That won't be necessary. They will be fine until things get wrapped up." A plate was placed in front of him, and he placed his napkin in his lap. "Won't you sit down? I want to hear what you have planned for the Society this year." He gave the person sitting to his right a look, and they instantly stood to make room for her.

"Maybe just for a little while." Abbie shot the displaced young man an apologetic look and sat down. "What can I tell you about?"

"What project are you personally working on?"

Abbie took a sip of her white wine. "I am making a value and condition registry of rural North Carolina."

"Does that have some personal significance?"

She took another sip. "Hmm?"

"Working in the rural part of North Carolina."

"It's an area that has so many great structures and great stories. I love the stories." She thought of the tattered sepia-toned photo sitting on her bedside table. Her mind created its own story of the young black woman quilting on the front porch while a black man stood on the cabin stairs looking out at a boat tied to a pier. She found it in the college library when she first started her research, and it became an obsession. One day she would find their cabin and their story.

"That sounds fascinating. Any plans to help research for my constituents?"

"We can certainly put that on the list for next year if you would like. I really appreciate your support. Now, I will let you eat your dinner while I go check on the next course. If you will excuse me?" she asked as she rose from her seat.

"Of course, I will talk to you a little later." He paused the slicing of his duck to give her a smile.

"Talk to you later." She made her way through the tables to step to the kitchen to follow up and take a breath.

The kitchen was moving like a well-oiled machine. The chef had already started plating for dessert. Abbie looked at the 250 white plates evenly placed on the large kitchen table. The uniformity of the dishes with a tiny sprig of mint looked like a piece of art in themselves. She stood a moment taking in the piping of chocolate moose and a swipe of ganache. It was time to take another walk with the guests.

She walked through the door and took a deep breath of the fresh air. Her hands went to her hair to make sure it was in place and then she stepped onto the lawn. She knew tonight was going to be the best year yet. Her eyes roved over the crowd and then stopped. There was no one at the bar. Oh man, where was Ruth?

Abbie slowly made her way through the tables. Hopefully, no one has noticed, but there was a line, and it was growing. The closer she got to the line a bad feeling grew in her stomach. She knew Ruth wouldn't let her down. Something must be wrong.

To be continued…

Coming in 2020

ABOUT THE AUTHOR

Tammera Cooper grew up on the Rappahannock River in Virginia watching the riverside community change with the times but remaining the same in spirit. The waterside lifestyle is in her blood and influences her writing every day.

Currently, she lives in Washington, North Carolina writing and sharing the small town's history with her readers. She is a member of the Pamlico Writers Group, Women's Fiction Writers Association, and Romance Writers of America.

You are welcome to touch base with her on her website: https://www.southernromanceonthepamlico.com/